THE FECKING FABULOUS FORTIES CLUB

FREYA KENNEDY

Boldwood

First published in Great Britain in 2024 by Boldwood Books Ltd.

Cover Design by Alice Moore Design

Cover Illustration: Shutterstock

This book is a work of fiction and, except in the case of historical fact, any resemblance to actual persons, living or dead, is purely coincidental.

Every effort has been made to obtain the necessary permissions with reference to copyright material, both illustrative and quoted. We apologise for any omissions in this respect and will be pleased to make the appropriate acknowledgements in any future edition.

A CIP catalogue record for this book is available from the British Library.

Paperback ISBN 978-1-83533-835-3

Large Print ISBN 978-1-83533-831-5

Hardback ISBN 978-1-83533-830-8

Ebook ISBN 978-1-83533-828-5

Kindle ISBN 978-1-83533-829-2

Audio CD ISBN 978-1-83533-836-0

MP3 CD ISBN 978-1-83533-833-9

Digital audio download ISBN 978-1-83533-827-8

Boldwood Books Ltd
23 Bowerdean Street
London SW6 3TN
www.boldwoodbooks.com

For
The Caravan Survival Club
Lisa, Julie-Anne & Marie-Louise
'Sure, we're only 27'
And in loving memory of my dear friend
Sandra Smyth

GLOSSARY

This book is set in my beautiful home city of Derry (also known as Londonderry, or Doire) in Northern Ireland. Although the television show *Derry Girls* has opened a lot of eyes and ears to some of our more colourful terminology, I know that some will still read as odd to those who are unfamiliar with our colloquialisms. To help a reader out, I have added a few explanations:

Boke – To be physically sick, to vomit.
Craic – A commonly used word across the island of Ireland, used to describe something being good or fun. It can also be used to denote news/ gossip or your personality. For example – 'The craic was ninety' means something was great fun. 'What's the craic?' is a way of asking if there is any news or gossip to be hand. 'Shite craic' or 'zero craic' means events were less than enjoyable. It can also be used as a descriptor for a very boring person. The absolute worst thing a person can be in Ireland, however, is a 'Craic-killer' – which is someone who actively tries to turn great craic into shite craic. Craic-killers are the Irish equivalent of emotional vampires. Avoid at all costs.

Craic never means high grade narcotics.

Dootsy – Something or someone old-fashioned and very much not on trend.

Dote – A term of affection, most usually reserved for children but also for kind-hearted people. In Derry it is very often preceded with 'wee' when referencing a child, or 'big' when referencing an adult. If someone is unwell, wee or big can be replaced with 'poor'.

Doting – Not to be confused with the above, if someone is 'doting' it means they are likely entering their older years and becoming a bit forgetful.

Gack – Someone who is a bit of an eejit, or behaves in an uncool, embarrassing way.

Going with – Dating or courting someone. Sometimes it more specifically means snogging someone as well. Teenagers were frequently asked 'Did ye go with him?' after a sneaky wee dance during the slow set on a night out.

Hoke/ hoking – A word used in place of having a nosy or trying to recover something from a small space.

The Maiden City – Derry is known as the Maiden City, which lore would have you believe is because the number of women here outnumber the men significantly. The truth is that Derry is known as the Maiden City because no one breached her city walls during The Siege of Derry in 1689, protecting her maidenhood.

Majella – Majella is a name given to a certain breed of Derry woman who loves her make-up, always has her hair perfect and wears the trendiest clothes. To be a proper Majella she must also speak very loudly, have oodles of confidence and love a bit of gossip. The popular girls in school were often known as the Majellas.

Quare – This one has a couple of meanings. It can mean large or substantial, as in: 'I had a quare feed of drink last night', it can also mean deeply satisfying or impressive as in 'It's a quare day outside today'. Sometimes it can mean all four of those words all at the same time. For example: 'You've a quare arse on you.'

Soupie – Soupie is a common nickname among the men folk, specifically those with the surname Campbell, as Campbell's make soup. Everyone in Derry knows at least one Soupie.

Sure (often followed by 'lookit') – In Ireland we don't believe in using just one word when twenty will do. Therefore, we like to add extra words at the beginning, or ending of sentences for emphasis. Sure is just a warning that we're about to say something of importance. NB: We always think we're going to say something important.

Tout – Someone who grasses or tells on another person.

1

A DOG'S DINNER

Rebecca
November 2023

'I'll call round in the morning,' I blurt down the phone to my mother. 'I'm just in the door and Daniel has had a good go at the chicken I'd been defrosting for dinner and it obviously didn't agree with him because he's been sick all over the living room rug and the smell would—'

'The smell isn't something I need to know about. Not when I'm just about to have my own dinner. It's chicken though and after that lovely picture you've painted, I'm not sure I'm quite in the mood for it any more,' my mother says, her voice intoned with the flourish of martyrdom she does so well. Of course, I know my mother does not like any talk of a delicate nature, and nor, for that matter, does she like Daniel, our oddly named but very adorable cocker spaniel, but as she phoned just as I'd come upon the gruesome tableau in partially digested raw chicken he had left me, I spoke without thinking.

'I'm sorry, Mum,' I tell her, as Daniel looks up at me with

sorrowful eyes that immediately make me feel guilty for calling him 'a disgusting ratbag' just minutes earlier. I give his fur a gentle stroke and hope that suffices as an apology for my anger as I continue to try to appease my mother. 'I hope it hasn't ruined your dinner. But I do need to get on and clean this up if I've half a chance of saving this rug.'

'Rebecca! Please! You know I've a sensitive stomach,' my mother laments. Of course I apologise again while mentally strategising the best course of action for the great clean-up. Kitchen paper, poo bags, that odour-killing spray and maybe even the carpet cleaning machine...

'Mum, I'll call over in the morning. I'm working from home so I'll nip round. Send me a text if you need anything over from the shops and I'll pick it up on the way,' I tell her.

'I will not send a text. I'll call you. All these people obsessed with their phones and no one knows what anyone's voice sounds like any more,' she says. The chance of anyone in my mother's acquaintance not knowing what her voice sounds like is somewhere between slim and none, but I am not going to poke that particular bruise right now.

'Okay, yes. Call me. Before half eight if you want to use the landline, or you can get me on the mobile after. I'll be taking Daniel out for his walk.'

'But you won't bring *that dog* here, will you?' she asks, in a tone that makes me realise once again that she sees Daniel as some sort of vicious beast and not just the slightly dopey dog he is – more likely to lick you to death than sink his teeth into your flesh. Unless your flesh is partially defrosted chicken that was supposed to be chopped up and cooked into a curry for dinner.

'No, Mum. I'll leave him home again before I call to yours.' Daniel gives me the wounded-pup eyes again and I swear he can understand what I'm saying word for word.

'Well so, I'll leave you a message on your landline and you can get it when you get home with *that dog*.'

I'm about to snap at her that she well knows *that dog* has a name and I'd prefer she use it. After all, it's been almost a decade since my then nine-year-old twin sons decided to give him a name that rhymes with his breed – and yet Mum's still campaigning to have him renamed Rover, Rocky or anything more 'dog-like'.

I don't think I have the energy to battle any more with her today, and that's with barely a five-minute phone call, so I just sigh. 'Okay, Mum. That's grand. Look, I'll see you then,' I say as I head to the utility room to gather the necessary supplies for the clean-up. My poor massacred chicken, or what's left of it, mocks me from the floor.

'Oh, before you go,' she says, and I feel my spirit leave my body. 'Did you hear who died?'

My mother lives for her at least once a weekly round of 'Did you hear who died?' She says once you get to her age ('seventy-six, not that I'm counting,' she tells everyone), finding out who has most recently departed this world becomes something of a highlight. Sadly, I have the same reaction to it as she does to tales of regurgitated chicken. Death makes me feel vaguely nauseous and panicky and this morbid game of *Guess Who?* my mother insists on playing regularly is the bane of my life.

'Mum, I really need to clean up after the dog,' I say in the hope that my words might will her into letting me go without too much of a fuss.

There's a deep sigh. 'Ah so, there will come a day Rebecca Burnside, when I won't be here to talk to on the phone and then you'll feel bad for rushing these chats,' she says.

'Mum!' I say and can't hide the exasperation in my voice. 'I love you, and I'll give you all the time you need tomorrow to tell me all the latest news on who is dead, and who is getting married and who is riding someone they shouldn't be—'

'*Re-bec-ca!*' she scolds and I'm sixteen again and my face is blazing because she's caught me singing 'Like a Virgin' while dancing provocatively in my bra pretending I'm Madonna on the Blond Ambition tour.

'Sorry, Mum,' I say, tears pricking at my eyes now. I'm tired. I ache. I have the period from hell and I'm so hungry I could eat the partially masticated chicken off the kitchen floor. 'I'll see you in the morning. Love you. I'm sorry. Bye!'

I hang up before the guilt trip ratchets up another notch and turn around to see Daniel squatting on the kitchen floor and emptying his bowels of whatever he hadn't managed to throw up in the living room. I contemplate just closing the door, lifting my car keys and going for a long drive off a short precipice, but I don't even think I have the energy for that right now.

So instead, I just scream... but not so loudly that it will upset Daniel and his watery bowels even more. The last thing I need is for him to take the zoomies through his own mess.

2

ME? A SWAN?

The person staring back at me in the rear-view mirror is not someone I recognise. Well, that's not exactly true of course. I know it's me. I haven't had some sort of catastrophic brain incident on the drive over here. It's just not the me I used to be or want to be, or the me I'd thought I'd be when I was finally all grown up.

The woman looking back at me is clearly old, tired, dehydrated and existing at the tail end of her very last nerve. She needs her greying roots done and could probably benefit from some Botox. She definitely could do with an eyebrow wax and maybe a personal shopper. A facial wouldn't go amiss either. What sick-minded creator of all that is human decided to throw adult acne into the menopausal mixing pot? I thought my days of applying seventeen layers of concealer over a spot that seems to emit its own radioactive glow were long gone. But no. I thought a time would come in my life where I emerged a beautiful swan after leaving aside the ugly duckling years, but it turns out there was no swan hidden inside of me, just waiting to glide majestically across life's pond. I have jumped from ugly duckling to dumpy old bird.

There is nothing chic or MILF-esque about the rather haggard figure in her well-worn slogan hoodie ('Tired & Needy') staring back at me. I look past my sell-by date. And if this is how I'm feeling now, before my mother gifts me with *her* opinion on how I'm looking and what I'm wearing, I have a feeling it's going to be a rough morning.

Of course, when I'd promised my mother that I would call round to see her this morning, I'd not known that I would have a relatively sleepless night. Daniel was still not quite able to be trusted with his continence after chicken-gate and I had spent the night on the sofa so that I could let him outside approximately once an hour to do his business. The sounds of his pitiful whines as he scrabbled at the living room door to get out left me under no illusion I, and my lovely woollen rug, would regret any attempt to ignore him.

How I wished the twins were home from university and able to share the night shift with me – even if I knew I wouldn't trust them to wake up in time to let Daniel out. But no, they are having the time of their lives in Manchester as a series of increasingly drunken messages sent between eleven and one reminded me. It's always nice to hear my children tell me they love me. It's not always ideal to hear it in a mumbled voice note after midnight accompanied by the sound of someone throwing up in the background.

Between that and a tsunami of night sweats, thanks to what I'm pretty sure – but don't want to accept – is the menopause, I did not have a peaceful rest. In fact, I'd almost fallen asleep in the shower this morning, dreaming I was being waterboarded by my old Latin teacher. I'm not sure what was the scarier part – the waterboarding or the teacher. Thankfully I jumped awake in time to stop myself slipping in the shower, sustaining a fatal head injury, and having my splayed naked body discovered weeks later after the flies had been at it.

Daniel's stomach has settled, thankfully, but instead of being able to finally take advantage of the calm after the storm to sneak in a quick nap, I've had to play the role of good daughter and check in on my beloved mother. Not for the first time I curse my sole sibling, Ruairi, for living on the other side of the country in Belfast. I love my mother deeply, but it would be nice to have someone to share the checking-in duties with.

I haul my tired and admittedly unfit body out of my car, and lift the bags of shopping I've picked up for Mum from the boot.

'It's just a few things, love. To keep me going,' she'd said as she started to read out her shopping list to me over the phone earlier. Twenty minutes later, the 'few things' had morphed into a full weekly shop plus some extras for Mrs Bishop (first name Emily, and her husband was called Harold. I kid you not!) next door 'to save her nipping out later'. I suppose I don't mind. Mrs Bishop is a lovely woman, and always has been. Her own children – now, like me, grown up with families of their own – have scattered to the four winds and left poor Mrs Bishop to contend with her increasing frailty on her own. Not that she will hear a bad word said against them.

I heft the bags up the garden path, deposit them on the front step and rifle in my pocket for my keys before letting myself into Mum's and carrying the shopping through to the kitchen. As usual, my mother has the thermostat in her house set to tropical heatwave and it isn't long before I can feel sweat gathering at my hairline, and starting to pool in the increasingly lower dip between my breasts.

'Mum!' I call, as I begin to unpack her shopping to put it away for her. Her kitchen may be as dated as shell suits and acid perms, but it's pristine and everything has its place. I find it quite soothing to tidy away the shopping in her well-ordered manner. It brings me back in time to my teenage years, huffing and puffing at being asked to help out and, on occasion, slamming cupboard doors shut because I felt so aggrieved that she had bought value label crisps when everyone else in school seemed to get Tayto in their lunch-boxes. God, but I was a brat to her at times – never copping on to the fact my parents bought Yellow Pack crisps because that was likely all they could afford. A cloud of delayed guilt swoops down on me, bringing with it an Unexpected Wave of Sadness because I might have made them feel bad, thirty-some years ago.

Unexpected Waves of Sadness have become an almost daily occurrence for me as my oestrogen levels have started to deplete. I can be having a perfectly lovely, sometimes even happy day, when all of a sudden they attack without warning like the doom-laden ninjas they are and my mood will sink faster than Philip Schofield's career.

'Mum!' I call again. 'Will I put the kettle on? I stopped in at the bakery on Ivy Lane and picked up some buns.' I don't mention that I ate a jam and icing turnover on the way over after another UWOS washed over me when I saw a harassed mother struggle to get her car seat clicked into the frame of her pram. That brought with it the realisation that I will never battle to transport another baby of my own from place to place ever again. At that moment, it felt like the most crushingly sad feeling I had ever experienced – so I carb loaded.

I'm filling the kettle when it dawns on me my mother hasn't actually answered. I'm just so used to this little routine of ours that I, it seems, take her replies for granted.

'Mum?' I call again, this time a question more than a greeting. I turn the tap off so I can listen for her response but the house remains silent. Prone as I am to random acts of extreme cata-strophising, there is a part of me that is already planning her funeral, convinced that I will go upstairs to find that she has expired in the hour since we last spoke when she told me to make sure to buy proper Rich Tea biscuits and 'not some sorry own-branded excuse for a biscuit'. I try not to let my repressed teenaged bitterness about the sorry own-branded excuse for crisps she bought sully the memory of what might have been my last conversation with the woman who gave me life.

'Mu-um?' I call again, and I hear a wobble of impending hysteria in my voice. I need her to answer. I am so not emotionally prepared to even think about losing her, never mind actually... I give myself a shake. I'm being ridiculous. Sure, she was fine an hour ago. Hale and hearty, as she would say herself. And just because I know how things *can* change in a heartbeat, it doesn't mean they *will*.

Reverting to the emotional neediness of an eleven-year-old, I yell 'Mammmmmmyyy!' in a strangulated voice, as I walk to the bottom of the stairs, poking my head into the living room and downstairs loo as I go. There is no sign that Roisin Burnside is in residence, except for the holy candle she has lit in her favoured holy candle spot on the mantlepiece. Roisin Burnside would never leave the house with a candle lit. No matter how important the intention.

With my heart now in my throat, I run up the stairs and stick my head into her bedroom. Her bed is made. The window is wide open to let in fresh air despite the near artic conditions outside. Everything is as it should be, and I suppose I should be relieved not to find her corpse on top of the bed but she's still missing and this is not typical mammy behaviour.

'Mammmmyyyyy!' I yell again, followed by a more plaintive cry as my chest tightens and the little hairs on the back of my neck rise. My deepest fears are doing their best to muscle their way into my head. This could be it. It could be happening. That's the thing when you have parents who are getting up the years a bit, you start to fear the worst. It stalks you constantly, picking off the parents of your friends one by one until you know it's only a matter of time before it's your turn to grieve.

I'm shaking as I poke my head into the bathroom, and still shaking when I look in the spare room – which I'm surprised to find isn't quite as perfectly ordered as the rest of the house. There are dusty boxes on top of the bed – my old bed – with a pile of clothes laid beside them. I recognise my father's familiar handwriting on the top of the first box – 'R's Childhood Memories' – and my chest tightens so much I wonder if *I'm* going to be the one who is found dead today. I've read that more women are having heart attacks than ever before – and younger too. Sure, Miranda Bailey had a heart attack in *Grey's Anatomy* and she's about my age, surely? I'll have to google it if I survive.

But as my breathing eases just a little, the distraction of Dr Bailey working its magic, it dawns on me that this is not a heart attack, it is just a visceral reaction to seeing my father's – my daddy's – handwriting again. Instinctively I reach out and touch it; my finger traces the curves and swirls of his penmanship. 'R's Childhood Memories' – as if a box could hold all those moments in one place ready for us to dip into whenever we wanted. If only.

If only time didn't steal so many of our memories or push them aside to make way for the flashier kind. The older I get the more I realise it's not really the big nights out, and the huge celebratory moments I long to recall with the most detail. Given the chance, those are not the days I would relive. It's the gentle, quiet moments I want. Like reading – just existing quietly – in the same room as my father, the sun streaming through the window, dust motes dancing in the air. Warmth, contentment, the rhythmic turn of pages. I wish I could remember what books we read. What we talked about between chapters. I wish I could remember what biscuits I gave him with his cups of tea.

I want those middle-of-the-night moments with my babies back, when the whole house was asleep but us. When I rocked them, feeling the softness of their downy hair against my shoulder, smelling the sweet, milky aroma of their baby breath. Oh, I would relive those moments in a heartbeat. I'd sacrifice a decade of whatever time I have left on this planet to relive just five of those quiet minutes.

A loud crash reverberates through the house, hauling me by the throat back from my internal time travel to the here and now, and my mother's voice as she shouts, 'Rebecca! Is that you! Can you come and help me here, love? I've got myself into a bit of a mess!'

It sounds very much as if her voice is coming from the small box room at the back of the house – my brother Ruairi's childhood bedroom which he remains bitter about to this very day. My parents were 'playing favourites' when they assigned the much bigger middle room to me, he says. I tell him he's talking absolute nonsense, but secretly I agree with him. I was a goody two-shoes. Ruairi was a wee shite.

'Mum?' I call, the relief that flooded my heart at hearing her voice already replaced by a sense of impending doom at just what this stubborn old goat has done to herself now.

'I'm in your brother's room!' she calls.

I'm already walking through the door to the smallest bedroom in Ireland, North or South, when she adds, 'Well, sort of, anyway.'

At first I don't see her, which, given the size of the room, is quite impressive. But I do see a battered cardboard box on the floor – which I'm going to assume is what made the godawful crashing sound – and a step-ladder. When I focus on the ladder and my eyes cast upwards, it's hard to miss the slippered feet dangling out of the hatch to the loft.

'Jesus Christ, Mum! What are you doing? How did you get up there? Have you a death wish on you? Christ alive, you could break a hip, or your leg, or take a funny spell and fall out of that damn thing and break your neck and then where would you be?'

'Well, love,' my mother calls from the cavern of darkness that is our loft. 'I imagine I'd be dead on the floor, but I'm not, I'm just a bit stuck. I dropped my torch, and my eyes are struggling to readjust to the light in the room so I can't really see the outline of the ladder and...'

'I was calling you!' I scold, in a voice I've only ever used before on my children when they disappeared in a busy supermarket and I immediately assumed they'd been kidnapped, only to find them hitting up strangers for pound coins to go on the *Balamory* bus ride. A mixture of relief and anger bubble forth from inside me. 'I thought you were dead!' I manage with a squeak.

'No,' my mother says, without a hint of acknowledgement of the mental trauma she has just put me through. 'I'd never die and leave the house in this state! I'd be mortified if the neighbours turned up to the wake to find my box room in disarray.'

'But I...' I try to find the words to tell her just how completely batshit crazy she is, but of course she interrupts me.

'"But I" nothing,' she says. 'Help me get down and then we can talk about you taking the name of our Lord your God in vain in front of your elderly mother.'

3

GUESS WHO'S DEAD?

With my mother retrieved from the attic, thankfully without any broken bones, we are sitting at her kitchen table drinking tea. My heart rate is almost back to normal after the whole thinking-my-mother-was dead-but-instead-finding-her-dangling-out-of-the-attic incident. I'm still completely baffled by her actions though.

'Why on earth would you think it was a good idea to try and climb up into the attic?' I ask while my mother examines each of the turnovers I brought with me to decide which one has the most icing and jam.

'It's my house and my attic. Who else is there here to go up into it but me?' She sniffs, turning the pastries over and tapping their bottoms as if she's Mrs Berry herself.

'I could've gone up. Or Ruairi. Or if you waited a few weeks the boys will be back for Christmas and they could've done it for you,' I say, my heart twanging a little at the mention of my boys who have been away from home for a full ten weeks now. While the upside of having twins is that you get the two for one bonus of only having to endure labour once, the downside has been that both my chicks flew the nest at the same time. The house is much too quiet without them.

'Nonsense,' my mother says, cutting through my thoughts. 'You've enough to be doing with your work and that dog. And Ruairi is even busier. Did he tell you he's turning people away now? Can't meet the demand. He's going to hire some new staff in the new year.'

I nod. Of course he is. Ruairi, once a wee shite is now a big shite, but a successful one. A solicitor with his own practice, specialising in claims, he's developed quite the reputation for getting big pay-outs for his clients. He's never been busier. Or richer.

'Right so, the boys. They'd have loved to help,' I say as my mother proffers the most icing deficient of the turnovers in my direction.

'Ah, when the boys come home, they'll be looking to rest from all their schoolwork and all. The last thing they'll want to be doing is helping their old granny out,' she says, before taking a bite from her pastry.

'It's the least they could do and don't let them fool you that it's all study and long sessions over the books,' I say. I don't mention their Instagram feeds which have showcased what can only be described as drunken shenanigans on a regular basis. An Unexpected Wave of Sadness washes over me as I wonder if I will ever, ever experience drunken shenanigans again. I mean, they'd probably kill me if I even tried them these days, but God I miss the recklessness of youth.

My mother shakes her head, dispelling any hint of criticism of 'her boys'. If my mother was able to let Ruairi away with murder when he was young, it would be fair to say she'd happily let Saul and Adam get away with a full-on killing spree. The sun shines directly from their arses – a belief I share when I'm in a good mood.

'That doesn't answer the question either,' I said. 'What was so important you had to risk life and limb to get hold of?'

'Sure, I told you upstairs. I can't be dying and leaving things in a state. I'm just trying to get my affairs in order.'

I feel the bite of pastry I'd just taken turn to ash in my mouth so I take a drink of my tea to try and wash it down, hoping it doesn't stick in my throat and end me prematurely. The absolute shame that would come from dying by turnover would be mortifying, especially given my need to lose a few stone.

'Getting your affairs in order?' I ask. 'Mum, do you have something to tell me?'

I know that I don't really want to know the answer. I am scared of it, but not knowing doesn't make it go away.

'I'm seventy-six, Rebecca. I'm not immediately planning to die but I can't escape the fact that it's out there. And let's be honest, I'm not likely to become more agile and able for climbing into attics as time goes on so I figured if I got it all done now it would be sorted and it would save you and Ruairi a lot of heartache when I do die.' She speaks in such a measured and matter-of-fact way you'd think she was discussing what bin to put out or what she was going to make for dinner, not planning for the aftermath of her own death.

'There's a will, of course. Your father made sure of that, but there's more than that to be dealt with. I don't want you two to have to go hoking through all my paperwork and belongings once I'm gone. If I declutter now, it will be as easy as giving me a good send off, selling the house and collecting your inheritance. As little fuss as possible. That's what I want.'

I stare at her, mouth agape, horrified by her calmness towards her own demise as if it wouldn't be utterly catastrophic for all concerned.

'Obviously, if I need nursing care or to go into a home before then...'

'You'll not be going into a home,' I interrupt. 'If you need care, you'll come live with me. Or I'll come here. We'll work it out. But you will not be going into a home.' Tears sting at my eyes at the very thought of Roisin Burnside in some grey and depressing nursing home, staring with vacant eyes out of a net-curtain-clad window into a soulless car park or something equally grim.

'No offence to you my love,' my mother says, 'but should the time come that I do need care, I don't want to burden you or your brother with that.'

'You'd hardly be a burden!' I protest.

'You say that now, Rebecca, but I'm still in my right mind and fully continent. Well, mostly continent,' she says with a small smile. 'I am seventy-six after all. You may well feel differently in the future when I need someone to wipe my bum or remind me not to strip in public or something equally embarrassing.' She's of course trying to make light of it, but I can see the worry the behind her eyes. Roisin Burnside is nothing if not a proud woman determined to keep a hold of her dignity no matter the circumstances. She cared for her own parents towards the ends of their lives and while I never saw her complain, I know it took a toll on her that remains to this day.

'Mum...' I say, ready to reassure her that I absolutely have no issue with any bum wiping or gentle reminding, but she raises her hand to silence me. I know better than to continue. When my mother is done with a conversation, it is categorically and emphatically over.

'Which reminds me,' she says. 'I haven't told you who died yet.'

Ah, the Derry Death Notices edition of *Guess Who?* I'd forgotten that treat was waiting for me. 'As long as it's not you,' I mutter under my breath, aware I'm skating dangerously close to the forbidden topic of conversation.

If my mother hears me, she chooses to ignore it. 'Mrs Bishop told me yesterday. Which reminds me, did you pick up those few items for her? Her hip is giving her awful bother at the moment and I didn't want to risk her going out in case it iced over. Last thing she needs is a fall right now, not with her lot at the other side of the world.' Mrs Bishop's two children live in England, but as far as my mother is concerned, they might as well be in Australia. Anything that requires crossing a body of water is too far away for my mother's comfort. She wasn't even terribly happy when I moved to the other side of the River Foyle after I got married.

'Yes, Mum. I got what you asked for and I'll drop them in next door when I'm finished with my cup of tea. I'll need to be heading back soon anyway – work to be done and all that!' I say, hoping she'll understand that I don't have all day to sit and chat.

'Yes, yes. I understand. You're very busy.' She takes another bite of her turnover. She is clearly in no rush to tell me who died. Or show me what it is she has found while Marie Kondo-ing her very existence. I raise an eyebrow at her in the hope she takes the hint.

'Right, okay,' she says. 'Well, Mrs Bishop told me yesterday that she had been down at Mass and the priest – that lovely young fellah with the beard and the Belfast accent – was reading out the deaths and I'm really sorry to be the one to tell you, but Kitty O'Hagan is dead.'

My blood really does run cold this time. My cup clatters as I drop it back onto the saucer.

'Kitty O'Hagan, as in, Laura's mammy?' I ask, my mind instantly flooded with memories of sitting around Laura's kitchen table having the mad craic before multiple nights out. Kitty O'Hagan giving us a lift into town, never once complaining at how rowdy or annoying we were being. 'Enjoy your youth, girls. It doesn't last long,' she'd say. Laura would roll her eyes and complain that her mum was being a craic killer. But her mum was never a craic killer. She was a bona fide craic bringer.

'The very same,' my mother says. 'Much too young,' she adds. 'It just goes to show we never know what's around the next corner. This is why it's important to get my affairs in order.'

My mother's sudden interest in climbing into attics makes more sense now, I suppose, but honestly, I'm still trying to digest the news that Kitty has died.

'Do you never see Laura any more?' she asks. 'I've not heard you talk about her in forever. I always thought the pair of you would make friends again. She's a lovely girl. I always liked her.'

'What happened?' I ask, my mind racing.

'Between you and Laura? Do you not know that yourself?'

'No. To Kitty. What did she die from?' I ask.

'No idea,' my mum replies. 'But I thought you should know in case you wanted to go and show your respects. You were always in and out of that woman's house when you were younger. Do you remember I used to joke we should just take your bed up there and let you move in? Regardless of whether or not you and Laura are speaking, you should go and pay your respects.'

I nod, my head already full of thoughts of Laura and what she must be going through. I know it well. The shock. The disbelief. The exhaustion as you push through the surrealism of it all. People in and out of the house and you just wanting to tell them all to go away – that you are broken and you understand they are sad, and they want to pay their respects but you are only just holding it together and you need to scream until you throw up. That you don't want people here to gawk at the coffin in the corner. To drink tea and eat sandwiches as if the most catastrophic event of your life isn't unfolding amid the Mass cards and sympathetic handshakes. 'We're sorry for your troubles,' they say and I've no doubt they are but there's a big part of them that is looking at you, witnessing your grief and thinking, 'We're just so thankful these troubles aren't at our door.'

'Do you know when the funeral is?' I ask. I'll have to call Niamh. She mustn't know yet. If she did, she'd have called me. She'd have picked up her phone and hit my number and made sure to speak to me. Some things were too important for a WhatsApp message.

'Well, from what Mrs Bishop said, she died on Wednesday night so I'd hazard a guess the funeral will be tomorrow, unless they're waiting for people to fly in,' my mother says.

In Derry we dispatch our dead with remarkable efficiency. There's a standard of two nights for a wake – where we bring our dead home to be surrounded by friends and family – before a funeral. If someone dies late in the day, those two nights will often extend to three. The same goes if family need to travel from wherever in the world they now live. People tend not to want a Sunday funeral Mass – where the service takes place as part of the ordinary weekly Mass and can feel less personal – so my mother is probably right. It is Friday morning and tomorrow one of the very best friends I have ever had in my life will be laying her mother to rest and I've not so much as spoken to her.

'You should've told me!' I blurt.

'I tried to tell you last night but you were more concerned with *that dog* and his business,' she says, her lips pursed in an expression which wouldn't look out of place on Maggie Smith playing a blinder as the Dowager Countess in *Downton Abbey*.

'You should've made me listen!' I say, guilt flooding my system that I didn't have the time yesterday to hear about Kitty O'Hagan's death. That I'm such a horrible person I've not been there to hug my friend and extend my condolences. She must be utterly devastated. Her brother, Conal, must be devastated too. It was always just the three of them against the world.

'Made you listen?' My mother sniffs. 'Rebecca Louise Burnside, in the almost forty-seven years you have been on this planet, nothing I have ever done has made you listen.'

She has a point, of course, but still. She should've tried.

'I'm sorry,' I say. The last thing I want to do on the day I hear Laura is mourning her mother is to start arguing with mine. 'It's just a shock... and I wasn't expecting it. She's so young. I just can't quite believe it.'

'Ach, I know,' my mother says, up on her feet without so much as a wince or an expression that her back aches. It's remarkable really. I'm thirty years her junior and have already reached the random-pain-noises stage of life. 'She was a lovely woman. A strong woman too. I'd never have thought it would be me who would outlive her...' She starts to clean up the tea things even though I'm not even finished my first cup yet. That means this whole thing has rattled her too. My mother always goes into super-clean mode when she's anxious. That she's decided to sort out her affairs too makes me think that Roisin Burnside is experiencing anxiety on a level she's not known before. There's been too much death around this last few years.

But Kitty O'Hagan was young, all things considered. She was ten years younger than my mother. Only sixty-six. Too young to be dead. The news comes at me again in another wave of disbelief. No, I do not like this stage of life where parents start to die and it feels like we're all on borrowed time.

How do I reassure a seventy-six-year-old woman, and myself for that matter, that she has years left when we've just been shown again that life can be so arbitrarily cruel?

My mind races back to all those days spent hanging out in Kitty's kitchen, or Laura's bedroom. We got up to so many stupid things – dance routines, applying make-up very badly, trying to learn how to walk in heels, which ended in a sprained ankle and a trip to A & E for Niamh.

And then there were the projects. There was the summer we spent designing our own magazine and fancying ourselves as revolutionary journalists. Of course, this was before computers were the norm, or able to do anything more than act as glorified typewriters, so we hand-wrote our stories, illustrated with our best markers and absolutely ripped off other magazines by sticking their pictures onto our pages. We kept Pritt Stick in business that year.

While other teenagers were out drinking two-litre bottles of cheap cider up on Derry's City Walls, we were geeking out designing our own range of super-trendy fashion. My daddy had brought a ream of 500 pages of crisp white paper home from his work and we spent a summer drawing as many rah-rah skirts, shell suits and bomber jackets as possible. We watched *The Clothes Show* each Sunday with the reverence we would have saved for Mass in the past and God love our parents, but they never laughed at us or told us to get a life. Kitty even managed to keep a straight face when the three of us, in our Dunnes Stores jeans, Primark T-shirts and Nicks (not Nike) trainers, described our style as 'Urban Funk'.

I wish I could remember the name of our fictional magazine or fashion house. I wish we still had those glorious projects to look at again now.

That's when another memory comes back to me. It was the summer of 1994. We were post GCSE, on the brink of womanhood and still dodging anything remotely cool. Although in fairness, both Laura and Niamh were making strides towards coolness by occasionally getting past the bouncers and into Squires nightclub. As such behaviour was very strictly verboten in my house, I instead doubled down on the dorkyness and suggested our summer project be putting together a time capsule.

'These are the formative years of our lives,' I had declared with all the conviction of a sixteen-year-old who thought she knew everything. 'We should keep a record of them. We should mark this occasion.'

So we did. And if I'm not very much mistaken, the resulting

creation is still buried in the back of the wardrobe in my old bedroom. Unless, that is, my mother has decluttered it in her attempts to put her affairs in order.

'Mum,' I ask. 'Do you remember that time the girls and I made a time capsule?'

'God, love, I barely remember my own name these days. And you lot were always up to something.' She fills the kettle to make more tea, even though she has just cleaned away the cups. She's definitely more rattled than she's letting on.

'You must remember,' I tell her. 'You came up with some ideas of what we could put it in. I'm pretty sure it's upstairs in my old room somewhere. Unless you've decluttered it over the years?'

She pauses for a moment as if trying to pull the memory from the back of her mind and place it in the here and now. I watch her closely, waiting for the 'penny dropping' moment to appear across her face. It doesn't.

'Nope. No memory of it. But I do know that I've not touched that wardrobe of yours. If you stored something in it then, chances are, it's still there.'

'Great,' I say, a little fizz of excitement bubbling inside me, mixed with a little bit of deep cringe at how utterly lacking in any kind of cool we were. What other sixteen-year-olds spent their summer holidays making time capsules – for fun?

Still, the cringe isn't strong enough to stop me from hightailing it to my old bedroom and starting to dig through the wardrobe. I come across old photo albums, which have half the pictures missing. I vaguely remember pulling them out at different stages to plaster on the walls of my university digs, or in my first flat. I'm not sure what became of them after that. I find a box of my old school books – my spidery handwriting in blotchy blue biro scrawling my class name and the name of my teachers. I swear there is still the faint whiff of the damp temporary classrooms at the back of the school. A mixture of mould, varnish and chalk dust. Another box yields the black pair of two-and-a-half-inch heels I wore to my school formal in Upper Sixth. I remember thinking they were so high I feared I'd topple off them. Today's formal attendees would laugh at me from atop their four-inch platform heels. Or they'd style it out and wear Converse under their prom dresses and everybody would think they were absolute style icons.

Eventually, at the very back of the wardrobe, under a fine layer of dust, I find it.

A dusty shoebox sealed with thick, now-yellowed sticky-tape. Pulling it out, part of me is surprised it doesn't disintegrate as soon as it hits the light. How long must it have been there, hiding away? If it was the summer after our GCSEs then that was 1994 which means... Oh God... it's almost time to open it.

Glancing down at the box, I see our names signed on the lid. There's me – spelling my name Becki, with an i, because I thought it was cool. There's Niamh's name, in purple biro, of course. Subtlety was never her strong point. And then, in swirly, feminine letters is Laura, with a little love heart drawn after her name. Just the sight of it is enough to make my heart break for what she is going through, and for the friendship we lost along the way.

It's then I spot the instructions, written in purple glitter ink, along the side of box. 'DO NOT OPEN UNTIL 2024! WAIT THIRTY YEARS!'

Close enough, I think.

4

PANDORA'S SHOEBOX

The time capsule is sitting on the passenger seat of the car as I drive home, still somewhat dazed by the news of Kitty O'Hagan's passing. She was the best of women – always delighted to see us arrive. She seemed to thrive when her house was full of rowdy teenagers and God love her, but she listened to all of our drama and never once told us to wise up. She was ten years younger than my own mother, and infinitely cooler. She had her hair bleached blonde and even had it cut like Rachel from *Friends*, whereas Roisin Burnside opted for a boring brown bob, liberally sprinkled with grey. My hand moves to my own hair, now a carbon copy of my mother's, circa 1994. I blush. Is that part of the reason Saul and Adam couldn't wait to get away? Because their mother is an old woman who doesn't even seem to try any more...?

No. No I won't make this about me. This is about Kitty and Laura. Poor Laura. I'll log into Facebook, which my sons fondly call Boomerbook, when I get home and look her up. Maybe I'll send her a message? But is a social media message appropriate in the circumstances? I worry just showing up at the wake to offer my condolences might be awkward. We haven't spoken in so long, and we didn't part on particularly great terms. I can't guarantee I'll be welcome. Then again, I'm sure right now Laura has bigger things to worry about than me showing my face. Maybe Niamh and I could go together though – and morally support each other.

I tap the button on my steering wheel that activates voice controls in the car and very slowly and concisely tell my car to 'Call Niamh', who will no doubt know the best way to handle this. A robotic voice booms through my car asking me if I mean 'Call Fergal'. My mind does gymnastics trying to figure out how on earth the word Niamh – soft and sweet – could possibly be confused with the double-syllabled harshness of Fergal. I also wonder who the hell Fergal is and why his number is in my phone.

'No,' I tell my car and repeat the instruction, slower and even more enunciated, to call Niamh.

'Did you mean Lesley?' it replies as I stop my car to allow an impossibly young and glamorous teacher help a group of children walking in pairs cross the road. I watch the children, holding hands and bundled up in big coats and hats laughing and chatting excitedly about whatever adventure they've just been on. I remember that used to be Laura, Niamh and me. We used to insist we be allowed to walk three abreast as there was no way we would want to be split up.

A shitstorm of emotion that has been building since my mother broke the news about Kitty comes pouring out of me in a verbal attack on a computer chip located somewhere in my car, or my phone or a satellite somewhere because Lord above knows I have no idea how technology works any more.

'No. I do not want to call fudging Lesley,' I shout. 'If I wanted to call fudging Lesley, I'd have said fudging Lesley, and not fudging Niamh but no, you can't fudging understand a Derry accent, can you? Because it's not fudging English or American and really, Niamh is a fudging common enough name here and through the entire island of Ireland, and I'm fairly fudging sure I speak in a fudging intelligible manner so maybe you should address your fudging bias!'

(For the purposes of clarity, I should point out that I did not use the word 'fudging' but I'm trying to tell this story politely.)

Red-faced with effort and a hot flush, I slam my hands on the steering wheel and take a deep breath just in time to see the afore-mentioned young and glam teacher staring at me through my windscreen, mouth agape, along with the last of her charges who share her same wide-eyed stare of disbelief.

Of course, I realise, I'd put the window of the car down to try and fight off the hot flush. Which meant those sweet innocent children have heard my tirade. Every fudging last word.

All I can do is babble a quick but heartfelt apology and drive off, embarrassment adding to the ruddiness of my cheeks. When I get home I send Niamh a quick WhatsApp message asking her to call me when she gets a free moment between classes, before taking Daniel out to the back garden to deal with his ablutions.

How he has anything left to evacuate from his body is a mystery to me, but he manages it all the same and I'm delighted to see it is solid in form and easy to scoop. I'm half-way through messaging my mother to update her on *that dog's* health when I remember her delicate stomach, and also that no sane person messages people about their dog's poo.

Is this what I have become? The mad, red-faced lady who swears in front of children and gets excited at a solid poo from my dog? It was bad enough when the boys were tiny and talk of poo – consistency, colour and odour – was par for the course among the mummy brigade. But I'm *forty-six* and this is a dog. He boops his wet snout against my hand in what I like to think of as a sign of affection and I look at his big brown eyes staring up at me with what I'd like to think is love. 'At least someone cares about me,' I say, self-pity knocking me sideways as I lead him back indoors and set about preparing him some freshly bought, definitely not poisonous, chicken and white rice to eat. That's when my phone rings and I see 'Niamh' flash on the screen.

'Is this about Kitty? I just heard in the staffroom. Awful news,' she says without so much as saying hello first. This is standard procedure for Niamh, and I admire it. I like that we don't have to go through the motions of small talk and can get straight to the heart of the matter.

'Did you hear any details? What happened to her?' I ask, feeling like a bit of a ghoul for wanting to know the ins and outs of what happened.

'Cancer, I heard. I don't know more than that, sorry,' she says. 'Except that the funeral is tomorrow.'

Cancer – the dirty big bastard. How I hate everything about it. I try to not think about Kitty being consumed by it – made smaller by it. Something catches in my throat.

'Did they know if the wake was open or family only? I'm assuming it's still on tonight? Are you thinking of going too?' I croak.

'Yes, the house is open and I suppose I should go. Are you going?' she replies.

'I suppose I should too,' I say. 'I was kinda hoping we could go together. Safety in numbers and all that.' I know that Kitty's house is likely to be busy this evening. It's the last night of the wake before tomorrow's funeral, and the final chance for people to pay their respects before the coffin is closed for the last time. But I still feel uneasy at the thought of walking in on my own, especially given how things are between Laura and me.

'That's a good idea,' Niamh agrees. 'We can just nip in, pay our respects, and leave again. We don't even have to stay for a cup of tea.'

'Unless Laura asks us to,' I say, thinking that it would be bad form to say no to any invitation issued by the recently bereaved. Whether she offers a cup of tea or tells us to get lost, we'll just have to suck it up, nod and do as she says.

'Of course,' Niamh says. 'I'm not sure she will though.' There's a nervousness in her tone. I can understand it. It might have been Laura and I who had clashed and caused the rupture of our friendship group, but Niamh had been a casualty too. She'd tried to play it like Switzerland and remain neutral, but the time had come when it was clear that simply wasn't going to work. She had to pick a side and I am grateful to this day that she picked mine. I know, like me, she misses Laura. I know she misses our joint friendship. But still, she picked me.

'Only one way to find out, and if she asks us to leave instead then we'll do it. But I don't think we can let her go through this without at least trying to reach out or something,' I say, as Daniel sits patiently at my feet waiting for his lunch. I give his head a little rub and I swear he smiles back at me.

'Same,' Niamh says. 'And I also really want to pay my respects to Kitty. She was the best.' There's a wobble in Niamh's voice and I get it. This isn't just about Laura, it's about this wonderful, vivacious and generous woman who welcomed us into her home day after day for years.

'She really was,' I say, my own voice wobbling. I must not cry. I must hold it in. I must be a good Generation Xer and bury my pain. It's what Kurt Cobain would've wanted.

'I suppose Simon will be there,' she says, her voice quiet.

'You're probably right. No show without Punch and all that.' Maybe I shouldn't be so caustic. Simon, aka the former Mr Me, is best friend to Aidan, the current Mr Laura. He is also absolutely the kind of person who loves a bit of drama and will no doubt be thriving in the role of dutiful best friend of the husband of the grieving daughter. Some would say the link is too tenuous to see him put himself front and centre of the grieving process – but that's not the kind of thing that worries Simon. He likes to be seen and to have attention drawn his way. If he could crawl into the coffin beside poor Kitty, there's a chance he would.

Niamh grimaces. 'You don't think he'll sing at the funeral Mass, do you?'

My ex thinks he missed out on a glorious career as a boyband singer and will happily tell everyone he was offered a place in Boyzone but turned it down 'because Ronan Keating is a gobshite'.

Neither is true but having told that story once while exceptionally drunk, Simon was so enamoured by the reaction to it that he has doubled down on it ever since, gilding this particularly noxious lily over the years with extra details. I'd hazard a guess he has told the story so often he's come to believe it himself.

'God, I hope not,' I tell Niamh. 'It will be tragic enough as it is without having to listen to him trying to hit the high notes.'

She laughs. It goes unsaid, as it does every time we talk about Simon, that to this day she doesn't understand how I ever found him appealing enough to marry and pro-create with. But that's the thing about Simon Cooke – he's a bit of a dick, but he's mostly harmless and he can be very charming when he wants to be. I was also just young, stupid and incredibly naïve.

'God forbid!' Niamh says. 'Kitty deserves better than that.'

And Niamh is right. Kitty does deserve so much better than Simon singing her to her eternal rest. This is not an occasion where he should be able to make it all about him.

'He must've known she was sick,' I say, as it dawns on me that it's something he and Aidan were likely to have discussed. 'I wish he'd mentioned it to me. You know? Given me the chance to see her before...'

There's a pause on the other end of the line. 'Love, if there is one thing time has taught us about Simon it's that he doesn't think of how things will affect anyone but him. I'm not one to defend him but he doesn't think the way normal people think.'

'I know,' I sigh, because I do know. All too well. I take a breath. 'But this isn't about him, or my feelings. We'll be there for Laura,' I say, the time capsule catching my eye as I speak. 'Oh, I've something else to tell you too,' I say but Niamh has already started talking over me.

'Oh, shit, sorry. Okay.' She mumbles. 'Becks, I have to go. I'm supposed to be meeting the head of department and I totally bloody forgot. I swear I'm losing it these days. I'll text you about this evening. Love you. Bye,' she says and with that she is gone and I'm left staring at the time capsule wondering if I should open it or not. I give a sigh that comes right from the depths of my soul and Daniel whines before pawing at me. 'Oh, I'm okay, dote,' I reassure him, crouching down to give him a nice big cuddle, but he doesn't respond with his usual enthusiasm for tummy scritches. No, he pushes away with his paw and lets out a low, rather grumpy grumble. I know it well.

'Okay,' I say, creaking my way back up to standing. 'Keep your fur on. It's almost ready. Let's get you some food and then I suppose I'd better get on with some work to distract myself.'

I leave the time capsule on the worktop, untouched for now. I've decided I'm not emotionally ready to examine its contents just yet.

5

FRIENDS REUNITED

Niamh picks me up at seven, on the dot. She is nothing if not punctual. I'm feeling a little frazzled having spent much too long trying to decide what to wear to the wake of my former best friend's mother. Obviously my 'Give Me Strength' hoodie and leggings combo was a non-starter, but nor did it feel like the kind of smart casual work attire type of affair either. I needed something in between. In the end, I settled for a black jumper dress and red ankle boots. Red boots probably weren't the most appropriate option but I didn't want to dress completely in black in case I was mistaken for a chief mourner and God knows that would be awkward. I did not need or want people shaking my hand and offering condolences. I brushed my hair into a sleek ponytail only to look in the mirror and see an uncanny resemblance to Miss Trunchbull from *Matilda* staring back at me, so I immediately took it down. I gave my head a little shake in the hope it would fall into a perfect 'just stepped out of a salon' beach-wave style, but instead it just sort of limply fell into a frizzy helmet of a style and I ran out of time to try anything else.

I explain all this to Niamh in an epic bout of verbal diarrhoea as soon as I get in the car. To give her her dues, she lets me talk before gently placing one hand on my knee. 'Becks, I think it's possible you might just be overthinking all of this,' she says softly. 'I understand why you're nervous, of course. I'm pretty much shitting bricks too. But we can do this. Kitty deserves this.'

'I know,' I say.

'And Laura does too,' Niamh says, and I nod but stay quiet because I'm not sure deserve would be the word I would use. I still have no idea how she will receive our arrival at her mother's house. She'd be well within her rights to turf us out, or at least turf me out, on our ears.

'I checked the death notices,' Niamh says. 'The funeral is at ten, from the Cathedral. We should go to that too, shouldn't we?'

'Let's see how things go this evening first. I wouldn't want to cause any further upset,' I say and Niamh nods before we both fall into an uncomfortable silence as we make our way through familiar streets to the home where Laura grew up. Both sides of the street are lined with cars so we park a short distance away and walk over, arms looped together. I know I should say something just to break the tension we are both feeling but for once I'm at a loss for words. My stomach twists the closer we get to the O'Hagan house and I can't help but wonder if it was just a very bad idea to come here at all. Even though it's a cold night complete with an icy breeze that would cut through a person, the garden outside the house is filled with mourners standing in small groups, their chatter rising on their cloudy breath into the night sky. I search their faces to see if Laura is among them but if she is then she's well hidden.

'Maybe she's not here,' I whisper to Niamh.

'We should still go in though,' Niamh replies although it's definitely more of a question than a statement. I think we might be playing wake chicken with each other – hoping the other will call our bluff and we can walk away safe in the knowledge it wasn't us who made the final decision to just go home.

'I didn't bring any flowers,' I say, spotting a row of floral tributes lined up against the front wall of the house, ready to be loaded into the hearse in the morning and placed on top of the grave. My heart thuds at the sight of them – something about funeral flowers makes me feel deeply uneasy. Watching them wilt and decay on a grave reminds me too much that beneath the soil there is more decomposition. My stomach threatens to turn. Niamh, picking up on my mood, probably because I've just squeezed her arm as if I'm trying to push a ten-pound baby out, squeezes gently back.

'It's family flowers only,' Niamh says. 'I checked. With donations in lieu to the Foyle Hospice. I made a donation in our name earlier. I figured that would be easier.'

I nod again and blink back the tears that are threatening to fall. She's right, it is easier and I'm incredibly grateful for her thoughtfulness. When we reach the door I see Conal, Laura's older brother, standing in the doorway greeting mourners and rehashing the same script over and over again.

'Thank you. It was good of you to come.'

'Yes, it was good for her in the end, you know. She'd been through enough.'

'You can never really can prepare yourself, can you?'

'Mum's in the front room if you want to go on through.'

And repeat.

We shuffle forward, still clinging together. 'Remember you used to have a mad crush on him?' Niamh whispers in my ear and, eyes wide, I look at her, announcing, 'I did not!' probably a little too loudly. I'm lying, of course. I was absolutely mad about Conal but as my best friend's big brother he was deemed off-limits. Not that he ever showed even an ounce of interest in me.

Heads turn to look at us, people I don't know or only vaguely recognise. I nod an acknowledgement to them, grateful for the dark night that's hiding my scarlet face. When they return to their conversations, Niamh whispers again, 'You so did. You even had a photo of him Sellotaped in your diary. I remember.'

'You remember wrong,' I tell her, adopting the patented Shaggy defence. Just like his hit song 'It Wasn't Me', I will deny all charges levelled against me until the bitter end.

She shakes her head, a cheeky glint in her eye – one that isn't entirely appropriate as we reach the front door and the alleged object of my teenage affections is taking us both in.

There's a slightly too long moment of silence before Niamh detaches herself from me and thrusts her hand forward. 'Conal, I'm very sorry for your troubles. Your mum was a brilliant woman.'

'Thank you, it was good of you to come,' Conan says, almost robotically and I wonder, does he even register any more who he's talking to? He looks absolutely exhausted; his skin is dull, his eyes red-rimmed.

'She really was one of the best,' I say. 'She always welcomed us in as if we were part of the family.'

Conal blinks and looks in my direction and then to Niamh before looking back at me. 'Becki?' he asks. 'And Niamh?'

We nod in unison like two absolute day-release cases.

'God, it's been years. Sorry, I'm not quite myself at the moment, you know,' he says with a nod towards the inside of the house. 'I think we're all just existing on fumes at this stage.'

We nod again and I will myself to speak but find I've reverted to the version of myself who became tongue-tied every time he walked into a room. He must've thought me to be a complete eejit.

There's a pause before Conal breaks the silence. 'Well, I imagine you're here to see my sister,' he says.

'Yes,' we chime in unison and I want the ground to open up and swallow me whole. 'She's with Mum, I think,' he says. 'In the front room. Go on through.'

After yet another awkward pause we move on down the hall, Niamh whispering in my ear, 'Well, that went well and wasn't at all humiliatingly awkward.' I have to hold in a snort of laughter, my nerves doing what they normally do in situations like this and threatening to bring on a fit of the giggles – which would be absolutely atrociously timed. The worst of it is, I can tell that Niamh is on the verge of a full-on nervous laugh fest herself and we absolutely cannot allow that to happen.

'Take a deep breath, and let's settle ourselves,' I whisper as we shuffle forwards towards the front room, with me thinking this really is the worst idea in the world and I'd have been better off staying at home with Daniel, picking up his poo. There would be less chance of a disaster there than being anywhere near an occasion as stomach-churningly solemn as this.

But, when I see Laura, and see her face masked with grief, my urge to laugh disappears. I feel Niamh stiffen beside me and I know she feels the same.

We three were inseparable once. We used to joke that when one of us felt something, all of us did. We convinced ourselves we had some special psychic bond. The truth was that we were all just a little prone to being over dramatic, or at least I *thought* that was the truth. Because now, when I spot Laura, it hurts to see her so clearly in pain. Even though we've not spoken in ten years, I feel the urge to go straight to her and hug her and tell her I know how awful all of this is and that she doesn't have to go through it alone. Even the fear of her rejecting me doesn't hold me back. Before I know it, I am in front of her and I am trying to tell her how very sorry I am for her loss but the words are caught in my throat.

She stares back at me, her expression a mixture of shock and grief and something I can't quite put a name on.

'Laura, we're so very sorry,' I hear Niamh say from where she's now standing beside me. 'We were so shocked to hear the news and we just had to come and pay our respects.'

Laura's gaze flits between the two of us while I stand here like a mute eejit, trying not to blink, knowing that if I do my tears will fall and if I start crying, I might not stop.

'Girls...' she eventually says and suddenly I'm looking at all the different Lauras I've known over the years: the precocious six-year-old, obsessed with Sindy dolls and My Little Pony; the eleven-year-old who walked into big school that first day holding my hand and telling me it would be okay; the teenager who had been the first of us to get her period and who thankfully didn't try to scare the life out of us with horror stories about how awful it was; the Laura who had been my bridesmaid, and Godmother to Saul; the Laura who, despite our estrangement, still had a life interwoven with mine, and with Niamh, and the Laura who I'm now pulling into a tight hug while Niamh wraps her arms around us both and all three of us sob.

God only knows what our fellow mourners are thinking at the sight and sound of us but right in this moment, I don't care. As we eventually pull apart, sniffling and shaking, I notice the room has emptied of everyone except us. And Kitty, obviously, who is lying in peaceful repose in her open coffin, hands clasped and a slight hint of a smile playing on her lips.

'She looks well,' Niamh says, softly.

'Well, she's dead, so to be honest she could be better,' Laura says with a watery smile and the three of us burst into laughter, already so comfortable once again in each other's company that we're immediately back in tune with each other's sense of humour. Grief is never very far away though, and while she is laughing, Laura is still wiping tears from her face.

'But yes, she looks well. A lot better than she did in her last few days, if I'm being honest,' Laura says, gently touching her mother's face. 'The cancer had left her grey, you know. Old looking, and she was never old looking. But she looks beautiful now. At peace, you know.'

The three of us nod. 'She does,' I say.

'She had a hard time,' Laura blurts, prompting a fresh flurry of tears. 'I wanted to call you both, you know. She'd have loved to have seen you. *I'd* have loved to have seen you. But it's been so long and I was afraid you might tell me to get lost. You'd have every right to. You especially, Becks. After everything.'

I swallow down the uncomfortable feelings those words bring. 'After everything' covers a multitude of things it is absolutely not the right time to start poking at.

'Look, the important thing is that we're here now,' Niamh says as I turn my gaze from Laura back to Kitty to break the tension between us. 'And we'll be here for you in whatever way you need us to be. Isn't that right, Becca?'

I nod and take a deep breath – this is not the time for a faint heart. Big girl pants are on. I look at Laura again. 'Absolutely, just say the word!' I tell her and she tears up again, as do I – which of course prompts Niamh to let tears fall as well. And once again, we find ourselves part of a triple-strength hug and it feels so nice, and so safe and so...

'Dear me, what's all this wailing about? Kitty wouldn't have wanted that!' bellows a voice that sends a chill through my bones.

Ladies and gentlemen, Simon – the ex-husband who has to be the centre of attention at all times – has entered the building.

6

JE NE REGRETTE RIEN – EXCEPT SIMON

I suppose a tiny part of me feels sorry for Simon as three pairs of eyes turn to look at him and he spots that one of those pairs belongs to me. I see the colour drain from his face to the point that lovely Kitty looks positively glowing with vitality in comparison.

'I didn't think...' he begins, which could pretty much sum up everything you need to know about my ex-husband. 'I was just trying to lighten the mood a bit.'

'It's my mother's wake,' Laura says, through gritted teeth. 'We don't need any mood lightening.' I'm glad it's she who has spoken and not me because I might not have been so polite. But then again, I've not remained besties with Simon for the past ten years, while it seems Laura has.

Simon and I function on a strictly need-to-know basis; that is, we are in touch with each other when, and only when, we need to be to discuss some issue in relation to our boys. The last time we had any contact with each other was before the boys left for university, to make final arrangements for their financial support, and I'm absolutely okay with that. He's not someone whose company I particularly enjoy – which is probably part of the reason it hurt so much when Laura chose him over me. Was I really that unsufferable? The thought nips at me and I have to push it down. My friend is in pain. She needs me. She clearly recognises that Simon can be a gobshite at times. I don't have to say a word. He is hoisting himself by his own petard and I have ringside seats.

'Sorry,' he blurts, his pallor now replaced by a fiery red glow of embarrassment. 'I didn't think I'd find Rebecca and Niamh here.'

I bet he didn't. I feel Niamh take my hand and squeeze it tightly – a friendly reminder to keep my cool.

'We just wanted to pay our respects,' I say. 'Kitty was a great lady. A real friend to us.'

'She was, for sure. There's no doubt Kitty will be greatly missed,' he says in a sombre voice that screams am-dram enthusiast. There's a lack of authenticity to him that irks me. Everything about him is a performance. Even grief.

'We wanted to offer our support to Laura,' Niamh says.

'That's very thoughtful,' he says, and I want to tell him we didn't come here for his approval. This has absolutely nothing to do with him. It's infuriating to me that his very presence can get under my skin this way. I feel Niamh squeeze my hand once again and I glance at Laura who looks more than a little uncomfortable. Now is clearly not the time to start digging into the train wreck that was my relationship with Simon.

I notice the faces of a few mourners popping in through the doorway – checking if the big emotional reunion is over and they are safe to re-enter the room. It seems like the perfect opportunity to grab onto to make our departure.

'We were just going anyway,' I say and Laura blinks at me through watery eyes.

'You haven't even had a cup of tea,' she says.

'You know me – not a big tea drinker,' I tell her. 'And I don't want to steal the attention from your wonderful mum. But we'll be there at the funeral. Unless you prefer we didn't come?'

'Please do,' she says, grabbing my hand and squeezing. 'It would mean a lot to Mammy and to me too. I think I need my girls,' she says.

'Then we'll be there, won't we, Niamh?'

Niamh nods. 'Of course we will. And if you need anything, just get in touch. You can find us on Facebook.'

'I can pass on Rebecca's number,' Simon, who clearly hasn't got the message that he's about as welcome as a fart in a lift, says. Maybe I should thank him for his offer, but I'm not feeling particularly generous towards him.

Laura nods. 'Mammy really thought the world of you both,' she says. 'She hated that we'd grown apart. She'll definitely be smiling down at us now.' We all glance skyward as if there's a chance we really will see Kitty smiling down from her heavenly cloud. Of course we can't.

'We'll see you tomorrow,' I say, and Niamh and I make our way towards the door – where Simon is lingering. I nod in his direction but don't speak, not until I see Conal again. 'We'll be there tomorrow,' I call to him. 'Mind yourself, and mind Laura.'

He gives me a sad smile. 'I will.'

* * *

'Well, that didn't go as badly as I thought it might,' Niamh says as she drives me back home.

'It could've been worse,' I agree. 'Bloody Simon didn't help. But I'm glad we went for Laura. And her mum of course.'

'And Conal?' Niamh asks as she raises one eyebrow.

'Keep your eyes on the road,' I scold. I will not be drawn into any discussion about Conal O'Hagan and the crush I refuse to publicly admit I had on him a long time ago.

'I believe he's single,' Niamh says. 'Divorced a couple of years back. Not that you'd be interested in hearing that.'

'Quite,' I say, my gaze firmly on the road ahead, refusing to acknowledge the warm feeling that information gives me. We drive in silence for a minute or two.

'It's sad though,' Niamh says. 'Kitty being gone. First there was your daddy...'

The mention of my father does what it always does – it blanks out all other noise and every other thought. It brings a fresh wave of grief. I do not want to talk about him. Not because I don't care, but because I care too much. It's too raw. The pain is too great. I don't know if it will ever feel anything but raw. If the mention that he is gone will ever not feel like a kick in the stomach. I don't want Niamh to continue down this particular conversational path. Kitty may be fair game for our chat, but I don't want to think about my father. Or about how this is what will mark the second half of our lives – loss and grief becoming a more and more regular occurrence. It's not a happy conversation or a positive train of thought to get caught on. Generally, it makes me cry, drink too much wine and eat too many Kettle crisps, and subsequently feel as if my own demise is only a matter of moments away for the next few days as my body recovers.

'I found our old time capsule,' I blurt, knowing it will shift the focus from my least favourite topic of conversation quickly.

'No way!' Niamh exclaims. 'Where? Oh my God! You still had it? I'd forgotten about that! Have you opened it? Is it super cringe?' Her previously sombre tone of voice has been replaced by a giddiness. I can't help but smile.

'No, I've not opened it. I only found it this morning when I went to see my mum. Truth be told, I'd forgotten about it too but then we got to talking about Kitty, and what we were like when we were younger, and I remembered our summer projects.'

'Oh Jeez, super cringe,' Niamh laughs. 'Do not ever tell any of my children about that. I'll never live it down. We were such gacks. Did you find the other stuff too? The magazine and all those awful drawings of awful clothes?'

I shake my head. 'Nope, just the time capsule. I think that's cringe-worthy enough.'

'God, what age were we when we put that together?' Niamh asks. 'Fourteen or fifteen, maybe?'

'Sixteen,' I say. 'Well, the box says 1994, and I know we made it in the summer holidays so... we'd all have been sixteen. Laura might even have been seventeen.'

'I can't imagine any of mine taking the time to make a time capsule at sixteen,' she says. 'Definitely not cool.'

'We were never cool,' I say with a laugh. I used to be mortified at my lack of coolness in my teenage years. I don't know why. It's not like I eventually reached a cool stage at any subsequent age. I've made my peace with that now.

'We were cool in our own way,' Niamh says.

'Being able to do the full rap from "Shocked" by Kylie Minogue doesn't count, Niamh,' I reply with a smile.

'I still know every word,' she says and for a moment I'm tempted to launch into it and see if she joins in. But then I remember I'm sober and forty-six.

There's another pause in conversation as we turn into my street. 'Will you open it?' Niamh asks as she pulls the car over outside my house.

'The time capsule? Probably,' I tell her. 'But it would feel weird to open it on my own. I mean, I know we put a lot of stupid mementos in it but if I remember correctly, we all put some personal things in too. Hopes and dreams kind of stuff. It doesn't feel like mine to open in a lot of ways.'

'Then we should open it together,' Niamh says. 'You and me, and maybe Laura too. If she wants to. If it's not too awkward.' I know what she means. I'm not naïve enough to think a quick hug over the top of a coffin will erase all the hurt of the last decade. It was a nice start but it might never be more than that.

'Yeah,' I agree. 'It would be nice if we were all there together. I'll not open it until we've spoken to Laura about it first.'

We make arrangements for going to the funeral together and say our goodbyes. I'm just about to open the car door to get out when Niamh reaches over for a hug. 'I know nothing about that was easy for you,' she says. 'So I just wanted to give you a hug and tell you I love you and you're the best friend a girl could want. Will you be okay? On your own? I have to get back to the younger ones. Paul is working and Jodie's staying up at college in Belfast this weekend, but you're welcome to come with me if you can stand it. The boys will probably just hide in their rooms and shout at the Xbox, but Fiadh is very good at hugs and making you feel good about yourself.'

At seven, Fiadh was the surprise later-in-life baby none of us, especially not Niamh and Paul, expected, but she had very quickly become one of my favourite people in the entire universe.

'I'd love to,' I tell Niamh, the thought of a Fiadh super-hug warming my heart. 'But Daniel has been sick and I want to keep a wee eye on him. If anything happens to him while the boys are in Manchester, my life won't be worth living.'

Niamh smiles. 'No worries. I understand.' And maybe she does, but I know I've not really been honest with her either. If anything happened to Daniel it would kill *me*. He's my sole company on many a day and the one creature on this planet who is always happy to see me.

'I'll see you in the morning,' I tell her before she drives off and I walk up the garden path to my home and the sound of Daniel barking enthusiastically at my return. I think I'll let him sleep at the end of my bed tonight. Again.

7

HOLY CANDLE IN THE WIND

I hate funerals. Every last second of them. I hate how performative they are, the formality a stark contrast to the friendly welcome of the wake.

I know they are by their very nature sad and solemn affairs, but when I think of Kitty, I don't think of the woman the priest on the altar describes. He calls her 'a faithful servant of the Lord' more than once. He doesn't mention her grandchildren. He doesn't mention that she had a singing voice that gave the lucky listener goosebumps. He doesn't mention that she was the worst baker known to man and there was many a birthday cake left untouched by even the bravest of children because we all knew about the one time everyone who ate her cake got 'the scoots'. He doesn't mention her beauty, or her sense of style. He doesn't even mention her *joie de vivre*.

It rattles me and without realising, I find myself muttering out loud that the priest hasn't the first notion what Kitty was like and he is a sour-faced old fucker anyway, which gets me a bad look from an old woman with a face like a slapped arse sitting in the row in front. I want to stick my tongue out at her but I don't. I will remain respectful. Niamh takes my hand in hers. I assume it's a sign of comfort or affection, but maybe she's just afraid I'll flip the bad-look-giver the finger. She knows how funerals wind me up.

'I'm not going to say anything,' I whisper, but in my head I play out a scenario where I storm to the front of the chapel and address the congregation on how women, especially this woman, deserve more. I play out imaginary scenarios like this a lot in my head. More so in recent times as the Unexpected Waves of Sadness have become more frequent along with their counterpart: Unexpected Waves of Rage. My doctor thinks it might be hormonal. She urged me to consider HRT. I've told her it's not because of my hormones, it's just that I've had enough of women getting a raw deal and I don't want to keep quiet about it any more.

She nodded sympathetically and handed me a leaflet on peri-menopause and HRT as I left. It's still at the bottom of my handbag, along with a crumpled tissue, a fuzzy Polo mint and an indiscernible number of wrinkled poo bags.

At least, I think, the rage is stopping me from feeling profoundly sad. I don't want to let that particular feeling in just now because I fear if I start crying, I might not stop for a long time. Rage is safer.

Laura looks wretched as she follows the coffin out of the church towards Kitty O'Hagan's final resting place. Exhausted and drawn, her pale face is particularly stark against the black of her dress and coat. Aidan, her husband, is holding her hand and the hand of their only child, Robyn. I've not seen Robyn outside of pictures since she was six years old and I'm struggling to reconcile the image in my head of the joyful bundle of life I remember with the solemn-faced emo holding her dad's hand. She is wearing thick, clumpy army boots, a coat that looks as if it's been through a shredder and long, black fingerless gloves, perfect for showing off her black nail polish. Even in her grief she looks assured and sure of herself. Kitty must have bloody adored her. *I* bloody adore her and wish I had been as cool as she is when I was sixteen. Instead, I was making time capsules and learning Kylie Minogue raps.

'Are we going to the cemetery too?' Niamh asks when the Mass is over. I nod because it feels like the right thing to do. Even though I really don't want to. The memories of my father's funeral and burial are starting to come at me thick and fast but as usual, I push them down. We start to shuffle our way out of the pew to follow the procession of mourners when Simon appears in the aisle, waiting for us.

'Close family and friends are invited to The Bishop's Gate for lunch after the burial,' he says. 'I'm sure you'd be more than welcome if you want to come along.'

Niamh and I look at each other. That feels like an invitation too far given our prolonged estrangement. 'I think we might catch up with Laura another time,' I say. 'She doesn't need to be worrying about us.'

He shrugs, his badly fitting suit bunching up and giving him the look of an eighties' throwback, and walks off.

'Does his jacket have shoulder pads?' Niamh whispers, eyes wide, and the thing is, I'm pretty sure it does. How did this man ever not give me the ick?

I'm feeling quite sombre when I get home. I make sure to call my mother and tell her I love her. She's immediately suspicious but I assure her I'm not looking for anything except to tell her I love her. For a moment I think that makes her even more suspicious until she remembers that Laura's mum has just been buried. She tells me she loves me too and that I'm to look after myself. I promise I will before changing out of my mourning clothes into leggings and an oversized hoodie that is in danger of becoming ordinary sized due to my fondness of biscuits.

Daniel looks at me longingly and so I slip on my trainers, my puffa coat and my knitted beanie hat and grab his lead. 'You win, fellah,' I tell him. 'Let's go walkies.' He reacts with such joyous enthusiasm that I can't help but feel my spirits lift.

So we walk around the Culmore Country Park four times, not even taking a shortcut when the heavens open and the rain starts to fall in sheets, drenching us both from head to toe. I walk until I'm tired, the light is starting to fade and Daniel is regretting his enthusiasm for walks, and then we go home. I stick the heating on, dry Daniel off, strip out of my outer clothes and escape upstairs to run myself a deep, hot bubble bath.

I even go to the effort of gathering and lighting some candles and pouring myself a glass of wine before I strip out of my remaining saturated clothes and slip under the suds. It's not quite giving the luxurious spa vibe I would've liked. The collection of candles is a bit eclectic to say the least – including one designed to clear cooking smells, three tea-lights, the dregs of a Yankee Candle, and a holy candle with Our Lady printed on the outside which my mother brought me back from the shrine at Knock in County Mayo. But if I just focus on the cosy glow they give off then it works. My wine is cold and delicious and the warmth of the water is bringing life back to my frozen toes. I close my eyes and rest my head back, grateful that the boys are grown and gone and long past the stage of automatically needing a poo every single time I dared to try and relax in the bath. Yes, I miss my babies. No, I do not miss my babies' refusal to give me any peace and quiet.

The tension is just leaving my body when I hear my doorbell ring. No. No, I am not getting out of the bath and schlepping it downstairs wrapped in Saul's old dressing gown only to find someone looking to talk to me about Jesus or sell me something. I choose to ignore it, hoping against hope that whoever it is will get the message and clear off.

They don't, but instead ring the doorbell for a second time, which only prompts Daniel to burst into the song of his people and bark as loudly as his little doggy lungs will permit. The tension that had started to leave my body does an immediate about turn and crawls under my skin and into my very bones with remarkable efficacy.

When the doorbell rings a third time, followed by a loud rattle of my letterbox and a shout of, 'We know you're in there!' I give up the ghost and haul myself out of the bath.

I recognise the voice from my letterbox, of course. What I don't know is why she's at my front door right now. And why she has used the word 'we'.

'I'm coming!' I shout, pulling on the dressing gown and slipping my feet into my incredibly non-sexy but very comfortable fur-lined Crocs (let's start a campaign to normalise comfortable footwear, please!).

'Hurry up! It's throwing it down out here!' Niamh calls. Or at least I think that's what she shouts. Daniel has moved on to the next song in his back catalogue and is howling and scrabbling at the front door. I wonder if I could actually train him to answer it for me?

Flustered, sweating and deeply uncomfortable about answering the door with nothing hiding my vagina except for an old dressing gown that could possibly get caught in a draught, I make my way downstairs. Daniel dances around my feet, showing way too much excitement for a dog who's just finished a substantial walk, and I have to shoo him away before opening the door.

The 'we', it turns out, is Niamh and Laura – the latter of the two still dressed in her black dress and coat, her face streaked with mascara and one hand holding aloft a bottle of peach schnapps. My stomach lurches at the very sight of it, remembering many a hangover born from peach-flavoured over-indulgence.

'For old times' sake,' she says, with a hiccup. 'It's what Mammy would've wanted.' Laura staggers through my front door, and wraps herself around me in a hug. Over her shoulder I see Niamh mouthing, 'I'm sorry!' before adopting her very best teacher voice. 'Laura arrived at my house, very upset and said she needed her girls to get her through this evening and that nobody else could understand how much she was hurting.'

'I'm so, so sorry,' Laura sobbed into my shoulder. 'I really let you down, and I'm sorry. Forgive me please,' she cried.

'There's nothing to forgive,' I say, tears springing to my own eyes. 'And of course we'll be there for you to help you through this. Can I just put some knickers on first?'

8

WHO KILLED LAURA PALMER?

I feel so much better when I'm wearing a fresh pair of knickers. There was no way I'd have been capable of holding a prolonged conversation with anyone with my vagina not put away behind a good cotton gusset.

I've put on my favourite grey sweatpants with matching sweater. I give my hair a quick blast with the hairdryer before twisting it up on top of my head in a loose bun. In my mind I look like an effort-lessly chic influencer who lives a life of brunches with the girls and exudes natural beauty. In reality I probably look like an inmate in HMP Maghaberry – and the kind who would cut a bitch at that. But now is not the time to think about vanity – my friend needs me and that is what matters.

By the time I get back downstairs, Niamh has already set up her very own *ad hoc* cocktail bar and has mixed us three syrupy sweet peach schnapps-flavoured drinks. Even the smell is enough to evoke a memory from the late nineties of great nights out and less great mornings after. There was nothing quite like the hungover sugar crash that came following a night on peach schnapps and pineapple juice. What on earth had we been thinking?

'Here we go,' she chirps, and hands me a glass. I look at her face, and at Laura, who has stopped crying for the moment but whose eyes are horrendously swollen and red. All three of us stare into glasses with trepidation.

'Remember when this was all we would drink?' Niamh asks.

'We thought we were so cosmopolitan. Everyone else got wasted on alcopops or cider and we were drinking this,' I say, my nose wrinkling at the smell.

'I can't remember the last time I had peach schnapps,' Laura says, her voice hoarse from crying, and I want to tell her there's probably a very good reason for that, and the reason is that it's not actually very nice. I keep quiet though. I am putting all my energy into the girding of my loins to drink this sugar-laden concoction.

'Well, ladies,' Laura says. 'Here's to my lovely mammy who will be smiling down from heaven at the sight of the three of us together again. Cheers, big ears!' she says and we all knock our glasses together before taking a drink.

The sweetness makes my brain hurt and I shudder. Niamh, meanwhile, has lowered her glass and is staring at me wide-eyed. I know that look well. The twins used to get that look in their eyes when they overdosed on Fruit Shoots. We were either heading for chaos or an emotional breakdown.

I'm distracted by a gagging sound to my left and turn to see Laura staring into her glass as if it has just personally offended her. 'Dear God, that's sickly sweet,' she stutters.

'That's a very polite way to say rotten,' I tell her with a grimace.

'It's worse than rotten,' Niamh says. 'It's hoachin'.' Now there's a word I've not heard in at least a quarter of a century. In our younger years it was a frequent flyer in our vocabulary as a descriptor for really, really, really rotten. It could be interchanged with words such as bangin', boggin' and mingin'.

'It probably wasn't my best idea,' Laura sniffed, on the verge of tears again. 'I was just trying to do something nice in memory of Mammy and...' I wrap my arms around her as she gives in to a fresh round of sobbing.

'It was a lovely gesture,' I soothe her. 'And luckily, I have wine in the fridge so we don't have to keep drinking it if you don't want to. But if you do want to keep drinking it, then we will be brave and persevere in memory of the legend who was Kitty O'Hagan!'

Laura lets out a little laugh and then cries a bit more before settling herself. 'No, I think Mammy would understand if we gave up on the peach schnapps and went for wine instead,' she says.

'Thank God for that!' Niamh says, not wasting any time in fetching a bottle of New Zealand Sauvignon Blanc from my fridge and three wine glasses from the cupboard.

'I'll get some crisps out too,' I say, realising that we are all old enough now that soakage is an absolutely essential survival tool in avoiding the dreaded three-day hangover that seems to wade in uninvited whether it's a skinful or a thimbleful of wine consumed. 'And then we can talk properly.'

I have my back to Laura and Niamh as I decant a few packets of my finest Tayto Cheese and Onion crisps into bowls, and I'm just trying to work how many crisps is too many crisps when I hear an exclamation from Laura – and this time it's not a sob, or a cry, or an expression of grief.

'Holy shit!' she says. 'Where on earth did this show up?'

I turn to face her and, of course, she has the time capsule in her hands and is examining it intensely.

'Is that it?' Niamh asks me. 'Oh my God! Let me see it!'

I'm not sure why I feel nervous as they read what we had scrawled on the outside of this box thirty years ago, but I do. It's the kind of nervous where I feel itchy under my skin and very much on edge.

'God, remember that! When you insisted we spelled Becki with an i because it was cool?' Niamh laughs.

'It *was* cool!' I reply defensively, even though I haven't spelled my name like that since circa 2001. There comes a certain stage in life when saying 'It's Becki with an i' makes you sound emotionally stunted.

'It was,' Niamh agrees. 'I was so jealous that you had all these variations of your name you could choose and I was stuck with Niamh. There aren't any ways to shorten Niamh.'

'Or Laura either,' Laura says. 'Apart from Laurs, and I hated that.'

'But at least Laura was a cool name. Like Laura Palmer in *Twin Peaks*,' Niamh says and Laura shudders.

'I hated that show. It scared the bejaysus out of me. Remember that creepy bloke who did all the killing... what was his name again?'

'Bob,' I say, thinking of the face of the supernatural killer who still haunts my nightmares.

'That's it! Bob!' Laura says. 'Absolutely terrifying.'

'We have to open it, don't we?' Laura says once we have talked over the bizarre moments of the original *Twin Peaks* and agreed that the recent updated series was just a fever dream that made no sense to anyone.

'I think it would be rude not to,' Niamh says.

'I think we *need* to,' Laura says, her voice a little more sombre. 'God knows I could use a distraction from today.' The sad look on her face is enough to give me the push I need to lift the box and agree it is time for the great opening.

'I think we'll need scissors or a knife,' I say, examining the very thorough sealing of what is essentially a box of tat. We really did want to protect our secrets, it seems.

'And a top up of our glasses,' Laura says, grabbing the wine bottle from the kitchen counter.

'We might actually need a second bottle,' Niamh grimaces. 'And more Tayto.' She retrieves another bottle of wine from the fridge, effectively wiping out my in-house alcohol content and leads the way through to the kitchen where she immediately plonks herself down on the rug in front of the fire – much to Daniel's disgust. 'That,' his epic side-eye seems to say, 'is my spot'.

I sit down beside her and start running the edge of one of the blades of my pair of scissors along the join between the lid and the box itself.

'Do you know, I'd forgotten about this entirely,' Niamh says. 'It only came back to me when you mentioned it, Becca. I'd never have given it a moment's thought, otherwise. I'd a very hazy memory in the back of my mind but if you told me I'd dreamt it, I'd believe you.'

'We made it in Becca's kitchen if I remember correctly,' Laura says. 'Though didn't we all write our letters separately at home and bring them over? God only knows what utter guff I wrote. I can only imagine if Robyn were to write one now. It would be full of teenage angst and woe. I don't think we were as woe-filled as teenagers nowadays. Even before Mammy got sick, my beautiful, happy wee girl had morphed into a walking streak of misery.'

'It will pass,' I reassure her. 'Both my boys went through the horrors of thinking the world was a bin fire and that their generation are the only ones who ever gave a shit or tried to change things for the better. They seemed to care a little less once they got money in their pockets, were able to get into a pub without getting ID'd and didn't live at home any more.'

'We had our own dramas though,' Niamh says. 'And who'd be a teenager now. What with social media and the pressure to appear to have the perfect life all the time. At least when we were that age, and making absolute dicks of ourselves, we didn't have to worry if we would go viral the next day.'

'And we didn't have to worry about the world and his mother seeing our geeky teenage years either – you know, when you're still growing into your face. I swear I looked like Mrs Potato Head from 1990 through to 1996,' I say as I slice through another layer of yellowed tape. 'This is harder to get into than Fort Knox,' I mutter.

'You're showing remarkable patience,' Laura says. 'I'd have torn into that by now.'

'I don't want to risk damaging anything inside it,' I say as the blade of the scissors finally slips under the lip of the box lid. 'God only knows what valuable treasures are hidden inside this box!'

The room falls silent as I slice around the final layer of tape until the lid is free and ready to come off.

'I really hope this isn't rubbish,' Niamh says, as three sets of eyes fall on the shoebox that holds a snapshot of the people we used to be and the dreams we used to have.

9

'POSITION OF THE FORTNIGHT'

It turns out we used to pretty much be the nerdy teenagers we remember. The box doesn't hold a wealth of surprises. There are a couple of editions of *Smash Hits* magazine – one with Take That on the cover and another with Dean Cain as Superman. The part of my heart that was insanely in love with *Lois and Clark: The New Adventures of Superman* does a little flip. God, that man was gorgeous back in the day. As was Teri Hatcher as Lois Lane. She was my first girl crush. I blush when I remember getting my hair cut in the same bobbed style she wore as if that would set the scene for a glittering career in journalism.

I lost hours of my youth daydreaming that Clark Kent and Fox Mulder would battle it out for my affection. I make a mental note to look up how they have both aged as if that will be the deciding factor now as to which one wins my heart. I don't allow myself to think about how much I've aged.

There's a copy of *More* magazine, which we roar with laughter flicking through, especially when we reach the page outlining the Position of the Fortnight. It was as close to hard core pornography as our teenage selves got. Niamh and I would hide the magazine from our mothers lest we be scolded for reading such filth. Laura didn't have to hide the magazine from her mum, because Kitty was cool like that, but she would hide it anyway having determined she would rather die than discuss 'The Wheelbarrow' with her mother.

Not one of us had so much as seen a penis in real life and yet each fortnight we read that article as if we were nymphomaniacs with PhDs in the *Kama Sutra*.

There's an empty bottle of West Coast Cooler in the box, which makes all three of us have the fiercest craving for the super sweet wine spritzer, but not strongly enough for us to actually do anything about it. There are a couple of tickets for Squires nightclub, which obviously had been placed in the box by Laura or Niamh because in the summer of 1994 I had yet to set foot through the hallowed doors of Derry's most popular hot spot. It would be another year, and some, before I would finally lose my Squires virginity and join the heaving masses on the dance floor, giving it everything to 'Things Can Only Get Better' by D:Ream. The fact that the lead singer of D:Ream is a Derry man gave that song a much longer shelf life in our pubs and clubs than anywhere else. In fact, I'm sure they might still play it now.

We poke through other detritus of our teenage years – bus tickets, button badges with the CND symbol on them, a pair of love beads. We fancied ourselves as free-spirited hippy types when the truth was that the closest we came to being hippies was choking on Sandalwood incense and having to convince my mother it wasn't in fact weed, as she suspected.

There's an empty tube of Rimmel Heather Shimmer lipstick – the remnants of the glittery shade scraped out. We made things last back then.

'You can still get that,' Laura says of the shade that was ubiquitous in every cool girl's make-up bag through the nineties.

'No way,' I say, immediately conjuring the colour in my mind's eye and remembering the smokey-eyed, dark-lipped look that made anyone with a truly Irish complexion look like the undead.

Laura takes her phone from her pocket and taps at the screen before turning it and flashing it in front of my face. 'See! Rimmel Heather Shimmer! Still on sale! I bought some for Robyn, but I don't think she was impressed. It's probably lying somewhere in the midden she calls a bedroom.'

'You should retrieve it and steal it for yourself. Go old-school vintage with your bad self,' Niamh says, with a laugh.

'I think I'm just regular old these days,' Laura says. 'Things are starting to sag that did not sag before. And hair is growing in all the wrong places. I'm afraid I'll wake up one of these mornings to a full beard. We'll not even talk about the grey hair...'

'I don't know why I never realised that the hair on your head isn't the only hair that goes grey,' I say, blushing.

'Oh yes!' Niamh says. 'I'm not over the trauma of having a badger stripe *down there*.'

I snort in response.

'Tell me this,' Laura says. 'When all our other hair is turning grey, then why do the beardy whiskers come in thick and black? And how do they arrive on our faces already two inches long as if they've been there for weeks or months?'

'As if we needed any further proof that God is a man,' Niamh says. 'No female god would put any woman through menopause and make us watch our bodies sag and wrinkle in front of our own eyes. And what do men have to deal with while we're in hormone hell? A finger up the bum once a year to check their prostate? There's men who would pay good money for that. Oh, and sagging balls. That's it. That's their lot!'

The image of a sagging ball sack dances through my mind and I grimace. Although, much like the virginal 'Position of the Fortnight' guru I was in 1994, I have no direct experience of sagging balls. In fact, it's been quite some time since I've had any experience of balls at all. Simon's were the last pair I had been up close and personal with and I've long come to accept that will more than likely stay the case for the rest of my days.

'Nothin' worse,' Laura splutters, choking on her wine. I watch her closely, seeing the moment she remembers, of course, that there are greater tragedies in this world than the natural life cycle of male genitals and sobers up briefly.

I reach across and give her hand a little squeeze. 'It's okay to laugh, you know. Your mum loved a good laugh – especially at inappropriate moments.'

'She did enjoy a good testicles joke,' Laura sniffs, wiping a tear from her eye. 'I was lucky with her, wasn't I? She was the best of them.'

'She was,' Niamh says solemnly and I nod my head, aware that we have missed out on so much of each other's lives. Here Laura had been caring for her mother in her final months and neither Niamh nor I had known about it until it was too late to be of any real help.

'Do you want to talk about what happened?' I ask gently.

Laura shakes her head and takes another long drink of wine. 'I absolutely do not want to talk about it, but at the same time I think I need to talk about it. Conal's been great. Even Aidan's been great, but it's not the same as talking about it with my girls.'

Guilt nips at me, knowing we have not been 'her girls' for a long time now, but I had felt I'd no choice back then. She had let me down so badly.

'We're always here when you want to vent,' Niamh soothes, and she's right of course, because regardless of what is nipping at me I know that Laura needs us to be her friends right now. She's just lost the woman who raised her single-handedly. The only parent she really ever knew.

'She was unwell for a long time,' Laura says. 'Breast cancer. We thought she had beaten it but the kind she had was a sneaky wee bastard. It kept creeping back and not giving her any peace. She fought as hard as anyone could've fought. Lost her breasts, and her hair. Never her sense of humour, mind. She kept that right until the end when it was all too much. I bet you didn't even realise that was a wig she had on her in the coffin? She told me she would come back and haunt me if I didn't put her best wig on her and make her look beautiful.'

Laura is speaking so tenderly and yet the pain in her voice is evident. I know it only too well. I had the same pain in my voice when my father died. It's the kind of crack in you that can never be fixed so you just learn to live with it and adapt to its sharp edges.

'She did look beautiful,' I reassure my friend who nods.

'It was the best she'd looked in months,' Laura said. 'Did I tell you that Robyn helped me do her make-up? The funeral home did all the foundation stuff – they've special make-up for that you know. To keep them fresh looking.' She grimaces slightly. 'But Robyn and I did her eyes, and her blusher and lipstick. It was very special, you know. Three generations of women together in the room. Just us. We joked we should go full goth or drag queen. I said I'd grab her old Dolly Parton wig from the cupboard and go all out. Mum would've loved that, I think. It would've given the neighbours something to talk about. But we decided less was more, in the end.'

The thought of Robyn having the maturity and wherewithal to help her mother with this most tender of tasks bring a tear to my eye. I look at the time capsule – at the silly mementoes of the care-free life we had at sixteen and I think of Robyn, the same age, supporting her mother so sensitively. It's hard to believe the babies who crawled around our feet are now well on their way to adult-hood and making us so very proud.

We three sit in silence, processing what we have just discussed, and where we are in our lives, until Laura jumps to her feet.

'Right, none of this crying and being miserable. Kitty O'Hagan would not be a fan of that!' She scrolls through her phone until the opening bars of 'Simply The Best' by Tina Turner blare out. It was her mother's favourite song.

'Girls, you know I've not a note in my head so you better get on your feet and sing this with me, for my mammy.'

Without thinking, I'm on my feet and Niamh is too and while it's fair to say none of us are exceptionally blessed in the vocal depart-ment, what we lack in talent we make up for in enthusiasm. We sing at the top of our lungs until the very last bars of the song, before plonking ourselves back on the floor and raising a glass to Kitty.

'She should've lived a bigger life,' Laura says. 'Don't you think? If she'd been born in our generation she probably would've trav-elled the world, gone to see Tina Turner in concert loads of times, been fabulous and eccentric and beautiful.'

'Maybe, but she always seemed happy with you and Conal and your home was always a happy one,' I tell her, thinking what use are ifs and buts at this stage of the game.

'Oh, she was,' Laura says. 'She told me she'd no regrets about her life and I believed her. She seemed content but sometimes I wonder if she was content because it was all she knew?'

Niamh shrugs. 'Possibly, but surely content is content. That's all any of us can hope for at the end of the day.'

The word bubbles over in my mind. Am I content? Is this the life I thought I would live? The time capsule seems to call to me, and I can't help but think of the sixteen-year-old version of myself, with all her hopes and dreams, and what she thought her life would look like when she reached my age. How she'd hoped to one day meet her own Clark Kent – which Simon most definitely was not. I don't think sixteen-year-old me thought she'd be living alone with a dog who had a sensitive gut, and wondering when her offspring would get round to calling her next.

I dig through the box and the remaining trinkets until I reach the bottom and see what it is I've been looking for. It's the girl I was all those years ago, speaking from the heart and sharing her hopes and dreams. Alongside the yellowed envelope are two more. One labelled with Laura's name and another with Niamh's. These are our love letters to ourselves, I think, as I pass them around, and this seems to be the perfect time to rediscover them. And it is almost 2024, after all, so we're not cheating by sneaking a look now.

My heart thuds in my chest as I recognise my own handwriting on the envelope, the memory of sitting on my bed writing this letter all those years ago flashing into my mind as clear as if I am watching it on a TV screen. Each of us had written our letters on our own, in our respective homes and had placed them in the box already sealed. We did not discuss the contents, instead agreeing that what went in the letters was as private and confidential as could be and we were in no way obligated to share them with each other. Not then, and not whenever we would uncover them again. Which, of course, is now.

'I'm not sure I'm emotionally ready for this,' Niamh says, staring glassy-eyed at her envelope. Laura has gone very quiet too.

'Me neither,' she says. 'And I think I definitely need to be sober.'

That isn't the worst idea in the world. Doing a deep dive into where I thought my life would be around now is probably not a good idea on the day of a funeral when I'm feeling fragile anyway.

'Tomorrow then, maybe,' I say. 'And we don't have to read them in front of each other. We made a promise, remember. What goes in the letter is between us and our god.'

'I think, actually, I need to get some sleep now,' Laura says and yawns, still holding her letter close to her chest. Of course, her yawn sets off a domino effect and Niamh and I soon join in the yawn chorus too. It's then I realise I'm already way past tired and that even climbing the stairs to bed will require significant effort.

'We should call a taxi,' Niamh says. 'Neither of us is able to drive.'

'You could stay here,' I offer. 'If you want. The boys' rooms are available and they're clean. I've been in with the hazmat suit on and gutted them after the lads went to university. There's new bedding and everything on them – I know how gross teenage boys can be.'

Laura gives a small smile. 'Teenage girls aren't much better. Believe me.'

'Seconded,' Niamh smiles. 'But yes, if you don't mind, the thought of climbing up stairs and getting into bed instead of schlepping across town in a taxi and into the loving but extremely demanding embrace of my family sounds great. Laura, what do you think?'

Laura is already fumbling with her phone and I assume she's calling a taxi, but she raises a finger to request we give her just one minute before she looks up. 'That is my husband and child informed that I'm having a sleepover. Now, direct me to my resting place. Or is that too morbid a way to put it after the day we've just had?'

'I think you get special dispensation for an inappropriate sense of humour on a day like this. Follow me,' I tell her, before leading my friends upstairs where I hand them some of my oversized T-shirts, and spare toothbrushes from the bathroom cabinet and bid them goodnight.

The mess downstairs can wait until morning, I think, as I carry out my evening ablutions.

When I get to bed I find that Daniel has been performing his usual bed warming duties, making sure I have as little space as possible on which to sleep, but I don't mind. It's nice having a warm body to cuddle – even if it is just a dog's.

If I expect to nod off straight away, I'm let down by my body's refusal to play ball. The envelope, now on the nightstand, is calling to me and I know I haven't a chance of sleeping until I've read it.

Frig it, I think. I'm going in.

10

---

* * *

15 August 1994

Dear Future Me,
    This feels really weird, but here I am, writing a letter to the me I'll be in thirty years' time. I'll be forty-six or forty-seven. FORTY-SEVEN — that's actually really, really old. Not like my-granny old, but you know, the kind of old where you're happy to sit in the house and watch Coronation Street or Casualty in your slippers and cardigan.
    Mum is forty-seven and she's always complaining about wrinkles and grey hairs, or her back hurting, or the change of life (which she whispers in case Daddy or Ruairi hear her and, I don't know, accidentally grow a vagina or something).

She's always telling me to enjoy my freedom now because once I settle down, I'll 'know what's sticking to me'. But, of course, she never lets me do ANYTHING so I'm not entirely sure what 'freedom' I'm supposed to be enjoying. Freedom to wash the dishes? Freedom to hoover the stairs?

Laura and Niamh are allowed to go out every weekend to The Embassy or Squires and I'm sure their parents know they're drinking too – even though they're only sixteen and took the Pledge on their Confirmation Day. Mum says she'll talk to Dad about letting me out, maybe when I'm seventeen and as long as I don't drink, have all my homework done for the weekend, and my grades don't start slipping. She's obsessed with my GCSE results and what A levels I'm going to study for. There are other important things in life!

The thing is, I don't even want to drink when I go out. I'm a bit scared of how it might make me feel, and what if it makes me make a complete eejit out of myself?

That's without even worrying about the fact it's illegal! I'm only sixteen. I don't need to get in trouble with the law. Knowing me and my luck, I'd get caught the first time I even tasted a West Coast Cooler and arrested and carted home in the back of a police Land Rover.

I'd never live down the shame, and I'd probably be grounded until I'm actually forty-seven.

Anyway, I just want to go out and dance and maybe meet someone. It's so embarrassing that I'm sixteen and not so much as had my first snog yet. I'm starting to think I might die alone.

Niamh says I won't because I'm a babe, but I think she might only be saying that to be nice. If I really was such a babe, surely I'd have snogged someone by now. Niamh has snogged four different boys already. And she was chatted up by a thirty-year-old in The Embassy. She told him he was old enough to be her da and to get lost.

Laura says there's not much talent to be had in Derry anyway. That's why she is mad about Soupie. (That's not his real name by the *way – he's called Colm Campbell = Campbell's Soup = Soupie). He's from Belfast and in Derry studying at Magee. He's eighteen and Laura is dying about herself because she's going with an older man, but not a creepy older man like the fellah in The Embassy.*

I wonder if Derry will still be called the Maiden City when I'm forty-seven? Will all the good fellahs here still get snapped up early by the Majellas? Laura says the ones left behind tend to have all the appeal of a mouldy banana. Still, it would be nice to find this out for myself.

But anyway, that's not what this letter is supposed to be about. This is me setting out what I want my life to look like by the time I'm forty-seven.

I don't want to end up like my mother who wears a sour face all the time, as if she's disappointed in the way her life has turned out. Cheers, Mum, by the way, for making one of your actual children feel like they annoy you just by breathing.

I want to live a fabulous life. I want to travel the world and walk along the Great Wall of China, or climb Kilimanjaro and watch the sun set from inside my tent high up on a snowy slope. I want to run along the moors in Yorkshire and imagine I'm Cathy's ghost searching for my Heathcliff. I want to wash my hair with Timotei shampoo under a water-fall in some tropical island before spending the rest of the day reading while swinging in a hammock, one leg lazily draped outside. I want to drive along Route 66 in a convertible car with my hair blowing wildly behind me, listening to Hootie and the Blowfish or the Gin Blossoms.

If I do get married, I want it to be to someone who looks like Fox Mulder from The X Files. But I'm absolutely not looking to get married any time soon. (And given that I haven't even had my first snog, that one is probably going to be easy to achieve.)

If I have the choice, I really would like to be in my very late twenties or early thirties – and will have done all my travelling and seeing the world. Maybe I'll marry someone I met along the way. A hunky Italian or something. That would make Laura pea-green with envy. After all, having an Italian lover would be way, way cooler than a boyfriend from Belfast.

Me and my gorgeous new husband would settle down in our beautiful home by the sea (of course) and maybe have two children – a boy and a girl. I'll not be like my mother. I'll be cool and chilled out and when my teenage children want to invite friends over, I'll let them order in pizza and not just get one of the cheap frozen ones out of the freezer instead. Those things never cook right. One minute they're still icicles, and the next they are charred remains of something that used to look like a pizza once, a long time ago.

We'll definitely have a den where the teenagers can hang out, so that my Italian husband and I – who will still be hopelessly in love – can snuggle together and drink wine in the evenings like the very sophisticated people we are. I will not walk around with a face like a slapped arse just because I'm having a hot flush.

Career wise? What I'd love is to be a journalist working on one of the big magazines like Cosmo, or More, or Vogue (Actually, maybe not Vogue. I don't think anyone who works there ever eats anything and I do like to eat, and I've never really had the kind of figure that could get away with size-zero clothes). Maybe I'll have my own column with a picture byline, and perhaps be invited onto TV talk shows, like This Morning with Richard and Judy. I accept I will never be size zero, but maybe this puppy fat will have disappeared – although given that I'm almost seventeen and it's still here, I'm starting to think it's actual full-on dog fat and it's never leaving. Laura is a size ten and Niamh is a size twelve. I'm a fourteen and feel like a mountain beside them. I hope it will even out and I'll be the kind of woman who can wear tailored suits and high heels and my Italian husband will really, really fancy me.

I suppose the only other thing I really, really hope is that Laura and Niamh and I are still friends like we are now. I've been friends with them *since our first day at primary school and I don't remember my life before they were in it. I just hope we'll always be there for each other.*

   Much love,
   Me xxx
   Becki Burnside, Aged 16

.

11

NOTHING BUT A HOUND DOG

If sixteen-year-old me was sitting here beside me in this room right now, there is so much I'd want to say to her. I'd tell her to be nicer to her mother for a start. And let her know than neither forty-six or forty-seven is old, thank you very much. I might even tell her that, in my experience thus far, snogging boys is more trouble than it's worth. Although that might send her into a depression cycle that could negatively affect the trajectory of her life – and God knows her life isn't jetting off to a happy-ever-after ending anyway.

Ultimately though, I'd apologise to the young Becki for letting her down so badly. It was up to me, after all, to carry the baton of her hopes and dreams forward and live the incredible life she'd imagined for herself.

Instead, what have I achieved? I am a divorcee, and have not so much as met Fox Mulder, never mind married him. I do not write for a major glossy magazine and nor have I ever done so. My career has only reached the dizzying heights of copy writing for a B2B marketer, where I spend my days writing and rewriting the same articles, just putting a slightly different spin on them depending on who our latest client is. It does not excite me or make me eager to get to my desk each morning. There are few, if any, perks outside of gifted branded mugs and pens from our clients. Although I did once get a really good golf umbrella which has been a life-saver on dog walks.

It's certainly not on a par, however, with sitting on the sidelines at London Fashion Week or writing a pithy monthly column à la Carrie Bradshaw.

I dare say Ms Bradshaw would have a stroke if she poked her head in my wardrobe and tried to find inspiration from my shoe collection. I doubt she ever had cause to pop her head into Matalan to pick up a new pair of heels before a night out, or ever whooped with joy at grabbing a pair of shoes for just £3 in the Primark sale.

As for teen me's ambitious plans to travel the world? I'd let myself down on that score too. Yes, I've been on a few holidays, none of which could ever be described as particularly inspiring. I've been to Spain and Portugal a handful of times, enjoying the best all-inclusive family fun offerings our budget would allow. I've even been for a week in a beautiful but absolutely arctic cottage in the Scottish Highlands, but aside from the cold, there really wasn't that much to write about. Scenery? Lovely. House? Freezing. Too remote to hear the lovely lilt of the Scottish accent half as much as I would've liked. The wine was good. The end.

I've never climbed a mountain – not even a small one like Mount Errigal in Donegal – or driven along Route 66. I experience 'the fear' driving on the M2 into Belfast, which is one of only a smattering of motorways that exist in Northern Ireland. Any road with more than two lanes going in each direction gets my IBS gurgling. I have sworn at my satnav much too often for comfort as I found myself trying to navigate four lanes of traffic to turn right only to be told to make a U-turn if possible.

It is rarely possible.

My world, and my life, is therefore relatively small. It's not much bigger than my own mother's has been if I really think about it. I've always put the grand adventures on the long finger. I'll do them when the boys have gone to university. I'll do them when I've lost a bit of weight. I'll do them when I can afford to take some extra holiday time. I've consoled myself all these years with the notion I have time to do things. But I'm not sure that I do any more. More and more I watch TV and there are adults on my screen who tell me they were born in the year I left school and I wonder how, in all that is under God, that is even possible. I've noticed that I'm slipping into that invisible stage of life that only a middle-aged woman can truly recognise. Too old to be noticed in the street, too young to be offered a seat on the bus. If middle-aged women were a colour, we'd be beige. Or worse still, greige. The kind of fad colour that everyone loves for a while and then gets bored of seeing everywhere so they just paint us out. Replace us with someone fresher and bolder.

I feel sad as I snuggle down under my covers, wishing I'd left reading the letter until morning. Nothing ever seems as bleak in the morning – not even the wistful witterings of a former incarnation of myself when compared with how my life has actually panned out.

I hope that Laura and Niamh have kept their own missives unopened. Today has been tough enough.

'I'm not sure I'm a fan of this being a grown up carry on,' I whisper into Daniel's ear as he curls his body against mine. I feel his paw touch my arm and try to convince myself it's his way of providing a reassuring hug. Chances are he just wants me to get out of the bed altogether so he can claim it all for himself, but I pretend not to be wise to his carry on and just give him an extra little hug back.

Nope, sixteen-year-old me definitely did not envisage that my only nocturnal companion at forty-six would be a dog with boundary issues.

12

A REAL FIXER-UPPER

I have realised I have a limited number of choices available to me at this time. I can choose to laugh at the letter and at how naïve young Becki was. I can scoff at her, fuelled by my years of life experience which have taught me that there are more than two certainties in this life. On top of death and taxes, there is also 'shit happens'.

I can then toss the letter in the bin and forget about it, and given my memory at the moment, that would probably happen quite quickly. I really must look into some sort of supplement to try and save what is left of my cognitive ability to remember anything at all.

If I'm feeling really dramatic, I can get the old metal bucket that normally lives in my shed, stick it in the middle of the garden and set fire to the damn letter in it. It could be some sort of cleansing ritual. I might even get some sage in and burn it to ward off negative vibes. Then I can forget about the whole sorry episode and continue on with my unremarkable life.

Or, is it possible this could be something positive? Maybe it's a celestial kick up the arse from Kitty or my dad, or my poor guardian angel who must despair of me at times.

I don't turn forty-seven for another ten months. That gives me oodles of time, or more accurately probably just one oodle of time, to try and achieve some of teenage Becki's life goals.

Okay, it's highly unlikely I'm going to get to travel the world, take an Italian lover, suddenly lose the puppy fat that has stayed my life-long companion, or get a monthly column in *Marie Claire* or *Red* magazine for that matter, but surely I can do *something*. Can't I?

I can fast-track this if I really put my mind to it. I can't argue that I have the distraction of children under my feet – unless we count Daniel who is a de facto child. My parents are no longer forbidding me from having any kind of a social life. I'm even old enough, and in possession of a house of my own, so if I wanted to invite friends back – and by friends, I mean a man – for some alone time together I can. That thought makes my tummy feel funny, but not in a good way. I have not had the right kind of alone time with a man since Simon left, and if I'm being honest with myself, there wasn't much alone time with him in the year or so before he cleared off either. No, he was too busy enjoying alone time with another woman whose name we do not mention. Ever.

It might be late on a Saturday night and it might just have been a long and stressful day, and I may be on the drunker side of tipsy on wine and peach schnapps but I suddenly feel more focused and awake than I have done in years and I know there is little to no chance that I'm going to get any sleep any time soon.

I read over the letter young me wrote once again, before grabbing a notebook and pen from my nightstand and scribbling down bullet points under the headline of 'Key Objectives'.

Live a fabulous life: Young Becki wanted to climb Mount Kilimanjaro or walk along the Great Wall of China. Middle-aged Becca already refers to her left knee as her 'bad knee'. She gets incredibly, irrationally angry when it is too hot or worse still, too humid. But that doesn't mean she can't still do some of the fabulous things.

I could definitely still go to Brontë country and feel the stiff breeze on the moors. It might even be more fun now I know the true hero of the piece was Brontë herself and not, as I thought at sixteen, Heathcliff. What a disappointment he turned out to be!

Wash my hair under a waterfall like in the Timotei ad: First of all, I must ascertain whether they still make Timotei. Secondly, I must research a fabulous tropical retreat – with really good air con – which has a waterfall shower so I don't have to stand under a freezing stream like I'm taking part in a Bushtucker Trial. Tropical retreat must have a hammock in which I can snooze/read.

Drive along Route 66 listening to the Gin Blossoms or Hootie and the Blowfish: No. Hours in a car with my post-twin pregnancy bladder is not a good idea. Nor, given my ability to get lost driving into Belfast, is giving me a car to drive across an entire continent. But, I suppose, I could do Ireland? Hire a convertible, turn up the Hootie and drive along the glorious Antrim coastline. I'm almost guaranteed not to get lost in those circumstances.

Find a love interest of Italian descent or who resembles David Duchovny in the early X Files *era*: As much as there is a little, tiny, teeny frisson of a long-lost libido eeping with excitement inside me at the thought of my taking a lover, there is a bigger, terrified screaming voice of my current libi-don't laughing hysterically at the very notion. I have become comfortable in my big knickers and free growth of body hair. I don't think I even remember how to snog, never mind perform any form of sex act. But would that be letting sixteen-year-old me down? Maybe I'll look into dating apps. How bad can they be?

Have a very fancy house by the sea, with a den and a luxury lounge: Not going to happen on my salary. Sorry Becki.

Have a glamorous career writing for a glossy magazine and attending fancy media things: It's a bit of a swivel to go from writing about the ten best ergonomic office chairs to getting a monthly column in Cosmopolitan. I'm not sure it's possible in the space of ten months, but maybe I could do something? A blog? Definitely not a vlog or TikTok. Perish the thought! Could I approach any local glossy publications? Maybe *Northern People*? Didn't one of my old school friends get a fancy job there? What could I pitch? Since *More* magazine is now defunct, maybe I could resurrect the Position of the Fortnight? But it would be Position of the Month, updated for menopausal women, and instead of sex it would be how to get comfortable enough to sleep despite night sweats and your bad knee?

Lose the puppy fat: No. Yes, I could stand to be a little healthier and not snack on all the lovely bad food so much. But I've been fighting this battle for almost half a century. Isn't it time to just stop hating myself or thinking I'll only be a decent person if I'm a couple of sizes smaller? I'm so tired of being so incredibly self-critical all the time. Maybe my goal should be simply to love the puppy fat, and myself, a bit more? Imagine how revolutionary it would have been to have embraced that message at sixteen. Maybe that's something I could pitch a column about?

* * *

After writing it all down, I feel invigorated and inspired. I feel grateful, even, that I have uncovered the letter and the time capsule with still enough time to at least try and achieve some of young Becki's goals. Maybe it's also about time I stop referring to her as young Becki. She's me. She's Rebecca Burnside. And my goals might have shifted a little, or got lost by the wayside but I still have goals. I can still achieve things. I don't have to ghost through life solely as a support act for the next generation. I'm not obliged to view myself like I would a carton of milk dangerously close to its use-by date – with suspicion and a reluctance to make any plans for it.

With my head buzzing with ideas and, dare I say it, hope, I snuggle down under my duvet and smile as Daniel shifts around and makes himself comfortable. I don't know what I'd been so afraid of. It was only a letter and sure, if it lights a fire under me to finally start doing big things then that's not a bad outcome.

13

___

HOLD UP, WAIT A MINUTE

It's been a long time since the three of us sat around a breakfast table, green to the gills and trying to figure out what we can have for breakfast, having examined the contents of my cupboards and fridge.

'The way I see it,' Niamh says, 'is we have two approaches. We play it safe and go with toast and coffee. No one ever died from toast and coffee. It will get us through these first dark hours anyway.'

I wash back two paracetamol with a drink of water before passing the box of tablets on to Laura who does the same.

'Or we could adopt the kill or cure approach. You've eggs, bacon and sausages there, Becca. I say we cook them up, along with the toast and the coffee. Make them into one dirty big toasted sandwich each and get it down our necks.'

Laura groans. 'I'm not sure I've the constitution for that,' she says.

'Nonsense,' says Niamh. 'It's long known that an 'Ulster fry' is the perfect cure for over-indulgence. What's the worst thing that could happen?'

'Well, erm, you did say it was a kill or cure approach, so I think the kill outcome might suck a bit,' I tell her.

'You make a fair point,' she says. 'But I'm sticking the frying pan on anyway. Just let me know if you want some.' I love that Niamh can treat my home like her own. It's true in reverse too. I know what belongs in what cupboard chez Niamh and I'm not above making myself a cup of tea and digging into the biscuits. It used to be like that at Laura's too, but I suppose it's different now. I look at my friend who is best described as a picture of misery. Her face is paler than normal. Her black dress is wrinkled and her hair is messy. She looks smaller than before, as if her grief is weighing so heavily on her it is compressing her.

'I'm so tired,' she says, and I remember that. It's not just that we had a late night or that we were drinking. I remember the exhaustion that comes after the funeral when the world goes back to normal and you're just left shellshocked by the last few days.

I could barely speak, let alone move around, in the days after my daddy's funeral. Every single ounce of energy I had was used to remind me to keep breathing, and to play different edits of the last few days over and over and over.

My phone ringing and my mother's voice sounding strange and strangled. How it took a moment for me to realise just how serious things were. How there was a lag in my brain as I heard what she said but didn't understand it. These words did not make sense. Not when it came to my daddy.

'Rebecca,' my mother had said, her voice tight. 'I need you to come home. Now. I need you to come home right now. Your dad... I don't think... well, he's not very well, Rebecca and I don't know what to do and I need you to come home now.'

'What's wrong with him?' I'd asked, the sound of my mother's voice enough to wrap a coil of dread around me and pull it tight. 'Can I talk to him?'

'No. No. No, love. You can't talk to him. He's not... He can't. Can you please come home.'

Her voice had cracked at the word please and I'd known then. I'd known he was gone even though we played the game for another while. I phoned an ambulance as I ran out of my house and to my car. I stabbed at the ignition with my keys but my hands were jelly, and the whole world was distorted and I knew nothing would ever make sense again. Not in the way it once had.

The ambulance hadn't arrived by the time I got there. I don't remember getting out of the car but I remember going in the front door which my mother had left open. I don't remember going up the stairs or down the hall, but I do remember the look on my mother's face. She looked scared, and small and vulnerable. My father looked at peace and I remember wanting to shout at him, 'Do you not know you're dead? How can you lie there so calmly when we need you?' He looked so at ease and if it hadn't been for the unnatural pallor on his face, or the way his mouth was drooped ever so slightly I'd have said he looked well.

I remember the thunder on the stairs, the call of the paramedics. I remember telling them he was gone as they ran into the room and started to examine him and I wanted to tell them they were wasting their time because he was not here any more. The energy in the house had shifted. The energy in the whole world had shifted. Because my daddy was dead.

I didn't have time to process it. The machine of death and dying took over. Neighbours offering to help. A doctor. A priest. An undertaker. Mourners. Shopping for black ties for the boys in Marks and Spencer and having a mini-breakdown by the fleece jumpers near the checkout. My daddy loved his fleece jumpers but he only ever wore the ones from Marks and Spencer. I had one lifted and over my arm to treat him before it really hit me that he didn't need it. He never would. Through sobs, I bought it anyway. It's still in the bag in the back of my wardrobe.

I remember cups of tea, and discussions about hymns, and some laughter and singing. I remember my boys sobbing like children over his coffin just before the lid was put on for the last time. These two six-foot-tall boys who had already become men even though they were just seventeen, looking at me as if I could make it better. That was my job, after all.

I remember just getting through it and then not knowing what the hell I was supposed to do when it was all over. Every cell in my body was frozen in shock and exhaustion and I recognise that now on Laura's face.

'Do you want to grab a shower while we make breakfast?' I ask her, remembering how the shower became my salvation. I could be alone, and cry and shout, and wash a little bit of the horror of the days that had been off me. No matter how dark the days that followed, I always felt just a little better after a shower.

She blinks up at me. 'I don't have any clean clothes. I think I'll just go home.'

'I have clean clothes,' I say. 'They'll be big on you but they are clean enough to help you feel more human again. I'll get you a sweater and a pair of drawstring joggers. They'll do in a pinch. I'm afraid any spare underwear I have might swamp you, so you might have to go commando.'

'I have spare knickers in my car,' Niamh says. 'We're the same size, aren't we? I can get them for you.' Both Laura and I turn to look at her.

'Spare knickers? You're going to have to explain that one,' I say. 'Is that something we're supposed to do?'

'They're in my go-bag. I have a full change of clothes, a multi-pack of new knickers, toiletries, trainers, power banks, some cash etc,' she says, as if it's a perfectly normal thing to have.

'A go-bag?' I ask. 'What's that? Are you on the run from the law or something?' I can't help but smirk.

'Everyone should have a go-bag,' she says, her face serious. 'You never know when you might find yourself in dire straits. It just means I'm prepared in case of emergencies. You never know what might happen in the world in this day and age. It could be anything.'

'What, like the zombie apocalypse or an alien invasion?' I ask, partially intrigued and impressed, and partially just very amused that Niamh has this secret survivalist side to her.

'Mock all you want,' she says, 'but come the day of the revolution I'll be chatting on my fully charged phone, wearing my new knickers and you'll be there with not so much as *Candy Crush* to distract you nor a clean pair of pants to wear. You know it makes sense.'

The depressing things is, she's not wrong. There's another thing to add to the list of worries that come with middle-age. Having to be the most adult adult in the room and be prepared for all eventualities.

'A shower would be nice,' Laura says, drawing us back to her. 'Fresh clothes would be nice. I think I might burn this dress. I don't see me ever wearing it again.'

'We can totally do a ceremonial burning of your frock if you want,' I say before remembering the black dress and jacket I still have hanging in the wardrobe from my dad's funeral and which I have not worn since. Every time I so much as see them, I come out in hives. 'And I'll burn my clothes from Dad's funeral too,' I add.

'That sounds like an idea,' she says, with the smallest hint of a smile. Even though it's sad and doesn't quite reach her eyes, I know she feels marginally better than she did first thing and that is a good thing. I give her shoulder a little squeeze and she reaches up to squeeze my hand back.

'Right,' I say. 'You come with me and we'll get you organised. Niamh – go fetch your go-bag and the new knickers.' They both nod and we don't so much as spring into action as gently amble in the vague direction of action. Hangovers never used to be this bad.

* * *

By mid-afternoon, I'm done in. It has taken all of my energy today to just keep putting one foot in front of the other. Laura had showered and dressed while Niamh and I had hammered together an artery clogging concoction that thankfully didn't kill us. I won't say it cured us either, but it aided the start of our recovery.

Once they'd left, I'd taken Daniel for a walk which I'd hoped would blow the remaining cobwebs away. It had almost blown Daniel away, never mind the cobwebs. I was worried he'd turn into some sort of kite/dog hybrid.

After battling to dry him off when we got home, I'm trying to gather strength enough to shower and change into my pyjamas even though it's not long dark and there are hours to go until bedtime. Drinking a well-earned mug of tea, my mind wanders back to the list I'd written in the wee small hours after reading the letter from the time capsule.

I wish I'd had the chance to discuss it with the girls but it didn't seem appropriate. Not when Laura was clearly struggling with the aftermath of all that had happened this week. We didn't even get the chance to burn the blasted clothes of doom – as we decided to call them – thanks to a pretty non-stop deluge of November rain making it impossible to set fire to anything successfully in the garden. Sadly, the fire in my living room is gas and enclosed, and useless for burning cursed items so we have decided to wait until another day.

So for now, the first part of my adventures will fall to me. Obviously, I'm quite limited as to what I can do on a rainy night in late November but I suppose it won't hurt to have a quick look at some of the dating apps.

I don't know much about online dating. I've heard it talked about on TV of course, and on social media. I know Tinder is viewed as a bit of a hook-up site. Bumble and Hinge are the two others I've heard talked about but are any of them suitable for a woman of my age and appearance? As I look at the pictures of fresh-faced, bubbly and no doubt sexually adventurous young things looking for love, I start to feel like I haven't a chance of getting noticed, never mind asked out.

If these apps were like Pet Rescue Centres, the gorgeous young things would be the cute labradoodle puppies that look like lead characters in Disney animations and everyone wants. Meanwhile I'd be the oldest, most cantankerous mutt in the pound. I can imagine the wording of my appeal:

Can you give this old girl a loving home?

Due to no fault of her own, this friendly, if a little skittish at times, mutt, has found herself without a forever family.

All Becca wants to be happy is a warm bed, regular exercise (not too much exercise) and toys to entertain herself. (Get your mind out of the gutter!)

Is good with other dogs but can be possessive about her food.

Mostly continent but given her age can have the occasional accident. Especially when she coughs or sneezes.

Are there dating sites for more mature ladies? I type in 'mature lady looking for love' and hit the search button. The first thing I see is an ad for one of the big-name dating sites. This encourages me, but the fee they charge puts me off. I'll keep it in mind though.

As I scroll, the options get worse, or I suppose better depending on your outlook. There's a site for cougars promising hot young men for 'thirsty' older women. A vision of some manchild who the twins went to school with showing up for a blind date with me is enough to keep me scrolling. I don't want a hot young man. I'll settle for a lukewarm, middle-aged man with a dad bod and a sense of humour. Actually I wouldn't even consider it settling. That would be ideal.

Next to pop up is a site for 'sugar mamas' which seems to have a similar premise to the cougar site, except it likes its female members to be rich. I know rich is relative, but a sum total of less than a thousand pounds in my bank account even on payday would not be considered rich by anyone's standards. And I've bills to pay out of that!

By the time I reach 'OldieGoldies', I'm losing the will to live. Their pitch could easily be adapted to match me with my undertaker of choice, or a carer to make sure I take my dementia pills. It's all 'twilight of life' and 'someone to warm your slippers' and pictures of couples in matching slacks with lap blankets and those little tray tables beside their matching lift-and-rise chairs.

There has to be some option out there. One that doesn't cost the earth or operate as an open invitation for scam artists to come and prey on elderly, rich, dementia-addled women. Maybe I'll get Niamh to ask some of her teacher friends which sites they use. Surely there are some single folks in her school.

Deciding that searching for love is making me quite depressed, I decide to work on another one of my goals. Scanning last night's list for inspiration, I decide to look at trips to Yorkshire. I'm not sure who I will be able to talk into coming with me, but I'm not averse to going on my own. I could even factor in a visit to the boys in Manchester. This is doable, I think. I can easily plan this and it will give me something to look forward to in the new year.

I'll visit Haworth and the parsonage, and of course the moors. I might even go all Kate Bush. I wonder whether I'll need a cloak. And even if I don't strictly *need* a cloak, might it just be fun to buy one anyway? I'll have to plunder my not-too-impressive savings but this isn't just for me, it's for sixteen-year-old Becki who was obsessed with *Wuthering Heights* to the level that she even went to see a production of it, on her own, in Belfast. While all her friends were sneaking off to pubs and concerts, she was sneaking off to go to the Grand Opera House to watch a play. Doesn't she deserve to have her moment on the moors?

I swear I can feel her in the room with me, vibrating with excitement as I research hotels and activities and oh my God, you can even stay in Ponden Hall – the house that inspired Emily to write *Wuthering Heights*!

I can feel my heart start to race, and my skin prickle with excitement. I can do this. I don't need to be a cougar, or a sugar mama or have a man at all to go and see a little part of the world that meant so much to me then, and still can now.

I'm taking notes, totting up costs and promising myself I will re-read *Wuthering Heights* for the umpteenth time when my phone rings. I smile when I see Saul's name flashing up on the screen. Of my two boys, he is the wildest of the pair and always has been. When he was young, I used to joke he had his own seat in the A & E waiting room due to the frequency of our visits. So far, he has managed to navigate his time at university without any major disasters but that doesn't stop me from living in fear that there is a catastrophe looming around the next corner. But even though he's fairly lax at calling me usually, this unexpected call on a Sunday night doesn't necessarily herald that bad things are afoot.

'Saul,' I say as I answer the phone. 'How are you, love?' A part of me always cringes that I've adopted the affectations of an Irish mammy and unconsciously add love or son to the end of my sentences when speaking to my boys. It feels like something a middle-aged woman would say and while I know I am middle-aged deep in my soul, I struggle when my status becomes so obvious.

'Hi Mum,' this deep man-voice booms down the line. Is this really someone I gave birth to? I swear I still expect to hear their high, light childhood voices when we speak. 'Look, I don't have long, but I need your help if that's okay?'

'Of course,' I tell him, simultaneously proud that he has come to me for help but also terrified of what his request might entail. I can manage if it's to guide him in whipping up a lasagne, or to check in his room at home for a forgotten textbook. I'm not sure I'll be able to react quite so calmly if he tells me he's phoning from the back of an ambulance or, worse again, the back of a cop car. None of those four scenarios would be beyond the realm of possibility for Saul. Not that he's a troublemaker, as such. The police haven't had reason to come my door. Not yet anyway.

'What do you need?' I ask him.

'Well, you know how I'm your favourite son?' he asks.

'My favourite first born, yes,' I tell him. I always answer my children in this way. Saul is my favourite firstborn and Adam my favourite second born. The true answer to that question, of course, is my favourite is whichever one is causing me least trouble at the time.

'Your favourite, son, yes,' Saul replies and even though I can't see him, I can hear that he is smiling. I can imagine the cheeky glint in his beautiful blue eyes. He's a handsome boy – a perfect combination of the best bits of my father and the best bits of Simon.

'Saul...' I say, my voice offering just enough of a warning to let him know I might not be overflowing with the cup of maternal kindness today. Call me a psychic, but I can see my fairly small savings pot start to disappear in front of my very eyes. I glance at my notebook and the excited doodles I've drawn on it and feel the heart that was so excited just moments ago sink to my boots.

'The thing is, Mum, that I've found myself a little financially embarrassed. You know there's a cost-of-living crisis, and the price of everything has gone up so much and I've been trying to be sensible. Honest. I've not been pissing it up the wall.'

'Language...' I chide, in a voice not unlike my mother's but he pays no heed.

'So look, I just wondered if I could borrow some money to get me through till I come home for Christmas maybe, or until my next student loan payment comes through.'

And there it is. My night in Ponden Hall gone. Over the past ten years I've become adept at doing boy-related maths very quickly. It's still a few weeks until the boys are due to come home for Christmas, and another three weeks after that until they get the next instalment of their student loan money. And I know that if Saul has to hand over an immediate chunk of that as soon as it arrives he'll find himself back to square one relatively quickly. And then there's the accommodation to be paid for the next term, and the boys' final year. I've already had to remortgage the house to fund their education – and that's with Simon helping and me saving as much as I could in their younger years. As it stands, the cost of their accommodation comes in at twice what my mortgage payments are. It's certainly not cheap to be a student.

I try and hold back my instinctual reaction of losing my actual shit by taking a few slow, deep breaths and reminding myself it's only money, and if Ponden Hall has stood this long it will stand a little longer until I can afford to visit. While I'm internally talking myself off a cliff, Saul tells me he has been budgeting and living off pasta and cereal and really, truly, he hasn't been at the Student Union in weeks.

'And Adam? What position is he in?' I ask, girding my loins for a double hit. The joy of having twins is that there has never been any reprieve since they were born. Every single thing I've bought has had to be multiplied by two. If one of them wrecked his shoes, the other would follow within days, if not hours. They grew together at a rate of knots. Getting ahead of myself financially was as pointless a goal as emptying buckets of water from the deck of the Titanic.

'He's fine,' Saul says. 'You know, Adam. The golden child.'

'You are both my golden children,' I say, even though at this moment Adam is definitely the shinier of the two. When he was home in the summer he worked all the hours God sent in Tesco and saved two thirds of his salary. He went back to Manchester with a healthy bank balance. Saul, on the other hand, worked two days a week in a pub and enjoyed spending his wages in the same establishment, or on clothes and a PS5. I had warned him he would be in for a rougher ride and now, here he is, dealing with the consequences of his own actions.

But what am I supposed to do? Leave him to starve? Tell him to suck it up?

'I feel really bad about this, Mum,' Saul says and the slightly cocky bravado appears to disappear. 'It's the last thing I want to do to come and ask you for help when you do so much for us anyway…'

He chats as I'm spinning beads on an imaginary abacus in my head. If I cut back on my own shopping, and hit my savings a little then I can help him out without bankrupting myself. Sure, it's a mother's duty, isn't it? To put her children's needs above her own. I have always wanted to be that kind of mum. The kind who remains close to her grown-up children. Who doesn't abandon her maternal responsibilities simply because they've turned eighteen. The kind who feels needed…

'Okay, son,' I say in my best Irish mammy voice. 'I'll send you £50 over now and you get some shopping in and have money to keep you going, and then I'll do some sums and come back to you about the rest of term.'

'There's just one more thing, Mum,' he says. 'I kind of spent the money you sent me to book my flights for Christmas. I didn't even realise I'd done it until it was too late and now the prices have gone up and...'

'How much?' I ask, starting to shiver with the cold of my wet clothes and with the fear of what this is going to cost me.

'One hundred and forty pounds would cover it, Mum. To get me home on the same flight as Adam.'

'Okay,' I say, doing my best to sound upbeat and not annoyed, because the last thing a mother wants to do is make her child – who is hundreds of miles away – feel bad about themselves. Especially not if their child is a teenage boy and in the demographic group most likely to harm themselves in any way. 'I'll book your flight as well,' I tell him, 'and I'll send you a message when it's sorted.'

'You're the best, Mum,' he tells me. 'You're an absolute legend. I love you.'

I tell him I love him too because of course I do absolutely love him more than words can say, and I try to bask in the feeling of being considered an 'absolute legend'. Even if I'm now an exceptionally skint absolute legend who will have to call her ex-husband to see if he can help with a bit of extra financial support.

14

THE UNBEARABLE SEXINESS OF MAGNUM PI

I don't often have to call Simon, especially now that the boys are older. With no more handovers of children at weekends, I rarely see him any more. That's kind of okay with me. We've long run out of things to say to each other – not that our conversations aren't amicable, they're just more businesslike. As if we are CEOs in the lives of Messrs Adam and Saul Cooke and have to discuss our strategy going into the next quarter.

Thankfully in most things parenting related, our values align pretty well although I am definitely the softer of the two these days. The boys moving away has certainly upped my generosity of spirit towards them.

But right now, my boys, or my one boy in particular, does not need my generosity of spirit. He needs my generosity of bank account. And his father's.

Calling Simon, it's hard to remember the days when my heart used to be all of a flutter waiting for him to pick up. Those days when we could talk for hours on the phone even though we'd spent the afternoon or evening together. It's hard to remember the funny, gooey feeling I got in the pit of my stomach when I heard his voice say, 'Hello.'

Now my pulse doesn't quicken when I hear his voice, I just get straight to business.

'Simon,' I say.

'Becca,' he says. 'What crisis have our offspring unloaded upon us now?' Oh, how well he knows me, and them.

'One of financial implication. Although to be fair, it's Saul who has an issue. Adam is doing fine,' I tell him.

'None of that surprises me,' he sighs. 'How big and bad is this issue? Because, you know, it's three weeks from Christmas and Santa still has a few things to sort here. Jessica is going OTT again.' He's trying to sound exasperated but I know he isn't. He's happy as Larry with the Cooke family set-up 2.0. Jessica is his wife of six years and, thankfully, not the woman he cheated on me with. She's lovely and she seems to find Simon lovely. I'm happy for them, honestly, and I'm not even jealous that Simon has had more children. Saskia is five and absolutely gorgeous. Theo is three and makes raising twin boys look easy. Wild is not the word. I couldn't imagine dealing with either of them full time again at my age.

'Well he's skint, and he hasn't booked his flight back yet. So I figured we send him a couple of hundred quid, and book his flight for him? If we can split that it shouldn't cost either of us more than about £160? Does that sound okay?' I hate asking Simon for money even though he has never once tried to make me feel bad about it. But still, I'm cringing as I wait for his response.

'Well, I'd suggest we send the money to Adam and he can help Saul budget a bit, otherwise he is likely to go on the mother of all benders and we'll find ourselves in this position again in a couple of days,' he says.

'Good idea,' I tell him. 'Thanks Simon.'

'No worries. And I'll have a word with him about his partying when he gets back. Nothing too heavy but just a gentle chat.'

'Thanks,' I say again.

'It was nice to see you at the funeral,' he says. 'I mean, awful circumstances of course. But nice you were there. For Laura. I know she misses you.'

His words make me sad, even though I know he doesn't mean for them to. I don't want to pick at this particular wound, certainly not with Simon.

'Yeah, Niamh and I were glad we could be there for her. So, look, I have to get on but if I send you my half of the money could you forward it all to Adam?' Yes, I am cutting this discussion off at the pass.

'I will do. Mind yourself,' he says, and in the background I hear a godawful crash which I can only imagine is Theo continuing on his one-man destruction mission. No, I'm really not jealous of Simon at all.

My bank account raided and my list set aside for now, I switch on the shower and prepare to soothe away the newly formed tension knots in my neck and shoulders. I'm dreaming of how good it's going to feel when I'm clean, warm and in my comfiest pyjamas in front of the fire. I might even order a takeaway for tea. Maybe a pizza. I know I shouldn't. Especially after having to dig Saul out of a hole of his own making. I should be switching to beans on toast or cornflakes for the next fortnight even though the texture of beans makes me feel sick to my stomach and it's much too cold to be living off cereal.

Teenage me would approve of the extravagance of ordering a pizza just for myself so I decide that I absolutely deserve a ham and mushroom thin crust from Paolo's Pizza. Even making that decision is enough to ease some of the tension in my aching muscles and to make up for the sudden removal of my dream of dancing across the moors.

I grab my phone and tap into the Spotify app. I'd like to say that my Spotify account is beautifully curated but the truth is it's a mess of random songs and genres all saved into seven different playlists, each called 'New' or 'New New'. It takes a few minutes to find the tracks I'm looking for and as Lizzo starts singing about being a 'thicc' bad bitch – which I've been reassured by the twins is a good thing – I open the shower cubicle and pretend the waft of steam that emerges is dry ice and I'm walking on stage to perform in my sell-out tour. I'm just stepping onto the stage (into the shower) when my phone bursts into life again. If I just let it ring out, I can check it when I get out of the shower and sure, I'm only going to be a few minutes anyway and it isn't likely to be anything so urgent that it can't wait a few minutes, I think, trying to resist the urge to look at the screen and see who's calling.

At the same time, I know that if I don't see who is calling, or answer, I won't be able to fully relax in the shower. No way will I be able to perfect the TikTok dance to 'About Damn Time' that I've been trying to get right for weeks, and I can't let my fans down!

Sighing, I close the shower door and look at the windowsill where my phone is propped up. My mother's name is on the screen and I know then there's no way I can ignore her. I live in fear of missing that one phone call where she tells me she has fallen and needs help and by the time I listen to my voicemail it will be too late. She'll be dead and it will all be my fault.

So, naked as the day she pushed me into this world, I answer the phone to my mother.

'Rebecca,' she says before I've had the chance to speak. 'Sweetheart. I need your help. Have you seen the weather outside today?'

I think of my walk with Daniel during which I was a little scared a White Walker might appear round a corner, and tell her that yes, I have indeed seen the weather today. 'It's a day for staying in and staying warm,' I tell her.

'Well, I agree with you but the thing is I've run out of milk and I'm low on bread and when I called over to Mrs Bishop to see if she was okay, the poor woman was sitting in the cold because her gas had run out. I said I would walk down to the shop and get her a top-up but then I slipped walking down the path and…'

My heart plummets to the pit of my stomach. 'You slipped? Oh Mum! Are you okay?' I ask, grabbing the clean underwear I had brought into the bathroom with me and quickly getting dressed, phone now on loud speaker.

'Well, I'm fine. A bit bruised you know. My arm… and my leg… and my ego…' There's a little wobble in her voice as she answers and I know this much to be true. My mother is not one to complain about her lot. Not even when Daddy died and I could see that her heart was broken clean in half, she would just say that he wouldn't want her moping around and she'd better get off her backside and get on with living her life. If there is a wobble in her voice, something is definitely wrong.

'When did this happen?' I lift my phone and carry it through to the bedroom where instead of putting on my comfy pyjamas I haul on a fresh pair of joggers and another hoodie. This one has the slogan 'Tired and Needy' plastered across the front and it could not be more accurate if it tried.

'Oh, a couple of hours ago. But I thought if I just took a couple of paracetamol and had a cup of tea, I'd feel a bit better and head to the shop then. Mrs Bishop has come in to sit with me, and to keep herself warm, so don't worry. I've not been here on my own,' my mother says.

Unsurprisingly, it's not as reassuring as she thinks it might be.

'Mum! You should've phoned me when it happened. You know I

would've come over,' I say, rifling through my drawer for matching socks. How on earth can I have an empty laundry basket and not a single bloody matching pair of socks to be found anywhere?

'I didn't want to be a burden. You've enough on your plate what with work, and the boys and then Mrs O'Hagan's funeral and...'

'You're never a burden!' I scold her and I feel tears prick at my eyes as yet another Unexpected Wave of Sadness assaults me – made worse by the hangover horrors. 'I just need to put my trainers on and I'll be round as soon as I can. I'll bring milk and bread so you get a nice warm cup of tea and then I'll nip out and get gas for Mrs Bishop and I'll put the code in her meter for her. Now, is there anything else you need? Painkillers? Arnica cream?'

'No,' my mother replies and her voice sounds small. 'You're very good to me, Rebecca.'

'I'll see you soon, Mum. Fifteen minutes or so,' I tell her and end the call before I sob down the line. What right have I to cry over my mother falling when she says she's fine? Maybe it's that I don't quite believe her or I know that she's hurtling towards eighty and a time might just come sooner rather than later when she isn't fine.

I abandon Lizzo and my dreams of headlining at Glastonbury and set out once again into the stormy day to rescue my mother and her neighbour.

Stopping at the shop, I pick up the essentials my mother asked for, and a Victoria Sponge which a good daughter would probably bake from scratch. Guilt makes me add a packet of McVitie's Chocolate Digestives to my basket as well. And some spuds, carrots, broccoli and chicken. I'll make sure to prepare dinner for Mum and Mrs Bishop before I leave again. Knowing my mother, she will argue that there is no need, and we might even end up giving each other all sorts of bad looks but reach a compromise that I've peeled and chopped everything and she will do the actual cooking part.

'Are you all right, love?' the woman behind the counter asks me. 'You look a bit pale.'

For the briefest of moments, I consider telling her exactly how I'm not all right. That I'm only just forty-six and swinging into the menopause at a rate of knots. That I'm divorced and haven't had so much as a snog in years. That my children have abandoned me and at least one of them seems to take me completely for granted and I only hear from him when he wants something. My mother is ageing and I'm terrified that she's not immortal and that chances are I'm going to lose her in the next ten to fifteen years and that's only if I'm lucky and she doesn't insist on offering to go to the shops for her elderly neighbour when it is icy and hailing outside. And to top all that, I'm absolutely hanging out of my arse for the first time in about three years and I'm pretty sure I'm now sweating 12 per cent alcohol Sauvignon Blanc.

'Tired and Needy?' she says before I've a chance to reply.

'Is it that obvious?' I ask, fighting with a plastic carrier bag to open it as a queue forms behind me.

'Your top,' the woman says, nodding to where my hoodie is partially exposed beneath my gilet.

'Well, if the hoodie fits,' I mutter with a half-smile that hides my urge to throw the damned plastic bag across the shop and throw a hissy fit that wouldn't look out of place on a two-year-old.

'Here,' the woman behind the counter says, gently putting her hand on top of mine before taking the bag from me. 'There's a knack to it,' she says. 'I'm always telling them they need to get better quality bags. Especially now people have to pay for them.' Her voice is soft and kind and I'm not sure why but once again I feel tears prick at my eyes and I will myself not to start sobbing in the middle of Eurospar. I give her a watery smile, not trusting myself to say anything in response to her kindness.

'I hope I'm not speaking out of turn,' she says, dropping her voice to a whisper, 'but you look around my age and… well… I've gone on HRT and it has helped me no end. I'm not quite so… well… tired and needy as I was before.'

I nod and mouth 'thank you', revelling in a moment of kinship with another woman. Maybe she's right. Maybe it's time I got proper, medically provided, help. Grabbing my shopping, I leave and make my way to my mum's, where I find two very contented women watching an old episode of *Magnum PI* as if they hadn't a worry in the world.

'You're a great girl, Rebecca,' Mrs Bishop tells me twenty minutes later when I have been out and topped up her gas meter before making them both a cup of tea, served with a slice of cake of course.

'She is, you know,' my mother says proudly. 'I'm very lucky to have her.' I feel just as self-conscious while also as warm and fuzzy inside as I did when I was a child and my mother would boast about me to her friends. 'She has the reading age of a fourteen-year-old! Can you imagine that?' She'd beamed with pride as ten-year-old me coloured beside her.

Leaving them to their tea and their chatter over the noise of the TV, I start preparing enough dinner for both of them in the kitchen. Now, maybe my hearing is a bit off, but I'm as sure as sure can be that I hear Mrs Bishop tell my mother she would 'climb that Magnum fellah like a tree' given half the chance.

'Ah now, he wouldn't be my type,' I hear my mother tell her. 'But that Harrison Ford? Now, he's a quare fellah! I wouldn't kick him out of bed for eating toast!' The loud peals of laughter that erupt between them warm my heart so much that I immediately burst into tears, and have to do my best to stifle my sobs so that I don't give my mother anything to worry about.

It's just been a long few days, I think. With a lot of emotions to process, not least the metaphorical face-to-face I'd had with my teenage self. I'll probably feel less emotional once I get a shower, something to eat and a long sleep. Surely that will make a huge difference to how I feel?

15

CHOOSE LIFE

It's almost seven by the time I get home. I use what little reserves of energy I have left to take Daniel out for a quick wee, feed him, and drag myself upstairs and into the shower. I'm too tired for the performance of a lifetime and Lizzo dance routines, so I simply switch my audiobook on and shower while the softy spoken narrator regales me with a tale of reinvention and true love. The now very tired and definitely very needy cynic in me mocks the romantic prose and the author's assertions that everyone can find the missing piece of them that makes them feel whole again.

I believed it once, I suppose, but now I wonder if anyone on this earth ever feels completely happy and content? The nature of life is such that things always change. It's foolish to get too comfortable or to assert you're finally happy.

People die. Children grow up. Pets die. Jobs are lost. Husbands have affairs. Friends make choices that have catastrophic consequences for the trust you had in them and we, us adults, get complacent about just about everything. We stop looking at the world in the same way we did when we were sixteen and full of hope and expectation.

God, I remember how *excited* we were just to grow up, my friends and I. As if we thought the process of ageing was all that was required to give us everything we ever wanted. We had it all mapped out – and by 'it all' I mean our twenties and thirties because we didn't really think too far beyond that. Very few teenagers lose hours fantasising about turning fifty and going for their first mammogram or joining the NHS bowel screening programme.

We'd go to 'uni', as the characters in *Neighbours* called it. It was only known as university before we all became virtual residents of Ramsey Street and picked up the Aussie slang.

After graduation we'd live in fancy apartments together like the characters in *Friends* – not flats, flats weren't considered glam – and life would be one big sleepover with big cups and purple walls. I was the Monica of the group, Laura the Rachel and Niamh was Phoebe, of course.

We imagined we'd spend our free time hanging out in chic cocktail bars and coffee shops. Booking girly holidays to Spain and Greece and getting our nipples sunburned under azure blue skies before plunging into crystal clear waters. We'd work hard and play hard – and let our hair down going clubbing. Choosing life as the *Trainspotting* soundtrack encouraged us to do, without really taking in the fact that the lyrics to that particular song are actually really bloody depressing and, it seems, prescient.

We didn't notice because we were too busy shouting and dancing in clubs through the late nineties – getting knocked down, and getting back up again, dancing while shouting 'lager, lager, lager' over and over again, even though we didn't drink lager. We were the original Bacardi Breezer generation. Pass me a couple of Lime Breezers and I was happy as a clam. We were the generation who grew up with girl power soundtracking our late teen years, and we believed Madonna when she told us that it would all be good if we just expressed ourselves.

But now, without realising how fast the years were passing, we find we're hurtling towards fifty and standing in the shower with greying pubes, stretch marks, and boobs that are starting to sag. That and the knowledge that we have ended up with only our own company to look forward to. Of course, that last one is deeply personal to me – the divorcee of our ensemble who has realised it has been *years* since I last had sex, never mind made love. The phrase 'making love' used to give me the absolute ick but now I'd kill to have someone make me feel loved, and desired. Damn it, I'd settle for a grope behind the bike sheds these days – something to give me that flutter in the pit of my stomach and to remind me that I'm alive and not a dried-up husk of a sexual being.

We never did live in a fancy apartment or get sunburn on our boobs – the latter not necessarily being a bad thing. We clubbed a bit, yes, but those years went so fast it's hard to pin down the memories of them now. It's all become a blurry montage of sitting drunk on a pub toilet feeling the music pound through our bodies, and standing in taxi queues regretting the open-toed high heels we were wearing. It's the hazy memory of the time we invented the term 'chipulary burns' when our post boozing sharing bag of chips on the walk home was much too hot. We used that expression a lot, and fondly, until we didn't any more, because we got into the habit of blowing on every single bite of food instinctively in case it was too hot for tiny mouths. This would become such a part of our identity that we would do it even if our children were nowhere near... or grown up and moved out.

We had jobs – careers even – and got married and had children, and the sense of routine we so looked forward to rebelling against in our teenage years became a survival essential. We prayed – and still pray – for the boring days and for a lack of drama, because life teaches you that drama is rarely a good thing and at times it feels relentless and you wonder how you're still standing.

But then you, as in I, get out of the shower and dry off, slipping into your comfiest pyjamas and woollen bed socks, slather on age-defying, criminally expensive face cream and don't allow yourself to think any more about what is now firmly vaulted in the past never to be repeated.

You plod downstairs, order the damn pizza you've been looking forward to all day and you eat it while watching *Casualty* on iPlayer and the only thing you allow yourself to worry about is that that you seem to be developing real feelings for Ian the paramedic.

Before I go to bed, I send a quick message to Saul, feeling guilty that I was annoyed earlier at his fecklessness. I tell him I love him and I have his back. I tell him we'll have a good chat about his finances when he comes home for Christmas. Then I message Adam and tell him that I've sent him enough money to cover the cost of his flight home too, even though I know he has already booked it. I feel guilty that I have given money to Saul and not him as well, so this goes some way to tackling that guilt.

I pop a message to my mother to tell her she is to call me in the future if she needs anything and she's not to risk going out in the ice or snow. The last thing either of us need is for her to break a hip. I've seen it on *Casualty* before, older people breaking hips and that marking the start of the final decline. Of course I tell her I love her but I don't tell her just how much I need her because it will only start me crying again.

Then I try to sleep, but it seems to be escaping me for now. There are too many thoughts dancing around my head and not one of them is conducive to a good night's rest. My pizza sits leaden in my stomach and I try not to think about how many calories are contained in the average twelve-inch pizza. I left one slice – a really skinny one – just so I can tell myself I wasn't a complete glutton.

It comes to me that I read once if you can't stop your mind racing, it's good to get your thoughts down on paper as at least that is them out of your head. It's worth a try, I think, sitting up in bed, switching on the lamp and fishing in my bedside drawer for a pen and a notepad.

I figure if I'm going to do this I might as well do this right, so I scrawl today's date at the top of page and then I begin. If a letter to my future self got me into this state, then maybe a reply can help pull me out of it.

Dear sixteen-year-old me,

First of all, you should know we go by Becca or Becks now. Mum still insists on giving us our full title of Rebecca. Or Rebecca Louise Burnside if we've done something to annoy her. (And yes, we are still a Burnside. We weren't for a while, but we reclaimed it about ten years ago. That's a very long story though – maybe best kept for another time.) Anyway, we dropped the Becki with an 'i' when we went to university to study journalism.

It was around that time we finally started drinking too, you'll be relieved to know. Sobriety does come to an end for you and for a while you embrace the clubbing lifestyle. With Laura and Niamh. Yes, you're still friends but it gets complicated a little in the middle. That's another one best kept for another time.

I've read the letter you wrote me and placed in the time capsule. I've reminded myself of all the hopes and dreams we had when we were younger. I think maybe we were a little naïve…

Nope. I score through that last line. I don't want to dash young me's hopes before I've even got started.

The truth is that life kinda got in the way…

Nope. That's not right either. I have to keep this upbeat!

Sadly we did not marry Fox Mulder but we do still have all our own teeth so that's a win, eh?

I score through this line as well, and the rest of the damn page. I think of my list. Of how I'm already intimidated beyond words at the thought of stepping into the dating pool once again. How even a relatively small trip might be beyond my financial means just now and for the foreseeable while my children navigate university and the ridiculous expense that comes with it. I think of all this and I'm tempted to tear all the scrawled-on pages out and roll them up to use as kindling to set fire to the clothes of doom, but then I think of Becki. I think of how I could imagine her vibrating with happiness earlier and I know that I'd be letting her down if I give up this easily.

I know I'd be letting *me* down if I give up this easily.

I don't need to write her a letter. I just need to give myself a good shake.

16

PHIL COLLINS AND THE GREAT TESCO MELTDOWN

Bleary-eyed and as grumpy as a toddler who's got past nap time, I'm sitting on the sofa working on a really exciting article on ten ways to increase productivity in the workplace. It's going about as well as writing the letter to my younger self went last night. What I want to write is 'pay your staff more and stop ripping the arse clean out of them with extra demands', but I don't think that would fly with this particular client – or any particular client to be honest.

Instead, I'm trying to sell some sort of grown-up version of a reward chart complete with corporate wank-speak, which doesn't so much as verge on condescending as have its own address on Condescension Street. Today's client offers £10 meal vouchers, branded company merch and 25 per cent discount on their software as incentives, which can be won by their extremely hard-working and undervalued staff. It's my job to make that, frankly insulting, attempt at employee motivation sound ground-breaking and aspirational.

This is not as easy as it sounds and I'm aware it doesn't sound easy at all.

'What do you think, Daniel? How would you recommend we

promote a culture of positivity and productivity in the modern workforce?'

Daniel raises one furry eyebrow, yawns and rolls over, releasing a profoundly unpleasant dog fart in the process.

'You're a great help,' I scold, before giving him a gentle pet and telling him that he is a very good boy and the best dog in the whole wide world. He responds by rolling onto his back and exposing his tummy to demand belly rubs.

'If only I could write that offering tummy rubs and being willing to live with noxious emissions could motivate all staff,' I tell him, before a flash of inspiration strikes me. What if I use this template – the boring old 'Ten Ways to...' that seems to make up the staple of my B2B work – to draft up a proposal for *Northern People* magazine? I'd flesh it out, obviously, beyond a bullet-pointed list so that I could inject humour and heart and realism into it, but it might work?

'Ten Ways to Survive Your Forties', for example? It might just work. In fact, I think it really could and I want to start writing it now, but I have to meet my deadline and then I have to check on Mum. It's still bitterly cold and icy outside and I don't want any repeats of yesterday's shenanigans. But later... later I can lose myself in writing something that makes my heart sing. I just need to focus on this list first. It's what young me would've done. She always was very studious and sensible after all.

Fifteen minutes later, I'm down to number six – 'give positive feedback' – when my phone buzzes to life with a notification that I've been added to a new group chat on WhatsApp called, rather unimaginatively, 'Becks, Laurs and Niamh'. Seconds later my phone buzzes again, with the first message to the group – from Laura.

LAURA
I read my letter.

NIAMH

Are we sticking to what is written in the letter is
between the letter writer and her God rule, or are
we allowed to ask for the deets?

NIAMH

Because I'm supervising in the sixth-form centre
just now so it would be a good time to get caught
up in a WhatsApp chat.

ME

I think it's up to the letter writer to decide whether
or not to share.

LAURA

I think I might need to share. But I think I might
need wine, or vodka, or something.

ME

That bad?

Laura replies with five crying face emojis.

NIAMH

Oh shit, I'm sorry, love. I'd pop over with a bottle
and a box of tissues but sadly the principal tends
to frown on that kind of behaviour.

ME

And I'm in B2B hell. But I'm here for you. Honest.
Do we need to schedule some sort of crisis
meeting about this?

There's a long pause where I can see that Laura has read my
reply, as has Niamh, but neither of them have responded and I'm
starting to worry I'm about to die from the worst possible humiliation of modern times – being left on read. But then my screen lights
up with 'Laura is typing' and I wait with bated breath.

LAURA

Can we? I know I've no right to ask after everything but no one is going to understand this like you two will. I tried talking to Aidan about it but he doesn't get it. He said I was only a child when I wrote it and I can't hold younger me to the same standards as grown-up me but

There's a pause and then the same 'Laura is typing' message pops up again.

LAURA

I think younger me had higher standards than grown-up me and I don't know what the actual fuck I'm doing with my life.

NIAMH

Just tell me where and when I need to be. My house is obviously not suitable because teenage boys are feral.

ME

My house is always free. If you don't mind the dog, who smells about as bad as a teenage boy in fairness but I can light a Yankee Candle.

LAURA

Tonight then? Even teatime? I'll bring chippy chips. Chippy chips make everything better.

ME

It's a deal. I have white bread, real butter and red sauce here so we can make chip butties.

LAURA

Perfect. Thanks girls. I'll see you then.

NIAMH

Hang in there, kid. We've got your back.

My phone falls silent and I resume my article, wondering if it would go down well if I wrote 'give your employees chippy chips, as this makes everything better'. This job would be so much easier if I could just cut through the bullshit and get directly to the heart of the matter. I bet more people would read chip-related advice than some nonsense about encouraging an atmosphere of flexibility and dedication to the customer base, which actually translates as sucking up worsening working conditions.

Maybe I'll add the chip-related advice to my 'Ten Ways to Survive Your Forties' pitch.

'Make sure to eat chippy chips, or pizza, or ice cream on a semi-regular basis. It won't kill you and it will make you feel like you're treating yourself. Diet advice is all well and good, but resist the urge to suck all the food-related joy out of life. Yes, a beautiful, from-scratch, low carb, high protein plant-based dinner can be tasty and can have health benefits but it's not a chip butty, is it? Sometimes you need to bring out the big guns.'

Or something like that.

Daniel lets out a low rumbling growl. I imagine he's telling me to quit dreaming about chips and just get on with my actual work and not my long-shot of a magazine pitch. Those tasty chicken chews he loves so much aren't going to pay for themselves, after all.

'Okay,' I tell him. 'I'll do it!'

He gives a half-hearted wag of his tail, which I read as 'Finally! A good decision!' before I focus back on the task at hand and he gives in to his sixth nap of the day.

But as much as I try to focus on my work, I can't help but think about Laura, and what it was in her letter that might have upset her so much. She's probably just having the same crisis of confidence that I am. With added grief, of course. I remember those raw early days only too well. They were a fever dream where I felt as if I'd had the very skin flayed from my body. Everything hurt. Every single thing felt like a personal attack. The chill in the air. The brightness of the sun. The songs that played on the radio. They didn't even have to be sad songs – in the thick of grief everything becomes sad and is assigned more meaning. Everything serves as a reminder of what has been lost. I bawled in Tesco when 'You Can't Hurry Love' by Phil Collins started playing because someone once told me my father looked like Phil Collins. He absolutely did not, for the record. I think that someone was talking about another person entirely. He certainly wasn't talking about my father who had been a tall, thin man with glasses, a thick grey beard, and zero drumming ability. But in Tesco, on that particular day, the rawness of my loss had me bent double.

I'd left my shopping in the trolley in the middle of the aisle and hurried to my car where I'd promptly had a panic attack. Saul and Adam got to order a pizza for tea that night and were delighted with themselves, while I'd done my best to keep the strength of my grief from them. The last thing they needed was to see me to lose my emotional shit on a regular basis. No, it seems I was saving that particular treat for when perimenopause kicked in.

I must make sure that Laura knows she doesn't have to keep any of her pain to herself. It's a shite truth that the only way to learn how to co-exist with grief is to allow yourself to live in it fully, feeling every awful shard as it comes. Just as you can't hurry love, you also can't hurry grief.

I bet you sang that last bit.

17

A LITTLE SPARK

'I probably shouldn't be eating this,' Laura says, loading a second slice of bread with thick, greasy chips which are scenting the air of my living room with their perfect vinegar-heavy aroma. 'I swore once the funeral was over, I'd get back to eating properly. Our freezer is full with lasagnes and casseroles that the neighbours dropped in to Mum over the last couple of months. There were so many we became the official overflow zone.'

'I do love a good lasagne,' Niamh says, squeezing the bottle of tomato ketchup so tightly it makes the same noise as a watery fart.

'You can have whatever you want from my house. Or Mum's freezer. She's not going to have much use for them now, and Conal says he can't bear to even look at them. He's taken to referring to her freezer contents as the "pot luck of impending death",' Laura says. 'I don't think either of us will be able to look at a lasagne the same way ever again.'

I nod. 'I remember from when my dad died. But it wasn't lasagne – he went too quick for the neighbours to start batch cooking and stockpiling. It was the egg and onion sandwiches that were made on an industrial level by my aunties and cousins to feed the mourners. I used to love a good egg and onion. Of all the food that gets offered to at a wake to go with your cup of tea, they were my favourite. I even liked them more than the pastries Erin and Flora at the bakery on Ivy Lane sent up. But now they just remind me of death.'

'They smell a bit like death too,' Niamh says, with a soft smile and a wrinkle of her nose.

'But they are lovely, all the same. Maybe you'll warm to them again in time,' Laura says before taking a large bite from her chip butty and immediately melting into a semi-orgasmic state as a trickle of melted butter runs down her chin. She wipes it away hastily, finishes chewing and laughs. 'Excuse me for being such a hallion. But these are so good, even if my waistline will regret it later,' she says.

I look at my friend, still just about as slim as she was when we were teenagers. Okay, she may now be nudging more towards a twelve rather than the svelte size ten she had been, but she's nowhere near needing to worry about her waistline. I, on the other hand, probably should be worried about mine, but in the spirit of helping young me love myself again, I'm just going to push the worry aside for a bit. I know I'm never going to have a flat stomach and I made my peace with that a long time ago. After all, I never actually had a flat stomach in the first place. The pot belly my mother lovingly referred to during my childhood just continued to grow with me, and then, after gestating the twins – both in excess of five pounds when they were born – I knew the battle was forever lost.

'Nonsense,' Niamh says, cutting through my thoughts. 'It's actual science that calories consumed during the grieving process do not count. And I'm a science teacher so I speak with authority.'

'See!' I say. 'So eat up and enjoy it.'

'Oh, there's no way I'm not eating it,' Laura says. 'It's just what I needed. Just like coming here to see you two was just what I needed too.' There's a pause. We haven't got round to discussing the letter just yet, having agreed that the hot chips had to be prioritised. I even reminded my friends of chipulary burns and we laughed. It has been easy to believe for just a while that everything is okay in our world and that we hadn't just unleashed the wrath of our younger selves on each other.

'Girls, honestly. I'm so grateful for you. I didn't expect for one moment you'd walk back into my life on Friday. I've wanted to call you both, to make this right, so many times, but I suppose I was just a coward.'

Niamh and I shake our heads even if part of me – the part of me who was so badly hurt by Laura's actions – thinks that yes, she was a bit cowardly. She had been cowardly at the time in not making it right and that had continued through the years. Maybe I'm just as guilty. I didn't have the time or mental energy, or forgiveness in me to try and make it better. Life moved on. Still, like the grief of losing a parent, it had a habit of jumping back up and biting us in the arse from time to time.

'We can't change the past,' I tell her, because ultimately, I can still be hurt or cross or angry, but it's not going to provide me with a time machine to go back and make sure things played out differently. And, truth be told, if I did have a time machine I'd probably go for something on a bigger scale – like warning the world of impending atrocities, or making sure my father had seen the doctor the day before he died instead of saying he'd wait and see how he felt in a day or two.

'That's true,' Niamh says. 'And I know because, as we've already established, I'm a science teacher and I can say with confidence no such technology exists.'

'You're a biology teacher,' I tell her. 'Unless time travel can be facilitated via a process of photosynthesis, I don't think it's quite in your field of expertise.'

'You won't be saying that when I suddenly have knowledge of all the winning sports fixtures next year and coin it in at the bookies,' Niamh says.

I can't help but laugh. 'You're not Biff from *Back to the Future* either.'

She simply shrugs and smiles before taking a slurp from her can of Diet Coke.

'Seriously though,' Laura says. 'I appreciate you coming to the wake. And reaching out to me. Just being there for me, you know? And I know Mum would think the same because she loved you both very much.'

'We loved her too,' Niamh and I say, almost in unison.

'And we love you,' Niamh adds.

Laura grabs a napkin and wipes her mouth, and then grabs another and wipes her eyes. There's a pause.

'So, the letter...' she says. 'I don't know what I expected from it but the truth is, it really unsettled me. Made me think about my life way too much. It made me question myself. Am I where I'm meant to be? Did I do everything I wanted? Becca, you read your letter, did it make you feel weird?'

'Yes and no,' I admit. 'I feel really disappointed in myself, I suppose. I've not exactly set the world aflame with my talent, have I? I'm single, heading for fifty and alone. But I'm still glad I read it.'

'And you, Niamh?'

Niamh gives her head a shake. 'Not read it. And I'm not sure I want to. I don't want to be unsettled or disappointed in myself. Thank you very much. I'm not sure any good would come from opening that particular can of emotional worms.'

'Emotional Worms would be a brilliant name for a rock band,' I muse.

'But sixteen-year-old us wanted now us to be able to read these, Niamh,' Laura interjects, ignoring my frankly brilliant suggestion. 'It was important to us at time so don't we owe it to our younger selves?'

'There are a lot of things that were important to sixteen-year-old us that we wouldn't touch with a ten-foot barge pole now. Tom Cruise, for example. He was the ultimate ride to young us, but now he gives me the dry bokes with all his Scientology carry on. I'm strictly Team Nicole and Team Katie,' Niamh says, in the voice she uses when she wants to make it very clear that the discussion is not one worth pursuing. I love my friend with every part of me and I would lay down my life for her in a heartbeat, but when Niamh has decided something, you can bet your life on it that the lady is not for turning. I have no desire to push this further and unleash her scary teacher voice.

'The worst thing in my letter,' Laura says, folding her chip paper over her remaining food and pushing it away, 'is that I said I wanted to make sure my mum got to live the life she missed out on by having us so young.'

Her voice wobbles and I feel a lump form in my throat.

'But that's lovely, that you wanted that for her,' I reassure her.

'It would be, if I wasn't such a sanctimonious bitch about it,' she says. 'I mean, I don't think I was purposefully mean, but you know how teenagers think they know absolutely everything and have 100 times the insight of their parents?'

'Oh God, yes,' Niamh and I say, this time in perfect unison.

'And just wait 'til we all get landed with Generation Z or whatever the latest iteration of crotch gremlins are collectively known as. I love Fiadh dearly but her teenage years are going to kick my arse,' Niamh adds.

'I will get my mum to say a novena for you,' I say, even though my lovely mum is not the novena-saying type.

'Can she say one for me that I'm able to survive to the end of term without losing it completely with Year 11?' Niamh asks.

'Of course,' I say, before turning my attention back to Laura who is obviously still struggling with the contents of her letter. 'Are you okay, love?' I ask.

Laura shrugs.

'I'm sure you weren't that bad,' Niamh tells her. 'And you can't judge grown-up you by teenage you's actions.'

Laura raises one finger to signal we should wait just one moment while she rifles in her bag and pulls out a folded sheet of A4 paper on which I immediately recognise the distinctive loop and swirl of her handwriting. She unfolds it, scans it for a second and clears her throat.

'I hope that you – grown-up me – have acknowledged all the sacrifices Kitty made to be your mother. She hasn't had half the opportunities you have and it must be hard for her to face the reality that her children are smarter and more worldly-wise than she is.'

I try to keep the cringe from my face, and I know Niamh is trying to do the same when I hear her cough and protest that her drink went down the wrong way.

'I – we – have a responsibility to help her expand her horizons beyond her own front door. I have realised that sooner rather than later...' Laura stops and takes a deep breath before looking at both Niamh and me. 'Hang in there, girls, this is a doozy,' she says. 'I have realised that sooner rather than later it will be my job to parent my parent and to become her educator. In fact, I think I might already be doing that.'

I want to assure Laura that it's not that bad. That's it's not patronising. That it reflected the kind of remarkable, hard-working and whip-smart woman Kitty O'Hagan was. But I can't. As well-intentioned as my dear friend was, this is pretty damn ropey.

Laura continues. 'I won't make the same mistakes Kitty made. I am already wise to the pitfalls of life. I already know I have one thing in my favour that Kitty did not – and that is a loving, fearless mother. And I'm going to make sure the pair of us live the big life we both deserve. I'll bring her with me on my life's great adventures.'

There is silence in the room – punctuated with sniffs and sighs – because we all know that Laura and Kitty did not set off on some grand adventure together and it's now too late for them to do so. This is a much more painful realisation than the smug bollocks of her teenage bravado-fuelled intro.

'So, you can imagine, I feel like shit. I *really* let her down. She didn't get to live a big life. We didn't travel the world together and I certainly didn't take her on my great adventures, unless you count getting her to babysit Robyn for me while I was at work. Girls, I think I treated my mother like the hired help and not like the legend she was. I can't stop thinking of the times I mentioned going to concerts, or away for city breaks with Aidan and she mentioned she'd love to do something like that sometime, and I never arranged it for her. Not that I even arranged them for myself all that often. It was so hard to find the time. I kept thinking I'd get round to doing it more and bringing her with me, but I didn't because I was too caught up in raising Robyn and trying to keep my marriage on track and working... I let her down in the end and I can't change that – unless we get that damn time machine,' Laura sobs.

But her words, and her tears, act as another spark to the kindling I set after reading my own letter. We can't change the past, but we're not dead yet and we can absolutely change the future.

And I should have realised as soon as I saw all three of our names on the top of the box, that I am not in this on my own.

18

NOT DEAD YET

It seems so blindingly, incredibly obvious that what I need to help my friends do is exactly what I myself have planned for myself.

If I can make changes and achieve the things I have written off somewhere along the way then why can't Laura and Niamh? Why can't we all support each other with the same vigour and verve we used to when we were in our late teens and early twenties?

Yes, we've moved on from letting each other copy homework, or holding hair back after one or more of us had one too many Bacardi Breezers but that doesn't mean we can't help each other in other ways. If the last few days have taught us anything it's that none of us know what's ahead of us or how long we'll be here for, or how long we'll be fit and able to do stuff for.

I've lost sleep in the past regretting the things I didn't do when I was young enough to do them. Like... I don't know... going on a Club 18-30 holiday even if the thought of a Club 18-30 holiday is my absolute idea of hell. Shagaluf? No thanks. But still, it would be nice to have the choice. Isn't that what ageing takes from us? The choices we had when we were young and not a bit appreciative of the possibilities that lay before us.

'What's that famous saying? The one about your biggest mistake being that you believe you have time? Or something like that,' I ask.

The girls look at me a little confused.

'I think we're all acutely aware that time is precious and we might not have as much as once thought,' Niamh says.

'Exactly!' I say, gathering up the chip papers and taking them through to the kitchen. I can hear my friends talk behind my back.

'Have you any idea what she's on about?' I hear Laura ask.

'Nope. But I do know Becca and she'll get there eventually and it will all make perfect sense. You just have to trust the process,' Niamh tells her, and I smile – smug in the knowledge my bestie has my back.

I grab a couple of notebooks from my completely unnecessary collection of unused notebooks – it's an addiction, okay? – and a few pens and walk back into the living room where the girls have hauled themselves back up onto the sofa, and Niamh is now lavishing a delighted Daniel with ear scratches.

'Oh God, she has the notebooks and pens out,' Niamh says.

'She hasn't grown out of that phase yet, then?' Laura asks.

'Girls, I am in the room and I can hear you! And no, I have not outgrown my love of stationery and I have no plans to do so,' I protest, with a smile.

'Yes, Monica,' Laura smiles.

'You can't hurt me by comparing me to the one and only Monica Geller. Everyone knows she was the best of all the *Friends*!' I protest. 'It doesn't hurt to have a few spare notebooks. You never know when they might come in handy,' I say, handing one to each of them before sitting down on the armchair by the window.

'True enough,' Niamh says. 'You might run out of loo roll or...'

I glare at her and she stops talking but I can't help but smile all the same. I love this banter and I have missed that Laura hasn't been a part of it for so long. There's something to be said for the kind of friendships where you know each other so well that you understand instinctively what lines can be crossed in the name of a good slagging.

'So,' Laura says. 'Are you going to keep us wondering or are you going to share just what is going on in that beautiful mind of yours?'

I take a deep breath and try to think of the best way to put into words the jumble of half-formed ideas darting around inside my head. 'It's what Laura said – we keep putting things on the long finger and thinking we'll get round to it, but we never do because, you know, life. And I was thinking about that and how I've been feeling that I have let young me down. I haven't achieved what she wanted. Nowhere near in fact. She certainly didn't expect to be sitting in her late forties, divorced, with an empty nest.'

Laura shifts a little in her seat. That's something we shouldn't put off too much longer either. Talking about my divorce and what happened. But not tonight. Not now. And anyway, I meant it when I said it's in the past. Didn't I?

I break my gaze, look down to my notepad page, where I wrote my list in the late hours of Saturday night, and then back up – and I will myself for this all to come together in my head in a way I can easily explain. Younger me would probably be firing ideas all over the place, older me – with depleting oestrogen levels and brain fog – needs a little more time. I want this to be my Jerry Maguire moment. I want to say it properly.

I straighten my back. 'Sometimes I feel like I've given up. That I've lived my young years and surely they are everyone's best years? You know, when you have energy and don't get three-day hang-overs. When you aren't tied down to mortgage payments or univer-sity fees? I think I sort of thought to myself "Well, you've had your chance, girl, and you blew it. It's time for the next generation to come through." I thought I'd made my peace with that,' I say. 'I mean, I have with a lot of things. I know, for example, I'm never going to marry Michael Bublé and as much as it pains me to accept that, I have.'

'Ah now, you never know,' Niamh says. 'You might. I mean, maybe it's the case that he just...'

'Don't say it,' I warn, my eyebrow raised.

'...hasn't met you yet.' She grins, delighted at her all too predictable reply.

I smile. 'Very funny, but believe me, even if he did, we're not getting married. Have you seen his wife? Stunning. Argentinian. I've seen pictures of her modelling lingerie. If I was faced with a choice between her toned body and sultry Latin vibes, versus my M&S multipack knickers, hot flushes and Derry accent, I know who I'd pick. And as I said, I've come to terms with that particular tragedy in my life. But I don't think I'm as okay with fading into the background or taking it easy for the rest of my days as I thought.'

They sit in silence for a moment. I can tell by the expressions on their faces they are thinking about what I've said.

'So when I read my letter, I wrote a list. Because, yes, I am a Monica as you pointed out. I was really bloody sad at first when I read it, and then I asked myself if I could change anything? Because in my letter I wrote about what I wanted to have experienced and achieved by the time I turn forty-seven and well, I'm not forty-seven yet. I know I'm not a kick in the arse off it, but I have time. We have time. Life isn't just for the young ones. Nights out and good times shouldn't be in our past.'

The girls look at me, rapt. To my surprise they aren't telling me to stop blethering on or to stick my notebooks where the sun doesn't shine.

Laura is the first to speak. 'So, what are you suggesting exactly? You're not suggesting we go out clubbing again because I'm going to be real with you, I would rather nail my boobs to the wall than set foot in a club.'

'Christ,' Niamh says. 'Me too! There is not enough alcohol in the world to make that feel like a good idea. Plus, our children are old enough for clubs now. Including the little darlings I teach. Can you imagine me giving it the full dance routine to "Spice Up Your Life" and my Year 13s or 14s watching.' She shudders.

'I hate to break it to you,' Laura says. 'But there are no clubs, except perhaps the very odd gay bar, that are playing "Spice Up Your Life" these days. You'd have to be giving it your everything to "Wet-Ass Pussy" instead. I'm sure Year 13 would love that.' She starts humming the tune to the Cardi B hit and to my shame I blush even thinking about the lyrics. Once again, the memory of me thinking I would die of embarrassment for being caught dancing to 'Like a Virgin' comes back to me. Meanwhile the youth of today think nothing of declaring how aroused their vaginas are. And they throw around the word pussy like it isn't the most cringe-making word in the history of words. What's wrong with referring to it as my generation did, with a simple 'down there'?

'You'll have to find space on the wall beside you for me to nail my tits as well,' Niamh says to Laura. 'Because there is no way in hell that I'm using the word pussy in front of Year 13. Not even if I am talking about an actual cat.'

'Okay,' I say. 'I think we're all agreed that clubbing is never going to be on the agenda. No one needs to nail anyone's boobs anywhere, or show anyone their vulva, or cat. But there has to be something? God, when we were teenagers we had all the plans in the world.'

'And they were plans that suited young, free and single types,' Niamh says. 'Like interrailing. Brilliant craic when you're eighteen. But when you're heading towards fifty, hostels and travelling with just a rucksack loses its appeal.'

'I don't know,' Laura says. 'I'm with Niamh on the hostels thing, but then again they gave me the heebies even when we were younger. I don't want to sleep in a room with strangers. I don't care how cheap it is – I wouldn't even do it for free. But I do kinda like the idea of packing a rucksack, or a weekend case on wheels, and going wherever the road or air or train track takes us. Sounds better to me than another fortnight in the Costa-del-all-inclusive-kid-friendly-waterpark-resort-from-hell.'

'Not a fan then?' I ask, with a smile.

'With Robyn as an only child, you can't imagine how many times I was hauled onto the stage at the kids' disco to accompany her. Aidan would be sitting there drinking his generic beer, laughing his legs off while I was left dancing to "The Ketchup Song" and "La Bomba".' She shudders. 'I'd love an adults-only holiday. We always swore we'd do a girly break at some stage but we didn't, did we? The furthest we got was your hen weekend in Bundoran, Becks, and if I remember correctly it poured from the heavens the whole time.'

Laura is not wrong. It had rained from the moment we arrived in the Donegal coastal town until the moment we left. Despite it being June, it was freezing and the heating in the self-catering apartment was on the blink. The whole thing was memorable for sure, but for all the wrong reasons.

'I should have read the signs from the universe,' I sigh. 'Between that and the thunderstorm on the day of the actual wedding, I'm wondering how I didn't cop on that the whole union was cursed from the start.'

There's a pause. Slightly awkward. Laura looks at her feet and I'm trying to think of something to say to take the awkward away but for the life of me nothing is coming to mind because it wasn't really me who made it awkward, was it?

'But sure, if you hadn't married him, you wouldn't have the boys and you wouldn't be without them for the world,' Niamh says, voice light and teacher-like in tone. It's a voice that says, 'We are moving on and let's just leave that elephant over there in the corner where she is perfectly comfortable.'

'True,' I say.

'So,' Niamh says. 'I think we can all agree that the first thing we are going to do to redeem ourselves to our younger selves is to plan a girls-only trip somewhere off the beaten track, but not too far off it. Because we want nice beds and clean bathrooms.'

'And cocktails!' Laura says and I see her look at her me, her eyes pleading with me to say everything is okay and keep the chat light.

'Sounds like a plan!' I say, because the great unmentionable aside, it actually *does* sound like a great idea. 'Now, let's start on the rest of your lists.'

19

ALL THE FEELS

So, we have a holiday on our joint list. Niamh is going to ask her eldest, Jodie, for some ideas because Jodie took a year out before university and visited as many countries as savings, an overdraft and a nice cheque from her granny on her eighteenth birthday would allow.

Jodie did it old school – trains and buses, hostels and the sofas of folks she met on her travels. Needless to say, Niamh nearly had a stroke when she heard about the latter which was thankfully kept a secret from her until Jodie was safely back in the bosom of her family. While she was lucky to come back with all her organs still intact and not stolen from her in her sleep, she was even luckier to come back with stories of great times and incredible sights. She'd avoided the tourist trail as much as possible to spend time walking the cobbled lanes of Sierra de Francia in Spain, Treviso and the Aosta Valley in Northern Italy, the bustle of Hanoi in Vietnam and the sun-soaked beaches of Thailand. I can't deny it took me a lot of introspection to come to terms with the fact I was brutally jealous of my own goddaughter.

But that will change once we set off on our own adventures –

after I figure out how to pay for them, of course. We might have to set our sights and our budgets a little closer to home than Thailand or Vietnam.

We've agreed that we will go to a gig. A proper outdoor gig. Maybe even a festival requiring tents, and a complete abandonment of our usual standards of personal hygiene. Laura says she will research who is touring and what is happening in the festival scene, as long as no one at whatever event we eventually choose to go to sings about their pussy.

There was a minor discussion about getting a tattoo – matching of course to signify our friendship – but we didn't ultimately decide on anything and to be honest I'm okay with that. Because the elephant, let's call her Nelly, in the corner of the room seemed to nudge me a little with her trunk as the discussion progressed.

I love Laura. I am happy she is back in my life and I am delighted that we can support her during this awful, awful time, but I'm not totally naïve. I know this repair to our friendship is still fragile. And while now might not be the exact right time to pick apart what happened in the big falling out of 2013, I know we will have to cross that particular bridge at some stage.

And that will be incredibly difficult because, when it happened, it almost broke me.

Actually, that's not true. It *did* break me. Losing Laura and our friendship, leading to the implosion of our triumvirate of BFFs, is the most painful thing I've endured in my life, next to losing my father. It hurt more than my marriage ending. The betrayal cut deeper. When my marriage had ended and Simon admitted he was in love with someone else, it was almost a relief. I knew we'd been flogging a dead horse for a long time and I had suspected there was another woman in the picture. I'd spent so long tearing myself apart, creating versions of what he was up to in my own mind that in the end, his admission felt almost anticlimactic. I'd almost replied: 'Oh that? Yeah, I knew that.'

But losing Laura? That hurt on a physical, visceral level. She was my friend. My best friend. She was the one who, along with Niamh, was supposed to be there no matter what life did to us. Relationships come and go, but friendships – the kind you make in your formative years – they're supposed to be forever. They're supposed to be unbreakable. We'd come so far – more than thirty years of friendship had embedded us in each other's lives in a way I thought was rock solid. We were supposed to be each other's person. She was supposed to be the Thelma to my Louise, the Christina Yang to my Meredith Grey, the Rachel to my Monica. To find out that simply wasn't the case was devastating. I have never felt so betrayed in my life. Laura had known, with certainty, that there was another woman. She had met the other woman. She had cooked dinner for the other woman... That was the real slap in the face in all of this. That was real pain.

I imagine it would have all been even harder to bear if we'd had permanent reminders of each other inked into our skin. I'm not sure I'm ready to take that risk even now...

The girls had left just after nine, each of us promising we would have a think about what else to add to our time capsule-inspired to-do list. I cleared up and took the rubbish to the outside bin so that I don't get up in the morning to the smell of stale chips, and I've been sitting on top of my bed since, trying to make sense of all the feelings currently buzzing around my head.

I'm nervous – of course. We discussed some things that will not just make me step out of my comfort zone, but will catapult me very far away from it, without a safety net.

There's a bit of excitement fizzing in the pit of my stomach too. Actually, it's more than just 'a bit'. Laura isn't the only person among us to long for a holiday that doesn't involve the 'Hokey

Cokey' or, as in more recent years for me, the company of two teenage boys who would literally rather be anywhere else than in the vicinity of their mother in a swimsuit.

But I'm sad too. For Kitty, I think, and maybe even for my own mother. For the generations of mothers who never put themselves first and didn't get to live out their dreams. I wonder what sixteen-year-old Roisin Burnside, née Moore, would have written if she had put together a time capsule with her friends. Or what Kitty O'Hagan would've written. Would it have been that different to what I did? Did either of them want to travel more, to get their dream career, or a tattoo with their friends that they wouldn't live to regret?

There's no way to ask Kitty those questions now, but I think that I really probably should ask my own mother. There's a lot about her that remains a mystery to me. I didn't even know that she fancied the arse off Harrison Ford until yesterday, for example. I may think I know my mother but I've always looked at her as the woman she is, and I never really allowed myself to think too much about the girl she was. I assumed that because I have always seen her as a strong, almost fearless matriarch, that she has always felt strong and never felt afraid. I wonder whether she has ever wished for more than the life she has. It makes me feel ashamed that we've never really talked about her hopes and dreams and another UWOS washes over me. Damn it, those feelings seem to be closer to the surface than ever now.

'I think we'll have to go and see Granny tomorrow,' I tell Daniel, who looks at me with his big brown eyes, perking up at the mention of going to see his human granny. I wonder if he knows she refers to him mostly as 'that dog' and swears she's not a dog person but keeps a jar of Markies treats in her cupboard in case he visits.

I give his fur a quick rub and he turns his head to one side and lays it on my lap, staring up at me with such trust that the Unexpected Wave of Sadness merges with an Unexpected Wave of Love for my furry best friend.

'Wouldn't it be great if you could write a letter and let me know what you want out of life too?' I say to him as I get under the covers and snuggle down. He immediately curls into me, one paw on my arm as if he's giving me an actual, honest to God hug and my heart swells. Oh, to be a dog and able to lift the spirits of those around you with a doleful look and fluffy cuddle.

* * *

I rush through my work while fielding calls from a very high maintenance client with a very limited understanding of what my remit actually is. No, I cannot get Lord Alan Sugar to agree to an interview in which he will extol the virtue of the client's medium-sized data analysis business. Especially since Lord Sugar has never heard of the client's business, let alone used it. No, it's not just a matter of 'asking nicely'.

Sometimes I do wonder how some people make it to positions of authority in business when they clearly haven't a notion of how the world works. I've come to the conclusion that it's generally because 1) The Patriarchy, 2) Some people are just very skilled at sounding like they know what they are doing, or 3) Sheer fluke.

In this case I'm pretty sure it falls into the sheer fluke category. However, as telling a client to 'wise the head' is generally frowned upon, I have to use much too big a portion of my daily mental energy working out how to explain Lord Sugar's lack of availability.

We reach a compromise just before lunch where he says he will email Lord Sugar himself, or send him a message on social media, to ask him directly. I wish him well on his quest and make a mental note to check the business mogul's social media feed later for any minor meltdowns.

I call my mum and tell her I'm going to call round, forewarning her that Daniel will be coming with me. 'Would you like me to bring you anything?' I ask.

'Am I allowed to say "not a dog"?' she asks, but I ignore her. She has to know by now that Daniel is like a baby to me since my own babies have cleared off and only really get in touch when they want money or need a pep talk.

'You love him really,' I tell her and she makes an indistinct noise which could possibly be interpreted as an agreement so I decide to take it that way.

'Have you had your lunch yet?' I ask her.

'I was just about to put on a tin of soup,' she says. 'Do you want some too? I seem to have an excess stockpile of them. Still can't seem to break the habit of buying for two,' she says. We both know chicken soup was my father's favourite and from October to March each year he'd have happily eaten it for his lunch every day. As soon as the temperatures started to dip he would start his annual overconsumption.

'Some soup would be lovely,' I tell her, knowing the smell of it filling her kitchen will bring me back to happier times. 'How about I pick up some crusty bread at the shop too? A tiger baguette?'

'I'm not sure my dentures could survive it,' my mother says, 'but God loves a trier. Let's do that.' I can hear her smile on the other end of the line as I say my goodbyes.

* * *

My mother's spoon clatters against her now empty bowl. She sits back and rubs her stomach while eyeing the remaining baguette. 'I don't suppose one more wee piece would hurt,' she says, cutting another slice and spreading it thickly with butter.

I'm tempted to go in for another slice myself but I already know

I've eaten more than I should and I can feel the bread bloats starting to kick in. It's bad news when my loose jeans start to feel tight. That's what I get for abandoning my trusty leggings in a bid to look more put together.

I watch as she slips a small piece of particularly buttery bread to Daniel, who is lying asleep at her feet as if he is her faithful servant. The turncoat.

'So, what brings you over here?' my mother asks.

'Is it so wrong for a daughter to want to spend time with her mother?' I ask.

'Of course not. It's just not all that usual for me to see you this often. What's this, love, three times in five days? I know I said I was getting my affairs in order and all but I'm honestly not planning on shuffling off this mortal coil any time in the immediate future. I know how you worry.'

I shake my head. 'Mum, I just wanted to see you. I worry about you, you know that. And for a woman who has no plans to kick any buckets you do like to live life on the edge sometimes. Falling on the ice or dangling out of attics.'

'Nonsense,' she says. 'I'm just living my life same as I always do. There's no good in me being a burden on anyone else when you all have enough in your own lives to be worrying about.'

'You are not a burden,' I say more firmly than I intended and with an unexpected break in my voice. I hate that she worries that I would ever consider her to be little more than an annoying obligation. I hate it because it couldn't be further from the truth, and if I'm honest, I hate it because I live in fear that my boys will see me that way in the future.

'You are my mother and I love you very much. If spending time with you is a burden, then load me up. I've got wider shoulders than the average woman and years of carrying two healthy boys around have given me an upper body strength well able for you, old woman, so enough of that talk!' I give her a watery smile as a damn traitorous tear starts to cascade its way down my face.

'Rebecca!' my mother says, her voice soft, concern written across her face. She gets up and walks to my chair where she pulls me into a hug and I let her. 'Pet, I didn't mean to upset you. I'm sorry.'

'No,' I say, 'I'm sorry. I'm so sorry. Yes, maybe I'm over a little more than I normally would be but, you know, these last few days I've just been thinking about a lot. You getting your affairs in order, Kitty dying, the time capsule, Laura... all of it. And I realised I've been so very selfish, Mum.'

'You have not!' she chides. 'You've been great, Rebecca. You've always been great. Neither your father nor I have ever had a bad word to say about you.'

'Not even when my marriage went tits up and I ended up a divorcee?' I ask, grabbing a napkin from the table to wipe my nose.

'Especially not then,' my mother says. 'You were brave and you got on with things raising those boys well. We were very proud of you. We still are.'

The words are both a joy to hear and so very difficult to absorb. I do my best to hold in my tears as my mother cuddles me close again, allowing me to feel the warmth of her body, the softness of her jumper, inhale the familiar and comforting scent of her Miss Dior perfume. She is hugging her forty-six-year-old daughter but a part of her is hugging every version of me that came before and I hug her back, embracing each version of the mother I have known through my life.

20

THAT LOVELY FELLAH OFF THE TV

My tears have abated and I feel calm again. Mum and I are now sitting side by side on her floral settee and as we chat, she allows me to lay my head on her shoulder. The gentle touch of her hand occasionally stroking my hair makes me feel safe and loved.

Of course it makes Daniel feel a little jealous. God forbid anyone else have their fur stroked other than him. He is doing his best to nuzzle in between us, but I just encourage him to sit on my other side where I can stroke him. Reluctantly he does as instructed, but the message in his eyes is clear. He thinks this is an extreme injustice and he would much prefer Granny's attention than mine. Well, too bad, Daniel – she's my mammy and my need is greater than yours.

'So, tell me more about these letters,' she says. I've already told her that there were three letters in the time capsules, all written by us for us, and that Niamh is yet to open hers.

'It's probably silly,' I say. 'But they're like letters to our older selves, detailing our ambitions and what we thought our lives would look like in the future.'

'And your life doesn't look the way you thought it would?' she asks and I nod my head.

'Nowhere near. I've totally let the sixteen-year-old version of me down,' I say. 'I'm not writing for some glam magazine. I'm not married to my teenage celebrity crush. I've not travelled the world or lived the high life. I'm here, where I started, single – no, worse than single, I'm divorced.' I grimace. 'My children are studying in a different country.'

'It's only England, pet. It's not like they've run to the other side of the world or like the olden days when you waved goodbye at the docks knowing you'd never see your family again in your lifetime. They could be home in a couple of hours if you needed them.'

I know she's making sense but still, while all that may be true, it is also a fact that the part of my life I cherished so much – the part where I was raising my babies – is now over. They might come back for high days and holidays, but I think I'm wise enough to know they're unlikely to ever make this their home again. I've seen it happen to so many friends. Opportunities are more plentiful in England or elsewhere and young people follow the work. But even if they do come back, they won't be coming back the same people they were when they left. They will have several years of independent living under their belts. They will be fully grown adults. Our relationship will still be forever changed.

'I know,' I say, feeling a little defeated by it all. 'But why does no one warn us about this bit? They want us to give our children everything and more and then we have to try and work out who we are when they leave. What's our purpose in life? Because I'm forty-six and I feel as if I'm starting all over again.'

'No one warns you because no one would do it if they did,' my mother says. 'It's not like the pain of childbirth. There's not a sweetener at the end of it – like a newborn to cuddle – to make up for what you've been through. If everything goes as it should, children will break your heart.'

Damn, I think. This is not the reassuring chat I was hoping for.

'So, I broke your heart?' I ask, ready for the onslaught of guilt to add to the already huge bag of guilt I carry with me wherever I go.

'You did,' she says and I tense. 'But, love, the story doesn't end when your children move out. See that heartbreak? When you have to let your babies go? Well, it's not forever. Things get better. Your heart gets better. If you're lucky – and I count myself as lucky – you get to build a new kind of relationship with your grown-up children, one that is just as rewarding but in a different way. And the added bonus is that you also get to discover yourself again.'

'I'm afraid there's nothing there to discover,' I say, and feel her hand stroking my hair.

'Rebecca, there is so much inside you that has just been waiting for the right time to shine. This is your time.' Her words are as gentle and soothing as her touch.

'Did you feel that way when Ruairi and I moved out? Did you feel like you were going to discover yourself again?'

I feel her shift awkwardly beside me and I sit up so I can see her face. If I'm not mistaken, she is blushing a little. 'This isn't about me, Rebecca,' she says, before calling Daniel over to lavish some affection on him. That's how I know, without a doubt, she is hiding something. A perfectly innocent mother would not willingly invite her arch nemesis to climb up beside her on the sofa.

'It is a bit,' I say. 'I want to understand your experiences too. So, how did you feel when we moved out?'

'Things were different then,' she says, as if we are talking about the 1890s and not the 1990s. 'My generation did things differently to you young ones. And I had your father in my life and as much as I loved that man with every part of me, he required quite a bit of looking after and mollycoddling. I didn't begrudge it, most of the time. He was a good man and we were very happy.'

'But did you feel you were able to reinvent yourself or chase the dreams your sixteen-year-old self had, once you were freed from the shackles of motherhood?' It sounds very dramatic when I put it like that but to be honest, it feels very dramatic now. Millions of women might move past their active mother stage every day the world over, but no one really talks about the seismic shift to your identity that comes with having to work out who you actually are once the apron strings have been cut.

My mother laughs. 'You see, love, that's the difference between my generation and yours. My dreams when I was sixteen *were* to meet a good man, marry him, keep a nice home and raise children. I lived my dreams, love.'

'Mum, there must've been other things...' I say.

'Like what?' she asks. 'I've had a largely happy life. There's many people not that lucky. I'd be churlish to complain about the less-than-perfect parts. No one gets a perfect life.'

'So you think I should be happy with my lot?' I ask her. After all, it has had its challenges and its heartbreaks but it hasn't been bad. Not really.

She smiles. 'You weren't made for the same kind of life I was. The world changed, pet. In the years between me being born and you arriving. It opened up. Your generation were promised you could have it all if you wanted it. I do remember thinking it was very exciting for you. That you'd do things I never would. And I remember that wee girl of mine who wanted to be Lois Lane. Who wanted to see the world and make things happen and I believed you would. But then you met Simon and you got married and had the boys and that was okay too. At first, I thought you were just a different kind of happy and were content to not reach the dizzying heights you used to dream about so I was happy for you too.'

'But then it all went to shit,' I say with a sigh.

'Language, Rebecca!' my mother gently scolds, before taking my hand in hers. 'But you're right. It all went to shit.'

I'm shocked to hear that word come out of my mother's mouth, and that she doesn't even drop her voice to a whisper to say it.

'Oh, don't look so surprised. I know a fair selection of bad words too, and I know when to use them,' she says, a wicked glint in her soft blue eyes. 'You don't live to my age without amassing quite the vocabulary. But look, that aside, Simon was not the man any of us had thought he was and he didn't deserve you or the years you gave him. Nor did he deserve those boys.'

She's right of course. Simon didn't deserve me, and even more so our boys. My boys, as I think of them, definitely deserved more than what they got with him. He's done his level best to make amends in recent years, but the mammy in me will never forgive him hurting them.

'You deserved to marry a man like your father,' she says, a little wobble in her voice. 'A good man and a great daddy too.'

'The best,' I say, squeezing her hand back.

'He believed in you so much and he was so very proud of you. And if he was still here, he'd tell you that you are just a young thing yet and if there is something you want to try, or somewhere you want to go then you should do it. He'd tell you that you'll be dead for a long time so get your living in now. So, love, do what makes your heart happy. Go work for a glam magazine, see the world, marry a celebrity. What about that Rylan fellah? Could you marry him? He seems like a lovely young man.'

'I don't think I'm his type, Mum,' I say, and smile. Far be it from me to explain to her just why we're not a good match.

'Nonsense,' she replies, straightening herself. 'Men like older women these days. I saw them talking about it on *Loose Women*. MILFs and cougars and what not.'

I'm about to tell her about the dating sites I stumbled across looking for sugar mamas when she starts to speak again. 'The Loose Women even said some men like a GILF, which is a Granny I'd Like To F—'

'Mum!' I say, shocked to my very core. But she isn't bothered by my interruption.

'Anyway,' she says, 'Mrs Bishop and I were joking we should get on that... what's it called... that Timber or whatever it is.'

'Tinder,' I say, floored that my mother and her elderly neighbour have been discussing dating apps I haven't even been brave enough to register on yet. Between that and the swearing, I'm starting to worry she may have had some sort of stroke.

'Ah, *Tinder*,' she repeats. 'I suppose that makes more sense. Like a flame of passion.' She nods and smiles, no doubt conjuring the image in her head. 'We thought they were just being really rude by calling it Timber. You know, because the men would get wood...'

'Mum!' I don't know whether to cover my ears, call for an ambulance or call for an exorcism because there is no way my seventy-six-year-old mother is discussing euphemisms for an erect penis without something being very much amiss. Stroke or demonic possession being the two obvious possibilities.

My mother laughs at my shocked expression, until tears start to slide down her cheeks. She looks beautiful, and joyous and happy and I can't help but start to laugh too.

'I told you I knew some things,' she says eventually as she wipes the tears from her eyes.

'I believe you! I don't need a demonstration,' I laugh. 'Just promise me one thing. Please don't go on Tinder. Because I really don't want to have to try and explain to you what a fuckboy is...'

'Rebecca!' my mother scolds. 'Language!'

21

THE MAGIC MONEY TREE

I stay with my mother all afternoon. She even accompanies me on a short walk around Brooke Park with Daniel, who thankfully behaves like the sweet angel baby he is and walks on the lead beautifully. We have one potentially worrying moment when he catches a whiff of a sausage roll emanating from Gwyn's Cafe close to the park gates. Thankfully, I am able to distract him with some cleverly secreted ham I put in a food bag in my pocket before we left the house, just in case of such incidents.

While the air is cold, it's dry and we're able to enjoy the fresh early winter weather. The sun hangs low and lazy in the sky and as Mum and I walk arm in arm up and down the well-tended pathways we reminisce about my childhood. We had so many picnics here on these lawns, before or after exhausting ourselves in the playpark at the top of the hill, or getting soaked to the skin in the large central fountain. The park was always so busy, so full of life and while it is still beautiful, I don't think it still attracts families for full days out the way it used to. I suppose we all have so many other options these days.

But we didn't need anything else when I was young. I know, I'm sounding like an old woman reminiscing about 'the good old days' but they *were* good. Laura, Niamh and I spent so much time sitting on the benches of this park poring over a joint copy of *Smash Hits* or taking turns to listen to Niamh's Walkman. One summer we upgraded to a boombox and would practice our dance routines on the grass, blasting out the hits of Stock, Aiken and Waterman. God only knows what the other people in the park thought at the sight. I imagine they thought there was a bit of a want in all three of us, but they were good times and innocent times when we didn't have to think about whatever else might have been going on in our home city or across Northern Ireland. Our parents, all of them, from Kitty to Mum and Dad, and Niamh's parents too, did their very best to protect us from the harshest realities of The Troubles. But we weren't ignorant of them – we just learned to live with them.

'Are you lost in your own wee world?' my mother asks as we walk towards the park gates to head home again. 'I thought I was supposed to be the one in danger of doting.'

I smile. 'I'm just remembering,' I tell her. 'And thinking how grateful I am that I grew up when I did. If you ignore what was happening politically, those were easier times.'

'Hard to ignore what was happening politically though,' my mum says. 'But I agree. You know, going back to what we were talking about earlier, about living your life differently... maybe the only regret I have, and it's a small one all the same, is that we didn't move away from here when things were bad. Then again, nowhere else would've felt like home.'

'Where would you have moved?' I ask her. 'If you could've chosen anywhere in the world. Where would you have gone?'

'I'm a home-bird, love. I'd probably not have moved further than Donegal, just over the border. And I'd have been content as anything there, as long as I could see the sea. Do you remember that year we rented a house down in The Downings? And the sun shone the whole week? I don't think you and Ruairi even had a cross word between you the whole time. We spent our days on the beach together. It was blissful. I'd have settled for that. Hey, maybe I'll go wild and book myself a week away down there – since we're all talking about living big and doing mad things!' she says as we walk through the cast-iron gates onto Creggan Hill where the immediate sound of the after-school traffic reminds us that as much as Brooke Park is quiet and calming, it is only an oasis in the middle of the city.

An idea comes into my mind that maybe I could get Ruairi on board with Caroline and the kids and plan a family break. All of us heading to The Downings. If we make sure it's when the boys are home from university then there's a chance we could all – the remaining Burnsides – be in the same place at the same time creating some shared memories.

By the time we're back at her house and I'm cooking her dinner I'm feeling positively on top of the world. The afternoon has been lovely. I can't remember the last time we laughed together so much or were so open with each other. This family break is something I shouldn't let slide. Then again, I still haven't figured out where I'm getting this magic money tree I'll need. A holiday with the girls. A holiday with the family. Going to gigs or festivals. Helping Saul with his expenses. Maybe it's time to consider selling some feet pictures on OnlyFans or something. I'd have to get a series of preparatory pedicures first and they don't come cheap though, especially not with my feet, which I have neglected over the years.

I might need to find some other way to make some cash.

The words my mother is sure my father would've said come to mind. 'You'll be dead for a long time, so get your living in now.' Maybe I shouldn't worry so much about raiding my savings. Not that I think there's that much in the account any more thanks to a broken-down car, Saul and Adam's accommodation costs and his emergency plea for financial assistance, but surely there has to be enough for a week in a cottage in rural Donegal? And if Ruairi is coming, he can chip in too. Lord knows he makes more money than I do, and his wife, Caroline, has a high-paid job with the Council.

I've made Mum her favourite dinner of mashed potato, peas and pork chops. To my surprise she instructs me to cook up the one left-over chop still in her fridge and feed it to 'that dog'.

'Sure, it will only go off if he doesn't eat it,' she says. 'And it's a sin to waste food.' But I notice her ruffling his fur and he nuzzles against her and I can see she is definitely less averse to him than usual.

Once I've washed up, I head for home – walking again, much to Daniel's delight. I'm pretty sure he thinks all his birthdays have come at once getting three walks in the one day. I only hope he's not going to expect this level of physical activity every day going forward, although it does cross my mind that if I really need to increase my income I could maybe take on dog walking. Daniel would love it, apart from the fact he can get a little possessive of me. But I could possibly make a few extra quid, and walk the legs off myself leading me to become a toned and lithe MILF instead of the walking Bird's Trifle I feel I'm morphing into.

I sigh, and Daniel stares up at me mournfully before nuzzling his head against my leg. 'I know,' I tell him. 'I shouldn't be body shaming myself. It's the patriarchy, Daniel. I can't help it. It's programmed in us to hate our bodies. But you're right. Haven't I promised myself I'll make peace with my body? I think I need to workshop that with the girls a bit,' I say, but Daniel has been distracted by a strong scent near some hedges and hauls me across the path so that he can liberally apply some Eau De Fox Poo on his furry little pulse points.

These are the times when I fully understand why my mother calls him 'that dog', I think, as I fight to pull him away from the godawful stench. My heart sinks at the thought of having to give him a bath when we get home. I'm definitely running on fumes right now and was really hoping to just curl up in front of the fire with the TV on while I scour my laptop for ideas on how women of a certain age can start to fall in love with their bodies before segueing into searching holiday homes in Donegal where I can take my mum for a much-deserved break. Instead, I will be up to my elbows in poo-infused water, trying my best to stop a slippery dog from escaping from the bath and causing unknown havoc as he bolts for freedom around the house.

I make a mental note to make sure whatever accommodation I book for my mother's break is also dog friendly. Daniel would love the chance to spend a week getting to run among the sand dunes and roll in all sorts of coastline unmentionables.

Yes, there's a lot to plan and a lot of things to think about just now but it's all good. This is me taking control. I am empowering myself. Becki would be proud.

As long as I can stay awake long enough to do so, I think with a yawn as we finally reach home and I shoo Daniel into the bathroom before he can rub his new favourite scent all over my sofa and rugs.

22

A FAMILY-SIZED BAG OF MALTESERS

To my shame, the rest of the working week zooms by at a rate of knots and my research doesn't go much further than falling down a number of online rabbit holes that started with good intentions but ended quite unproductively.

Where I started to look into holiday rentals in Donegal, I ended up – somehow – watching countless true crime cases online of sociopaths luring unsuspecting holiday makers to their demise. When I started to research tattoo ideas I ended up watching six episodes back to back of *Just Tattoo of Us* and wondering why anyone would subject themselves to getting a tattoo done that they hadn't personally approved and which could turn out to be pretty offensive.

With these frequent side quests away from what I am supposed to be doing, I've come to realise that the menopause might just be affecting my ability to focus on the task at hand – along with everything else.

Maybe this is the reason a lot of women my age no longer live big and crazy lives and become perfectly happy just to get through each and every day, and maybe reward themselves after with a nice cold glass of wine each evening.

My 'Ten Ways to Survive Your Forties' article has stalled at number five which, at the moment, is just 'surrender to the ageing process and sleep more'. It's not quite the mixture of inspiration and humour I was hoping for.

Maybe I've been too ambitious with my transformative plans. It's too much to expect me to suddenly go from just about holding my shit together to arranging a completely new supply of shit to deal with on top of everything else. I should accept that I have shit-holding-together limitations and cut myself some slack.

Maybe women like me, who can see fifty waving at us from the top of the hill, should just be happy with our lot. We should leave the adventures to the youngsters and invest our energy instead into finding comfortable cardigans and stylish yet functional footwear.

Perhaps I don't have to reinvent myself simply because last week was exceptionally emotional and my feelings were stripped raw and easily manipulated. Surely I don't have to change my current existence because of a letter I wrote thirty years ago. Who would be daft enough to take life advice from a sixteen-year-old, teetotal virgin who loved making up dance routines with her friends in public in the local park? But when I try and tell myself that I can just be me and I'm under no obligation to change for anyone, a little voice whispers in my ear.

'You are being a complete and utter tit,' it says. 'You know you've been feeling past it for a while now. You know you've wanted more. Stop talking yourself out of it just because you're tired. Don't you realise you're tired because you've allowed yourself to get too comfortable?'

The fact that the voice sounds very much how I remember Kitty O'Hagan sounding is not lost on me. And when it's not Kitty giving me a good talking to, it's my father's turn to speak to me from beyond the grave. 'You'll be dead a long time,' he says over and over again. 'Have you done everything you wanted to? And by the way, your mother really does deserve a nice holiday.'

By Friday afternoon I am semi-delirious with it all. Between the true crime watch-fest, the tattoo trauma, and being haunted by Kitty and my father – who seem to be tag-teaming me like a modern-day Marley and Marley – I am feeling more than a little overwhelmed. (Yes, I know in the book there is but one Marley, but in *The Muppet Christmas Carol* there are two, and I will always, always defer to the Muppets.)

In fact, I'm feeling so overwhelmed that when I see Niamh's name pop up on my phone screen I do the unthinkable and let it go to voicemail. I don't have the physical or mental energy to have actual voice conversations with anyone I don't absolutely have to today. I've answered my phone when work have called, because I want them to keep paying me at the end of every month. I answered my phone when my mother called, because it's simply easier and quicker to get to the point over the phone. Occasionally she does try to message me instead – Adam having installed WhatsApp on her phone before he left for university – but she tends to get a little flustered, over rely on autocorrect and take at least fifteen minutes to draft even the most basic reply. We have both agreed that voice calls are both our preferred options for communication, even if today that meant my listening to her give a running commentary of *Homes Under The Hammer* before getting to the point that she wondered if I could take her, and Mrs Bishop, for a wee run up the road to Strabane so that they could have a potter around Asda for Christmas bits. I agreed, of course, and we're going at eight tomorrow morning because older people tend to get up at stupid o'clock and always have to get on the road as early as possible – even if it's only a twenty-minute jaunt up the road to the nearest Asda.

All things considered, this means by the time Niamh calls me, I have exhausted my ability to form coherent sentences out loud. It's already dark outside and I've just drawn my curtains against the blackness. I am lying prone on the sofa like a pyjama-wearing sloth. I don't even feel the desire to have a glass of wine, but I am fully planning on eating the full family-sized bag of Maltesers I bought earlier, and I refuse to feel guilty about it.

When my phone rings again fifteen minutes later, and Niamh's name flashes up once more, I can't hold in the yell of, 'Only psychopaths phone people instead of messaging them,' before squeezing my eyes shut and waiting for the call to ring out. I know there's an option to reject call immediately and send them directly to voicemail, but I don't want Niamh to think that I'm actively avoiding her. It might be true, but it's not personal. I'm actively avoiding everyone right now.

I think about switching my phone off or to silent but I know in my bones the moment I do, I will tempt the gods of ill fortune to bestow something catastrophic on either my mother or my two boys. I have imagined the scenario in which I miss a vital, possibly life-saving call countless times and I know it never plays out well for anyone. It's simply not worth taking the risk.

When, half an hour later, my phone rings a third time, Daniel lets out a volley of barks that seem to indicate that he is fed up with my non-phone-answering shenanigans and wants me to take the call before he gets really annoyed and pees on the rug or something.

'Only psychopaths phone people instead of messaging first,' I say without even offering a hello. 'I apologise for saying that if this is a legitimate emergency, but if it's not a legitimate emergency then I will be ending the call quickly.'

'Define emergency,' Niamh says.

'Something life-threatening, unexpected baby in the uterus area related, or involving a real-life sighting of Michael Bublé – without his beautiful wife – in the city centre,' I offer.

'Hmmm,' Niamh says. 'It's none of those so I suppose I should probably just let you end the call...'

I role onto my back and sigh. She has me over a barrel here and she knows it. I'm too nosey and she is calling my bluff fair and square.

'You're on the phone now, you might as well tell me,' I say. 'But I'm going to warn you, I'm in a kind of funky shitty mood and I might not respond appropriately.'

'Fair enough,' she says. 'I get it. It's been a fun Friday for me too. If we ever get access to that imaginary time machine we discussed, can we go back in time far enough to give me a good shake and tell me not to go into teaching because in 2024, Year 11 will suck the very life from my bones?'

'It's a deal,' I say. 'So spill. About why you're calling. Not about Year 11. Unless that's why you're calling, obviously.'

'No. This is not school related. It's more exciting than that. We're going to have a pamper day tomorrow. It's all booked so you can't argue. And it's my treat so you really, really can't argue. Let's call it my Christmas present to you. And Laura.'

My stomach sinks with that familiar feeling of guilt that someone is intending on spending their hard-earned money on me. No. This isn't right. I pull myself up to sitting. 'Niamh, you can't do that. It's too much,' I protest.

'Look, every birthday and Christmas for forever, Paul's mum has got me gift vouchers for that fancy spa on Ivy Lane and I never use them because I tend not to like people hoking and poking at me but look, they're doing this City Girl pamper afternoon thing and I thought, "There's a sign if ever we needed one. Frig it. We have to book that!" So I did, for the three of us at three in the afternoon. Do you remember when we were teenagers and Kitty lent us *City Girl* to read and then we all became obsessed with wanting to be like Devlin and Maggie and whatever the other one was called...'

'Caroline,' I say, recounting the characters in the iconic Patricia Scanlan books we had adored in our teen years and into adulthood. 'I still love those books.'

'I still want to be like Devlin when I grow up,' Niamh says wistfully, 'and if a City Girl pamper afternoon wasn't a sign from Kitty herself to be more Devlin then I don't know what is. Sixteen-year-old us would be absolutely wetting themselves with excitement at the thought of a makeover.'

'Hang on,' I say as her words sink in. 'A makeover? What do you mean by a makeover? I thought this was just a pamper thing? You know, maybe a facial and a rub of our shoulders? A makeover sounds a bit more dramatic?'

Already I'm having visions of becoming the human equivalent of one of those awful *Changing Rooms* transformations in the nineties. Everyone would smile awkwardly at the camera at the end, but clearly, we'd all look awful and be dying inside.

'I'm sure it's not. It's just a bit of pampering with cocktails thrown in. Imagine we could walk out of there looking like actual MILFs,' Niamh says and I cringe at the thought. I don't want to look like a MILF. I just want to lie on my sofa, in my pyjamas and my Oodie and eat my family bag of Maltesers like a normal middle-aged woman.

It's then I remember my mother and Mrs Bishop and our planned outing to Asda.

'Shit!' I say. 'I've just remembered, I promised to take my mum and Mrs Bishop up to Asda tomorrow to do a bit of Christmas shopping and there's only three weeks left until the big day so I don't want to put it off. Neither of them get out very much and I know they'll be looking forward to it.' I'm aware that I am laying it on heavy, but I know that while Niamh rarely takes a 'no' from me, she wouldn't do anything that would risk annoying or upsetting Roisin Burnside.

'Ah, really?' she asks, disappointment evident in her voice.

'I only arranged it this afternoon,' I say. 'And you know she had that fall last week, and Mrs Bishop hasn't a being near her to look after her so I really wouldn't want to call her back and let them both down. If I know them they'll be making their shopping lists already and have themselves all excited for the trip.' I'm aware I'm only talking about Asda and not an all-expenses-paid trip to the Seychelles, so I tell myself to reel the drama in a bit. 'And you know how my mother loves Asda and thinks there's no place like it.'

'I know,' Niamh says. 'In fairness I could do with a wee run up to Asda myself. It's great for getting clothes for Fiadh. How about I come along too? We can make it an intergenerational girls' day of fun.'

How Niamh has the energy for this level of enthusiasm at the end of the working week is beyond me, but here she is nonetheless, rallying the troops for a trip of a lifetime... to the supermarket.

The only problem is, if I say yes she will learn quite quickly that we're leaving the house at eight in the morning and she will also work out that even on her best days my mother isn't able to manage more than a couple of hours at the very most in Asda. Which, of course means she will work out very quickly that we will definitely be home in time for our City Girl makeover appointment. I've really landed myself in it this time.

And that's how I find myself agreeing to whatever in God's name a City Girl makeover is – as long as no one comes at me with hot wax, all should be good.

23

EMBRACE THE FULL BRIEF

Taking my mother and Mrs Bishop around a supermarket three weeks before Christmas reminds me greatly of what it was like to take the boys out when they were wee and totally feral. Both women went straight for the big trollies after plotting their plan of action on the drive up from Derry to the border town of Strabane. Niamh was very impressed. 'I thought older people liked to take their time and have a dodder about the place,' she said. 'Those two are something else. I wouldn't be surprised if they slipped on some camo gear to go full guerrilla operation.'

'I'm not sure camo gear would blend in with the sparkles and bright colours of the Asda women's wear department,' I say. 'Otherwise, I'd agree with you.'

My mother is a creature of habit. Each year, even though we are both almost fifty, she insists on buying new pyjamas and socks for Ruairi and me. She also buys new pyjamas for my twins and for Ruairi's two girls. This is a tradition that cannot be broken, not even when I tell her the boys aren't really big into pyjamas and are more likely to sleep in their jocks and a T-shirt than anything. 'And if there was a fire, would they run out into the street in their pants?'

she argues. 'I think not. So a decent pair of pyjamas they can wear in an emergency is a good thing to have. And what if they had to go into hospital? Sure, you wouldn't want to be scrambling round trying to buy them pyjamas then. No, Rebecca. I have bought them pyjamas every year since their first Christmas and I am not about to stop now. Let me do things my way!'

So I do. I watch as she enters the store, goes straight for the escalator to the first floor and starts throwing pyjamas into her trolley as if she's on *Supermarket Sweep* while Mrs Bishop is zooming up and down the aisles like a demon selecting an array of Christmas jumpers, socks and pants. I didn't know Mrs Bishop could move that fast.

Meanwhile Niamh and I are standing beside the children's clothes while she tries to pick out some new bits and bobs for Fiadh – aka the fussiest child in the world – while my dying ovaries are having one last gasp of longing at the sight of the teeny tiny onesies declaring it is 'Baby's First Christmas'. I think of my boys – both of them standing at over six feet tall, hairy and beardy with deep voices and size-twelve feet and I marvel that they ever fitted into a onesie in their lives. It's even madder that at one time they both existed in my uterus together. And now look at them, with their men-feet and their chest hair. I'd give my right ovary – not that it would be much use to anyone at this stage – to be able to spend just ten minutes with them as the wee boys they used to be. I know I was permanently exhausted and my house looked at all times as if it had just been carpet-bombed but oof, the feel of their wee chubby, often sticky, hands on my face or holding my hand. It made me feel like the most important person in the world.

'Rebecca, should I get you a 14-16 or an 18-20?' my mother hollers loud enough that I can hear her over the Christmas croonings of my one true love, Mr Michael Bublé, on the shop's speaker system.

I feel a sea of eyes turn in my direction and run their way up and down my figure, all asking themselves the same question my mother has just asked me and I want to crawl inside my own body and die. This brings back a very vivid memory of her announcing to both my father and my brother that I was 'a woman now' when I got my first period circa 1989. In those days, in our part of the world, a period was talked about then as if it were some giant, dirty secret and it was a fate worse than death for a boy to find out you were bleeding *out of your vagina*. That my mother relayed this news to my father and my one-year-older-than-me brother over our evening meal of potato waffles and Turkey Jetters – with a side salad because we weren't heathens – was utterly mortifying. Almost as mortifying as my mother announcing what size she thought I might be in Asda, even if anyone with eyes could probably have a fair guess at it without being prompted. As I hurry across the shop floor to tell her that the 14-16 would probably be okay, but maybe just go with the 18-20 for extra comfort, I wonder if matricide is always morally reprehensible.

'Mum!' I hiss. 'Do you have to announce my size to the whole shop?'

'Everyone is too busy worrying about their own problems to worry about what size of pyjamas a stranger in a shop is wearing,' she says. I really hope that's true.

'You shouldn't let what other people think annoy you,' she adds. 'You're perfect the way you are. Now tell me this, if I'm getting you some new underwear would you like a full brief this time? They are so comfy and easy on the old menopausal tummy.'

I know she is trying to be lovely and supportive and I don't want to be cross at her so I agree to get the big knickers and resolve to order myself something a little more alluring from Marks and Spencer when we get home. If I am going to enter the dating arena, I'll need something sexier than a full cotton belly-warming brief.

My humiliation complete for one morning, I saunter back to Niamh who has adopted a one-of-everything approach for Fiadh.

'I figure if I buy it all, she can choose herself and I can return whatever she doesn't like. It just makes it easier. I'm going to pick up some toys for her Christmas presents too,' she says. 'Is it okay if I leave those in your house so madam doesn't find them? I think we've only one or two Santa years left and I don't want to risk getting discovered.'

'Of course,' I tell her.

'I don't know what I'll do when we've no Santa to worry about any more,' Niamh says, a little misty-eyed. 'It will feel like the proper end of an era. Why is everything speeding up so fast just now? The years just fly in.'

In the background, Michael Bublé is singing 'Have Yourself A Merry Little Christmas' – a song that reduces me to a mess at the best of times – and I'm watching my best friend get emotional. And Niamh Cassidy never gets emotional. Not the sad kind anyway. She's famed for her ability to laugh in the face of adversity and not let the times life has served her a shite sandwich get her down. I both admire her and fear her because of it. In my darkest moments I've wondered if she is some kind of sociopath. I mean, she has never ever cried at *Grey's Anatomy*. Not even the 007 scene at the end of series five.

I watch as she glances down at her trolley, filled with clothes that seem aimed at the tween market as opposed to the cutesy little girl market. There are no pretty party dresses or traditional tartan smocks. It's skinny jeans, slogan sweaters and a pair of high-tops.

'Our baby is growing up,' I say, tears pricking at my own eyes. Fiadh, being the very unexpected surprise that she was, has felt a little like our communal child these last seven years and I have revelled in her childhood in a way I didn't have the patience for when the twins were young.

'You don't expect it to go so fast,' she says. 'Even when it feels interminable, and you want to swing for every single fucker who tells you childhood goes by in the flash of an eye. But it really does go so fast.'

I reach out to give her a consoling hug but in a moment she seems to switch back to Niamh mode and shake off her tearfulness.

'Oh my God,' I tell her. 'You've just had an Unexpected Wave of Sadness!'

'A what?' she asks. 'Wise up. I'm not sad. I'm fine. Just fine. There's no wave of anything. Just a moment which was perfectly justifiable and understandable given that I've just put a top with the slogan "*Sassy*" on it in my trolley for my seven-year-old. But it's done. I'm fine. Now let's go to the toys and see if they have the Blue- tooth karaoke mic she has my heart broken asking for. And before you say anything else, you will be coming over on Boxing Day so she can perform the entire set list from Taylor Swift's Eras Tour for your listening pleasure.'

'I don't mind,' I say. 'As long as she lets me join in to "Cruel Summer".'

'I've already told her that you and I will be her backing singers. She didn't take that news well.'

With that, Niamh marches off towards the toy section. I can hear my mother shout, 'Rebecca, would you like a thermal vest?' as I add *worry about Niamh* to my to-do list. Something is not right in her world and it's not just Fiadh getting older. I know Niamh, and this is something more than that.

24

A WOMAN'S TOUCH

Niamh is back on form when we arrive at Sonas Spa and is happy to take the lead while I eye the price list on the wall and try not to suffer a myocardial infarction. (I've checked, by the way and Dr Miranda Bailey was in her early forties when she had a heart attack in *Grey's*, so it's entirely possible that one might befall me too.) While Niamh chats to the receptionist, who she apparently taught five years ago, Laura explains the different arrays of facials to me. It seems our Laura is no stranger to pampering sessions. That's probably why she looks a good five to ten years younger than both Niamh and me. I'd been putting it down to the fact she only has one child whereas I've endured twin boys and Niamh has four of the little darlings. Given the fact Niamh works with teenage children all day every day too, it's a wonder she doesn't look as if she's in her nineties. I'm convinced young people thrive through sucking the life force directly out of surrounding adults.

Laura is explaining something to me about how collagen and skin elasticity should be key areas of focus for menopausal women but I'm only half listening. My skin care regime, if I could be so bold to call it that, has only recently moved on from baby wipes and the occasional sweep of moisturiser. I only switched up my routine because I'd noticed my skin was suddenly drier than the Sahara desert in the middle of a heatwave – and when I say 'switched up', I switched to Dove soap and a regular sweep of moisturiser. I've never had a proper facial in my life and the last time I had a full manicure was just before my wedding when I went all out and got false nails with a French Polish. They had felt so alien on my hands that I'd hauled them off on the plane to our honeymoon and it had taken months for my natural nails to recover. Not realising I was only peeling off falsies, Simon also took months to recover from thinking I had lost the run of myself and was tearing my actual nails from my fingers.

I probably should have realised then that Simon Cooke did not have the stomach to spend a lifetime of forevers with me.

I'm pulled from my reverie with the arrival of what looks like a literal child carrying a tray of tall-stemmed glasses, filled to the brim with Prosecco, and a plate of chocolate-covered strawberries. I could get used to this kind of pampering, I think, wondering if I could just request that I be allowed to lay on a chaise-longue, drinking fizz and eating chocolate-covered fruit while Niamh and Laura get all their treatments done without me.

The childlike figure, who it turns out is the salon owner, speaks in a soft, angelic voice as she welcomes us to her spa and the City Girl experience. Combined with the soft background music and the sweet smell of essential oils in the air, her voice actually has quite a soothing effect. And as I drink more of the chilled-to-perfection Prosecco, I start to think this sweet angel child could convince me to try anything. Even hot wax.

Thankfully for me, her and my unkempt pubic region, she doesn't.

Instead she tells us that we will each enjoy a soothing rejuvenating facial, perfect for menopausal skin.

'Does it have collagen?' Laura asks and the salon owner, whose name is Gabby according to the shiny badge on her tunic, nods that it does. She adds, 'Gold star for you!' and Laura beams with pride while I feel a little jealous that I don't appear to be Gabby's favourite.

'Along with your facial, you will each enjoy a hot stone massage to ease any tension from your bodies and a luxury manicure with gel polish.' It sounds quite lovely.

'And the makeover part?' I ask, wondering how on earth Gabby and team of angels can fit all those treatments into our three-hour slot.

'Well I hope you won't be too disappointed,' Gabby trills. 'But your friend Niamh here explained you were a little nervous at the thought of a transformation and maybe could benefit more from our rejuvenation and relaxation package so we did a little rejigging and poof – no need to fear we'll go in heavy handed with the foundation and blusher. Although, don't worry, you'll still get your Prosecco and snacks!' She smiles but I'm wondering just how awkward it was for Niamh to explain my reticence. Could that be why she was in a funny mood earlier?

'Well, that sounds like exactly what the doctor ordered,' Laura says.

'Yes,' Gabby replies in a tone of voice that oozes empathy and sympathy, 'Niamh tells me it has been a tough time for you. Don't worry, we'll help ease some of that tension in your body and have you floating out of here a new woman.'

'Thank you,' Laura says a little tearfully. I look at Niamh to thank her too and see she's also a little tearful, but when she sees me looking she quickly adopts a smile and claps her hands together to attract all our attention. 'Right then,' she says, in her best teacher voice. 'We should get going with all this carry on, shouldn't we?'

'Thank you,' I tell her. 'For organising this. You're a star.'

'Sure, I know,' she says. 'And when I thought about it, the last thing any of us need is a massive makeover. Before you know it, we'll lose the run of ourselves and dye our hair Menopause Magenta, start wearing really thick glasses frames and dungarees with DM boots.'

'Menopause Magenta?' Laura asks.

'It's a thing,' Niamh says. 'I've seen it. You *must* have seen it. Women having mid-life crises start dying their hair wacky colours and experimenting with different looks and, you know, fair play to them if it makes them happy. But it's not you, girls. It's not what you need and it's not what sixteen-year-old you would have wanted either. Sixteen-year-old us would want us to feel good and look good and put ourselves first for a bit. So get your holes into those treatment rooms and get pampered for Christ's sake.'

There's something a little manic about how she's talking but I'm certainly not crazy enough to pull at this particular thread any further just now. I sense that my darling Niamh might just be on the edge. So I nod, say, 'Yes, miss,' like the good girl I am and get my hole – as she so delicately put it – into the treatment room where Gabby hands me a dressing gown and instructs me to strip down to my knickers and get ready for stage one of my pampering, the hot stone massage. I start to reluctantly do exactly as she tells me, even though it's been at least ten years since anyone has seen me without a bra.

'I'll just leave the room while you get ready,' she says before I have my top lifted enough to reveal that I opted for comfort not fashion with my underwear today. 'You can put your clothes on that chair and then lie down on your tummy on the table and I'll be in shortly. I've left you a little blanket there to pull up around yourself to make you feel more relaxed. The massage is concentrated on your neck and back. It's all very discreet.'

I breathe a sigh of relief. Thank God. No enforced nudity.

Gabby looks at me. 'It's okay to find this a bit unsettling,' she says. 'Especially if you're not used to pampering yourself – and you'd be surprised the number of women who are not at all used to pampering themselves. Some even find it very emotional. It can be a form of release.'

I feel a little bubble of something I can't quite name rise up inside me and I immediately try to dampen it down. I don't want to be feeling 'feelings' in front of a virtual stranger. I don't want any form of 'release' – whatever that means. A fart, after all, is a form of release.

'I'm only saying,' Gabby continues. 'What happens in here, stays in here. Consider it to have the sanctity of a confessional. And there is no body issue, lump or bump I haven't seen before and dealt with before. So relax and let me take care of you for a bit.'

I don't think I have ever wanted to hug a stranger more. Gabby exudes a calmness and I immediately know I can trust her as she gives a small smile and gestures towards the door, indicating she is leaving. I strip off in peace and quiet and climb up on the table which – oh my God – is heated. If they could, I'm sure my boobs would sigh with relief as I rest them on the gently warmed towelling surface, then place my head on the cushioned headrest. I haul the soft blanket Gabby left for me up over my back and then I allow myself to let go, relax and embrace the calming sensations of this dimly lit, fragrant, almost womb-like treatment room.

To some women these spa visits are par for the course but for me it's a revolutionary act of self-care – something I put to the bottom of a very long and never-ending to-do list. Massages and facials, and even a gel polish, are not something I've had the time or money for as I tried to raise my boys and just get through each day.

If I had extra money it went to treating the boys. Or my mum. Or paying a little extra off a bill.

The wobbly feeling returns. It dawns on me it's guilt, even though Niamh is still insisting on covering the cost for this afternoon. Could it be that I feel guilty simply for putting myself first?

I remind myself to breathe through it. It's okay to put myself first for an afternoon, isn't it? It's okay to relax enough to enjoy a massage, and a facial and a gel nail polish. I might even go for slut-red even though I have no one to be a slut for.

There's a knock on the door and Gabby lets herself back in and asks if I'm comfortable in a voice that is even softer than it was before. I wonder if it would be appropriate to ask her to make me a recording of her reading a bedtime story that I can play to lull myself over to sleep each evening.

Sadly, I'm pretty sure it isn't, so I say nothing and simply allow myself to relax while she gets to work. 'I'll do a light massage first,' she whispers in her little angelic voice. 'Just to loosen you up a bit. Then we'll place the hot stones on acupressure points along your neck and spine. This will help release any further tension and anxiety your body might be holding on to, and it may ease any pain you may be experiencing in that area. Do you suffer from back pain?'

'I'm forty-six,' I tell her. 'I suffer from back pain, knee pain, hip pain and just general all-over pain.' I say it in a jokey voice even though I'm not joking. Every month a new ailment seems to get added to my list of ongoing ailments. Injuries no longer heal quickly and they leave their mark as you edge closer to your demise.

Gabby gives a little angelic tinkle, which I think is a laugh. 'Forty-six is hardly old,' she says. 'You've a lot of living left in you.'

'Maybe,' I say. 'But sometimes it feels old. You'll understand in time, probably. What age are you, Gabby?'

'Oh, I'm twenty-eight – the big three-oh is looming! Eek!' she says. I want to cry. I can barely remember my own big three-oh these days. I just have scattered images in my mind of a meal out with Simon and friends, drinks and then wishing I'd skipped both when dealing with two boisterous toddlers the following day. Simon, if I remember correctly, had a terrible hangover and had to take to his bed.

'Anyway,' she says. 'By the time you walk out of here today we'll have you feeling re-invigorated and hopefully minus all those aches and pains.'

'If you achieve that I'll be calling the Vatican to have you lined up for a sainthood,' I joke.

The touch of her hands on my back makes me jump even though I've been fully anticipating it.

'Sorry, is that a little cold for you?' she asks, but no, it's not cold. Her hands are perfectly warm and lovely. The feeling of them pressing into my tired muscles and drawing down along my spine just feels so good.

''S'fine,' I say, my words already a little slurred with the blissful sensations flowing through my body right now. I stifle a moan, afraid to let it out in case it sounds a little like a sex moan. Not that I remember too much about sex moans. It has been a long, long time since I moaned about anything other than housework and Donegal drivers.

It's been ten years since someone touched my bare skin in so tender yet purposeful a way. Of course, the more I try to hold in the moans of pleasure and release, the greater my need to vocalise how I am feeling grows. Never in my life did I think I'd have to start trying to remember the names of all the Walton children to stop my body reacting involuntarily to being caressed by another human. Dear God, is that what Gabby meant when she said someone people find it a form of release?

John Boy, Jason, Mary Ellen... who comes after Mary Ellen? It better not be me, that's for sure. It's not Jim-Bob. I know that much. Or the youngest girl – Elizabeth. I run through my 'Goodnights' to keep my mind focused on not humiliating myself as Gabby's hands run the length of my spine.

'*Erin!*' I finally gasp out loud, with great relief.

25

_____

BRINGING SEXY BACK

'How did that feel for you?' Gabby asks as we finish the massage and she hands me a glass of iced water to drink.

'Well, it was quite lovely,' I tell her, my face still flushed with embarrassment at how my body had reacted to her touch. Am I the female equivalent of a dirty old man? I wonder. Then again, there was no inappropriate touching. I didn't ask her for a happy ending and while I may have called the name 'Erin' out loud I think that might just have coincided with her unknotting a muscle in my back. Honest, guv. I haven't had some kind of lesbian awakening on the massage table, my body has just remembered what it was like to be touched in a tender way. It wasn't sexual, but it was nice.

And it made me realise that maybe having someone else – someone I'm attracted to – touch me in a tender way might be nice as well. It might be worth taking a chance on the dating apps after all, even if the thought terrifies me. Niamh will no doubt ask me what I have to lose, but I don't think she'll be happy when I reply, 'My last remaining crumbs of self-worth.'

I have generally accepted that no one with an ounce of wit would find me attractive in that way. This was compounded by

Simon taking up with another woman while we were still very much married. It reaffirmed that I don't bring a lot to the table in that regard. That's been a tough one to shake.

Maybe if I tried a little more – didn't exist in my hoodies and leggings and hadn't fallen under the spell of my fur-lined Crocs – I'd feel more confident in myself.

Or if I was the kind of woman who didn't want to tear acrylic nails from her hands five minutes after spending a fortune to get them done. If I found the notion of a Brazilian wax to be appealing and not my idea of an actual nightmare. Splayed on a hard bed with someone tearing hair from my poor, tattered and Frankensteined-back-together perineum? No thanks!

Maybe if I was a gym-bunny, or a super bendy yoga girl. Daniel gets me out walking with him but he's such a plodder it hasn't succeeded in helping me transform my post-twin babies' pouch into a toned, flat stomach. I didn't even have a toned and flat stomach before I had the twins, so I suppose it was always going to be a big ask of the universe to expect I could earn one afterwards with minimal effort.

But there's a little voice inside me that screams at me that I have to stop tearing myself apart. I've a body that grew two wonderful human beings and brought them into this world. My hoodies and leggings are comfortable, but I do have other clothes. Or I can get other clothes. Maybe I could get Laura to help me with that. She seems to pull off effortlessly stylish well. She looks trendy but isn't a living example of mutton dressed as lamb. Or Niamh's Jodie might be able to help – if I want to push myself completely out of my comfort zone.

And as for intimate hair removal, well that's a bridge I can cross if I ever get to it but even I know other options exist outside of parboiling your genitals in hot wax.

A little shiver of something long forgotten in the very pit of my stomach reminds me that somewhere inside I am still a woman with needs. It's just been so long since I even allowed myself to consider any form of sex life, I've grown to live without it, and stopped even trying to send sexy vibes out into the universe.

Could it be fun to do a full Justin Timberlake and bring sexy back? I hum the tune as I have my nails painted a vibrant red, as if I'm a harlot. I'm surprised how good it makes me feel to look down at my fingers and see a splash of colour instead of my plain, short, unremarkable nails. Who needs fancy rings when you have pillar-box red, glossy gel nails? Already I feel a little sexier. Maybe that's the key. Attractive is as much about self-belief as it is about nice clothes and toned tummies. Nothing is as sexy as a confident woman.

Sixteen-year-old me desperately wanted to know what it was like to get a boyfriend and be kissed. It seems forty-six-year-old me feels just about the same – and she owes it to her younger self to start believing she's worthy of both.

I feel as if I'm floating on a saucy little cloud by the time Gabby has finished. She has treated my skin to quite the makeover and she didn't even make me feel bad about my absolutely awful skincare regime. Instead, she complimented me on how youthful I looked even though a part of me knows she is playing the role of a bloody good salesperson and I probably look like I was a passenger on the Ark along with Noah and his cast of animals.

So when she makes her helpful suggestions about which quite spendy skincare products she would recommend for me, I gladly let her fill her beautiful paper shopping bag and stuff the top of it with an essential oil scented tissue paper. I manage not to stroke out when she tells me how much it all costs, reminding myself that thanks to Niamh's generosity I'm not actually paying for my treatments. But surely that means I should treat Niamh to something as a thank you? So I double up on some of the spendy products and Gabby beams with delight at a job well done all round. I resolve to worry about balancing my books on a future date and allow myself to feel glam, sexy and wealthy with my perfectly prepped and preened skin and my beautifully wrapped packages.

I'm sitting in the lobby area relaxing when Laura appears from her treatment room, glowing and looking as if the weight of the world has been lifted off her shoulders. She hugs her therapist and I'm sure I hear a little muffled cry from both of them, before she joins me on the sofa and lifts a freshly poured glass of Prosecco to her lips.

'You know, that was exactly what I needed and what I absolutely hadn't realised I needed until I was right there in the middle of it. That poor girl had to deal with me snivelling and wailing like a banshee. There's something magical in her fingertips,' Laura says. 'Whatever she did, it unlocked a lot of... well... grief and feelings and guilt.'

There's something in the way she is looking at me as she says the world guilt that makes a chill run down my spine. And it's not a sexy nice chill, like the one Gabby unlocked in me earlier this afternoon. It's a very real reminder that we still have much to discuss. But not here and not now.

'I'm glad you found it beneficial,' I say. 'And when I have a couple more glasses of this fizz, I'll tell you what happened to me during my massage.'

She raises her eyebrows in curiosity. 'You have me intrigued,' she says as there is the sound of another door opening. A smiling Niamh walks out but I can't help but notice how pale she is.

'All okay?' I ask her as she sits down opposite us.

'Oh yes,' she says. 'That was lovely. Totally relaxing. I even fell asleep at one point. I'm told I didn't snore but I don't believe that for a second. Paul says I'd wake the dead at times.' She laughs but I know my friend, and I know that something just isn't sitting right about this whole scenario. She's hiding something.

'Here,' Laura says. 'Enjoy your Prosecco – you might as well get your money's worth and besides, we're on a mission to get Becca here drunk enough to reveal her deep dark secret to us.'

Niamh lifts the glass and brings it to her lips, taking the smallest sip. 'A deep, dark secret?' she asks, raising her own eyebrow so that it perfectly twins with Laura's.

'Drink first, major revelations later,' I say. There is no way I'm revealing to these girls, in the front lobby of a prestigious spa, that getting a massage awoke things in me that had long since dried up and been blown to the four winds.

'So where shall we go on to once we're done?' Laura asks. 'Bishop's Gate, or The Blackbird?'

'Wherever is dimly lit,' I say, aware that while I feel amazing my facial has stripped my skin of any make-up and left it with a slightly oily glow as it absorbs the rich products Gabby slathered all over me. 'And wherever we can get a couple of cocktails. We can pretend we're the *Sex and the City* girls and sip Cosmos and discuss how fabulous we are. It would be exactly the kind of afternoon that sixteen-year-old us would've loved.'

'I don't know,' Niamh says. 'I don't want to be a party pooper, but Paul has been with the kids all day and I don't want to take the piss by staying out too long. And I've marking to catch up on. The life of a science teacher isn't an easy one,' she says with a small smile. 'Especially coming up to Christmas. We've just had the end of term assessments...'

I can't help it. I'm a little disappointed. The thought of extending our afternoon into the evening with cocktails and giggles is so appealing, but I guess we still have our responsibilities.

It's hard to remember sometimes that Niamh has three children still at home relying on her – and if Jodie isn't home for the weekend, she and Paul have to divide their down time. Leaving the teenage boys to look after young Fiadh would be a disaster in the making.

'I suppose I should probably get home to Daniel too,' I say, even though I left him with food, water, the heating on and the TV on so he could watch *Dogs Behaving Badly* all afternoon, and maybe learn a thing or two.

'Are you sure you couldn't stay out?' Laura asks, looking from me to Niamh and back again.

'I'm sorry,' Niamh says, and I notice she puts her Prosecco glass back down on the table still full to the brim. 'But there will be other times – and didn't we all have a lovely time getting pampered?'

'We did!' I say. 'And I got you a little something to say thank you.' I hand her the beautifully styled gift bag and blush to my roots when I see her tear up a little.

'Oh, this is lovely,' she says. 'But you didn't need to. This was my treat. I wasn't expecting anything in return, it's too much.'

'Nonsense,' I tell her with a warm smile.

'How about I grab a bottle of wine and we go back to yours,' Laura says, pulling my attention away from Niamh.

'I'm not sure,' I tell her, already feeling the shift in the mood in the room. Right now, even though I feel relaxed, all I really want to do is get into my pyjamas and give Daniel a giant belly rub. What I don't want to risk is a head-to-head between Laura and me. Not tonight. 'I'm starting to feel really tired now,' I tell her. 'All those essential oils must be doing their work. I've not felt this relaxed in ages.'

It's a blatant lie but one made with kindness at its very heart.

'Okay,' Laura says mournfully, lifting Niamh's untouched Prosecco and making pretty decent headway on knocking it back. 'I suppose I should probably spend some time with Robyn and Aidan anyway. But we'll do it another time?'

'Of course,' I say and Niamh chimes in to agree.

'And you'll tell us about whatever it was that happened to you during your treatment?'

'We'll see,' I say with an elusive smile.

As we hug our goodbyes a short time later, I hold Niamh a little tighter than normal. 'You'd tell me if something was wrong?' I whisper. 'Because you know whatever it is, I'll have your back.'

'I'm fine, Becca, honest,' she says, giving me a perfunctory squeeze back. When she doesn't so much as glance back in our direction after climbing into her taxi, I know more than I've ever known anything before that my best friend is lying.

26

THE BOYS OF THE NYPD CHOIR...

'*Mu-um!*' Saul hollers into his phone. He is FaceTiming me, but as I can only see his chin and the ceiling of what I think is a pub, I'm not sure why.

'Saul?' I say, raising my voice in the hope he will be able to hear me over the din of the revellers wherever he is out now. It's clear, however, that he's not at home in his student digs watching his bank account to try and scrape it through to the end of term.

'Mum! It's "Fairytale of New York",' he bellows before lifting his phone so close to his face that I can see up one nostril.

I love this song. We love this song. My boys and I. We sing it every year together. I feel a moment of longing for them pull at my soul – until, that is, Saul belches loudly before declaring he's going to be sick and the FaceTime call ends suddenly.

'How am I supposed to not worry about that boy?' I ask Daniel, who simply gives his eyes a bit of a roll which I take to mean, 'You're fighting a lost cause there.'

Saul has always been a bit of a dreamer. He takes life much less seriously than Adam and while at times that's quite admirable, at other times I worry he will never get his act together. He only just managed to get a place to study in Manchester thanks to the power of Clearing.

I know there is no point in calling him back. He's worse than useless at answering his phone when I call at the best of times, never mind when he's out with his mates and three sheets to the wind. I have to trust that he will be well able to get home safely – but I'll make sure I check his location on 'Find My Phone' during the night.

How on earth did my parents cope without this new-fangled technology that allows us the ability to contact or track our children at will? I can't imagine the abject horror I'd feel if the boys were reliant on a public phone and a topped-up phone card to stay in touch with me – as was the case when I was at university in Belfast all those years ago. The world really has transformed in the last three decades, I think, as I scroll to Adam's number and call him. It's probably unfair to put responsibility for his sibling on his shoulders, but I can't pretend it's not helpful to be able to have someone have eyes on Saul when the need arises.

When Adam answers, I can hear a similar din in the background although it's a little more muted. 'Hang on, Mum,' he calls. 'I'm just heading to the smoking area where it's a bit quieter.' There is muffled chat as I wait for him to speak again. I'm actually quite relieved to hear that he is out and enjoying himself. Adam has a bit too much of my sensible approach to life about him and it worries me at times. I don't want my handsome boy to reach forty-seven years of age and find himself worrying about the things he could've done and the fun he could've had.

'Right. Hi, Mum. I'm here. What's up? Is something wrong? Is it Granny or Daniel?' The worry in his voice upsets me. I should've known he'd have gone straight to the worst-case scenario. He is his mother's son after all.

'No. Nothing is wrong. Everything's fine. I'm just checking in,' I say and feel guilty for the lie.

'Well, I'm out tonight. Christmas drinks with friends,' he says and he sounds a mixture of relieved and jubilant. 'You'll never guess who's here!'

'Is it Saul?' I ask, thinking it would be better if I just get to the point. 'Because he's not long off the phone with me and he seemed to be enjoying himself a little too much maybe.'

There's a sigh and new guilt piles on top of my old guilt. I recognise the weariness even in the sound of his breathing. 'Yes, Saul is here,' he says, a little deflated. 'And yes, he is enjoying himself a lot, just like Saul always does. But don't worry, Mum. I'm keeping an eye on him. As usual.'

It could be that I'm paranoid and all my feelings are floating dangerously close to the surface but I feel his annoyance radiating down the phone in waves and I realise I've not asked about him or let him tell me who is there and he must sometimes feel like the invisible child. Having Ruairi as an older brother, I know that feeling only too well myself.

'You're very good,' I say. 'You really are. And are you okay? Are you enjoying yourself? Who is it that's with you?'

There's a pause – it's not particularly long but it's long enough to make me worry that he is genuinely and irreparably annoyed with me, prone as I am to catastrophising.

'I'm good, Mum,' he says. 'I'm having a good night. And a great weekend. I took time off work because Jodie is over.' There's a little something in his tone that grabs my attention.

'Jodie? Jodie Cassidy? Niamh's Jodie?' I ask. She's certainly the only Jodie I know and the only one he's ever mentioned to me before.

'What other Jodie is there?' he asks and this time there is no mistaking things. That sounds very much like the voice of a man with a crush. They've been friends their entire lives and he has never expressed any sort of romantic interest in her. I wonder if that has changed? I'm about to try and wheedle some more information out of him when I hear the music get noticeably louder in the background and there are a flurry of excited voices all chatting over one another.

'Mum... I've got to go. I'll keep an eye on Saul. Don't worry. I'll call you tomorrow if I get the chance,' Adam says and he is gone before I've even had time to draw breath enough to answer him.

How strange though, that Jodie is in Manchester with my boys and Niamh didn't mention it during our day together. Not when we were in Asda shopping, or in the car, or at Sonas this afternoon. Once again it nips at me that something was not as it normally is with Niamh and it annoys me that I don't know what it is. Niamh and I have always shared everything. We have had no secrets. That became even more the case when our terrific trio became a dynamic duo after the great falling out of 2013. We normally discuss every worry together – and none are too small or too big. Having an absolute mental breakdown over what to feed the children for tea? This was fair game for an hour-long messenger conversation between us. The time Niamh found a lump in her breast and was terrified while waiting for her hospital appointment to come through? I was there by her side, having a good old feel of her boob every time she was worried the lump had got bigger or changed shape. Thankfully, it turned out that she just has – as the doctor called it – 'lumpy breasts', which were thankfully, in this case, nothing to worry about. We had quite the relieved laugh about that afterwards as we tried to make lumpy breasts sound like something to be coveted. 'It's the latest trend, darling, don't you know?' Etc.

If she's keeping quiet now, I don't like it. And I don't like that she hasn't mentioned that Jodie is over with the boys. There's no way she won't know where Jodie is. They speak umpteen times a day.

Surely it can't be the case that she thinks my boys are not good enough for her precious first born. Although in fairness with Saul, she might have a point. He'll wise up and settle himself eventually but for now, it would take a brave and/or stupid woman to take him on.

No. It can't be that. It has to be something more serious than that. My mind drifts back to the lumpy breast incident. Could it be another health scare? A new lump? Could it be that she fears something more than hormonal fluctuations are behind a new lump? It's scarier now, what with Kitty dying just last week from breast cancer. It has brought it all into our minds in sharp focus. I've even made sure to give my boobs a thorough examination in the shower twice since hearing the awful news. No. It can't be that. The timing would be too cruel.

The familiar clutch of fear tightens around my middle. I think I could handle almost anything else except Niamh getting sick. She is my person. The most positive and loving friend a woman could ever ask for. The universe would be a complete bastard to foist an illness on her just as we all made a very conscious decision to embrace our lives to the full.

Then it comes to me that she still hasn't opened her letter from the time capsule. In fact, she seems really, really unwilling to do so. Could it be that she doesn't want to read about the hopes and dreams she once had when she knows she may not have much time left? I feel the Prosecco I so enjoyed earlier churning in my stomach ominously. The room takes on a slightly fluid feeling as waves of worry come at me.

Still, my phone sits, silent and dark, on my lap. I don't know if I should text or call her. I don't know how she would react to being questioned. If she wants me to know whatever it is that is bothering her, then she would've told me. Niamh doesn't like being put on the spot, but she might really, really need a friend right now and I'm not sure if I just need to be more forceful with her.

Before I even realise it, I'm crying. Daniel sits up and is doing his very best to lick the salty tears from my cheeks. There must still be a trace of whatever gorgeous products Gabby used on my skin though, as he stops, grimaces and jumps down off the sofa. He ambles across the room to, presumably, get as far away from me as possible, and gives me the filthiest of looks. How dare I season his favourite snack?

To my shame, I give him the finger in return. 'I'm allowed to feel my feelings,' I tell him. 'And get lovely facials.'

I'm done holding everything in and pretending I'm fine when I'm not. I'm not making myself uncomfortable just to make life a little easier for someone else. Even if that someone, in this case is 'just a dog'. He gives a little bark in response. It's more of a 'whatever' than anything with any real malice behind it, and I know he still loves me. So at least that's something.

I probably should just call Niamh and then I can stop this super spiral from spiralling any further.

I have the perfect opener. A simple, 'Ooh, I didn't know Jodie was visiting Adam and Saul,' would ease us into the conversation where I beg her to be okay and not be battling cancer. However, my gut is telling me to play this one carefully and the fact my subconscious is sending me warning flares just makes me more worried about the entire situation.

I try to apply rational thinking. I have no concrete reason to believe Niamh may be deathly ill or going through some similar-level life trauma.

Maybe it's just the case that it's been a long and emotional day. Between my mother shouting my size all over the supermarket, my near orgasmic experience in the spa, worrying about my son and now this anxiety about Niamh, it's entirely possible all my emotional stability features are off-kilter and misfiring all over the place. That's what I get for drinking in the afternoon and allowing a child to realign my chakras for me.

I'll get an early night, I decide, and thankfully Daniel is forgiving enough not to stay in his huff but instead pads dutifully up the stairs behind me. To distract myself from worrying, I run through the list of the seven Walton children, prefacing each name with 'Goodnight' as I get changed and crawl into bed.

I resolve to call Niamh first thing in the morning.

27
_____

THE CASE OF THE MISSING BFF

Niamh is not answering her phone. I have tried to call her three times this morning and I have sent four WhatsApp messages and a number of really very funny Instagram reels featuring dogs trying not to look guilty after destroying their homes. Normally, something among this would garner a response, even if it's only a laughing face emoji, but no. There is nothing. She hasn't even read the WhatsApp messages, which is very unusual and on any other occasion I'd probably consider it rude. There's an unspoken agreement between us that we never leave the other hanging.

I don't want to keep pushing her to reply though. There must be some reason behind her quietness and whatever it is I am sure she will tell me when she feels ready and able to.

I just hope she doesn't leave it too long.

Thankfully I don't have to endure the same lack of contact from my boys. Adam sent me a message shortly after midnight to say he and Saul were back at their digs, and he had put his brother to bed with a pint of water and a basin at his side. This morning, I saw my eldest (by ten minutes) son post on his Instagram that he is 'hanging out of his arse', complete with a picture of him looking positively grey while a mammoth Full English is on the table in front of him waiting to be demolished. Resolving to have a chat with him about his wilder ways when he gets home at Christmas, I focus my attention on Adam instead. Thanking him for letting me know they were both home safely, I ask him about Jodie.

ME

> That's a bit of a surprise about Jodie being over in Manchester. Is she visiting old school friends or on a shopping trip? It's nice that you met up.

ADAM

> She came over to visit me and Saul, Mum. She's staying with us.

ME

> I hope you cleaned up that flat of yours before she arrived.

ADAM

> *rolling eye emoji* Of course I did, Mum. I even bought a new toilet brush, and cleared out the shower drains so that mouldy smell went away.

I cringe, imagining the particularly potent boy aroma that my darling offspring can generate. That is not something I've missed since they've been away. In fact, my house would be beautifully fragrant at all times, were it not for Daniel and his sensitive tummy.

ME

> I'm very proud of you. And surprised Jodie is over. Is there something you need to tell me?

ADAM

> What do you mean?

ME

> Well, the last I knew you were both very firmly in
> each other's friend-zone. Has that changed? Or
> has it changed with Saul?

Immediately I'm imagining Niamh and me together, proud mothers of the bride and groom in clashing hats and fancy frocks at their wedding.

ADAM

> Saul? Get a grip, Mum! Jodie has more sense than
> that.

ME

> But you haven't answered my question. Is there
> something going on between you and Jodie?

ADAM

> If I tell you will you promise not to go all Rebecca
> Burnside on me and completely overreact?

ME

> Go all Rebecca Burnside? Whatever could you
> mean? *curious face emoji* But that means there is
> something going on, doesn't it?

ADAM

> Mum! It's new. It might be nothing. Please don't
> overplay it. We're friends – and we both think
> maybe we could be more. But we don't want to
> jinx it, so please, keep it quiet. Don't tell Dad. Or
> Granny. Or Niamh. Not yet, anyway.

My boy sounds so mature and sensible that I am both very proud of him and also sad for him that he can't just enjoy himself without worrying about all the possible ways things could go wrong. Sadly, he did not lick that particular trait off the stones and I must accept the blame for passing it on.

ME

I won't. Promise. Go and have a lovely day together, son. And tell Saul I'll talk to him later when he isn't hanging out of his arse as much. Love you.

ADAM

Thanks, Mum. Love you too xxx

I instinctively touch his words on the screen with my fingers before kissing them. It's the closest I can get to giving him a hug just now, and it will have to do until he comes back in two weeks and I get to spoil him for real.

Of course, now what I really want to do is call Niamh and discuss this latest development but Adam has asked me not to get overexcited about it, and Niamh isn't answering her phone or reading my messages anyway. Feeling the need to distract myself, I start cleaning. We're in December now and I suppose I should be thinking about putting the Christmas tree up – it would be nice to have it in situ for the boys coming home. The only problem with that is the fact the decorations are all in the loft and it's normally my very tall, very fearless boys who climb the ladder to get them down for me. I don't do well with either ladders or lofts. Ladders immediately engage my fear of heights and lofts immediately engage my fear of dark spaces, insects, ghosts or creepy mass murderers who have been watching me sleep for months. No. I will not be retrieving my Christmas decorations myself. And yes, I do feel embarrassed by that – especially when I conjure the image of my seventy-seven-year-old mother dangling out of her own loft just over a week ago and wish I was half as fearless as she is.

Abandoning the plan to decorate the house for Christmas, but still not having heard from Niamh, I pull on my thickest, most unfashionable but exceptionally warm coat and lead Daniel out into the sleet and cold of a wet December day so that he can get some exercise.

I'm hopeful that by the time we have walked around the park and back home Niamh will be ready to chat or that if she isn't then I'm too busy trying to warm up my frozen and saturated limbs to be able to go into full-on panic mode about it.

Because it is cold. And wet. And windy too for that matter. Where are the crisp, bright winter days that I've read about? The kind where the frost twinkles on the branches and my breath mists in the cool air. Where is the kind of weather I've seen in Hallmark Christmas movies where everyone can dress in non-waterproof clothes and return from their walks with their hair and make-up still perfect?

This is head down, shoulders hunched, collar up and hands firmly in pockets kind of a weather. Not that Daniel minds. He's in his element by the time we reach the otherwise deserted park. With no one else around I unhook his leash and let him enjoy burning off some of his copious energy with a dose of the zoomies up and down the pathways. As I watch him frolic in the long grass, I think to myself that at least someone is having a good time.

I'm still battling the elements with my trusty companion never too far from my feet as we turn the corner into a more densely wooded area. Clearly catching the scent of something most likely disgusting, Daniel takes off like a rocket. Within seconds he is out of my sight but as I start to call his name, the wind seems to pick up speed and I'm now really quite worried that my voice might be carried away on the breeze and he won't hear me. Honestly, with the increase in the wind strength, I'm also a little worried Daniel himself might get carried away on the breeze.

'Daniel!' I call, doing my best to make it sound sing-songy and appealing but unable to hide the underlying panic in my voice. '*Daniel!*' I yell louder as I start to tramp between the trees looking for him. I wore comfortable shoes but not suitable-for-wading-through-mud shoes and my feet start to squelch and stick in the muddy woodland ground. I keep calling and looking while ten minutes pass and there is still no sign of my dog or anyone else.

I'd like to tell you I'm not hysterical by this point, but I'm pretty much hysterical by this point. 'DAN-IEL!' I scream with all my might, not caring if anyone does hear me although there still doesn't seem to be another being around.

Daniel has never disappeared from my view for this amount of time before. He always comes when he is called. Being the kind of person I am, I am starting to panic that while it's relatively unlikely he will have been carried off to Kansas, Toto style, he might have been injured by a falling branch, or stuck in the mud like the sad horse was stuck in the Swamp of Sadness in *The Neverending Story*. Every single person who was a child in the eighties knows that particular scenario doesn't end well.

My heart is threatening to beat right out of my chest as I keep walking until I'm almost back at the car park and there is still no sign my lovely wee dog and my God, I cannot stand the thought that I might lose him.

It's then that I see a figure emerge from behind some trees, his dark coat buffeted by the wind, his hand pulled down over his head, his arms cradling a rather muddy but definitely very much alive Daniel.

At his feet a small black dog bounds along happily on the end of a leash.

'Did you lose something?' I hear the man ask, as I fight the urge to grab Daniel from his arms and hug him like never before.

'I did,' I say. 'He picked up a trail and off he ran, and then the wind and the rain and God knows...'

Daniel, who looks absolutely delighted with himself, wriggles and jumps free from the man's arms and I crouch to stroke him, not caring if I too end up mucked to the eyeballs. I can barely speak, I'm so filled with emotion.

'I think he might need a bath but apart from that he seems unhurt,' the man says. 'We found him wandering about like a lost soul near the bridge. I thought it'd be best if I brought him back here or maybe to the vet to see if he was microchipped.'

'Thank you,' I say, my voice shaking, glancing up only long enough not to be rude and then focusing my attention back on Daniel to make sure he isn't hurt. 'You're such a rascal for making me so scared, Daniel!' I scold him.

'Erm... Becki?' the man asks. 'Is that you?'

Becki.

Hang on.

I look up, blinking in the fading light, and see that, as luck would have it, the man who has found Daniel, and who has since found me, semi-hysterical, dressed like the Michelin man and now covered in mud, is in fact Conal.

Yes, just like waiting for a bus, there has been no sighting of him for years and then it's Conal everywhere I look. Not that I'm not incredibly grateful for him in this very moment.

Having clipped Daniel back on his lead, I stand up and try to muster whatever dignity I can to thank him. The adrenaline currently coursing through my blood stream makes me want to grab him and hug him but I won't. I hold myself back. Instead, I mutter his name, and not in a sexy romantic heroine way. My voice is so thick with emotion that I sound just like the boys did when they were fourteen and their voices started breaking.

'I didn't recognise you,' I manage to stutter afterwards.

'To be fair, we're both so wrapped up it would be hard for anyone to recognise us. It's only when you spoke to the dog that I clicked. There can't be too many dogs called Daniel in Derry.'

I explain to him how the boys thought it was hilarious to call him Daniel The Spaniel and he laughs.

'That's brilliant,' he says.

'What's your dog called?' I ask.

'Oh him? He's Lazlo. After one of the vampires in *What We Do in the Shadows*.'

'I love that show!' I say. 'I'm a big Nadja fan myself.'

He smiles as Lazlo sniffs around my feet, the rain gets heavier and the daylight really starts to slip away.

'Well,' I say. 'I think we should probably get home before this weather gets any worse.' I want to say more. I want to ask him more. I want to invite him home with me just to see if it feels as weird as I'm afraid it might to have Conal O'Hagan in my own house. But I don't. Because deep inside of me, there really is just a little too much left of timid and shy Becki Burnside.

'I think you're right,' he says. 'But it was nice seeing you, Becki,' he says.

Like an absolute dick, instead of telling him it's nice to see him too or complimenting him on his rugged good looks, or thanking him for saving my dog, I correct him.

'Actually, it's Becca these days,' I say.

'Sorry. It was nice seeing you, Becca,' he says, before tilting his head and walking off, Lazlo nipping at his heels as they go.

'Well, you fucked that one up,' I say out loud, addressing both myself and Daniel.

* * *

Back home, I try to warm myself up with a cup of tea while Daniel scents all my soft furnishings with Eau De Freshly Washed Wet Dog. I try not to continue picking apart every last moment of my interaction with Conal, wondering if that would make for a good

'Ten Ways' column for my pitch. 'Ten Ways to Still Behave Like an Awkward Teenager in Your Forties' perhaps? It could work.

Niamh still hasn't been in touch so inevitably I start to worry about her again, my interlude with Conal clearly only being an interlude before the main event of having a full breakdown about my longest standing and very best friend.

Still, I don't want to annoy Niamh by badgering her even more, so I do the only thing I can really think of doing short of driving over to Niamh's and breaking her front door in. I call Laura, in the hope that our recently repaired friendship triangle will mean she might at least know what's going on.

'Becca,' she answers, her voice a little hoarse. 'How are you? I'm feeling a little delicate. I think I went too gung-ho on the Prosecco at Sonas yesterday. My head is not thanking me for it. Doesn't help that Aidan and I demolished the best part of a bottle of red when I got home.'

'Poor you,' I say. 'Thankfully I'm not hungover but I was just out walking Daniel so I need to thaw out a bit. It's bitter out there today. We're not long in from a walk and we were both absolutely drenched. We met Conal in the park walking his wee dog.'

She sighs. 'He can't sit still at the moment. Has to keep busy. That poor dog has had the legs walked off him. Conal just doesn't want too much time to think about things, you know? I'm heading over to Mum's soon to help him go through some paperwork and start clearing the house. There's nothing I'd rather do less,' she says and I can hear the trepidation in her voice. I don't blame her. It's a horribly cruel job to hoke through the detritus of a life knowing that is all that is left behind.

'I'm sorry,' I say. 'It's not easy. At least you have Conal to help. I'd have been lost without Ruairi, for all our fighting, when Dad died. I'm afraid I sort of fell to pieces a bit.' The memories of that awful time come flooding back and I close my eyes tightly to push them away. No, I have enough to be worrying about without slipping back to the worst of times.

'Conal has sort of fallen to pieces too,' Laura says mournfully and I'm floored with guilt about not asking him how he is and focusing on Daniel instead. 'I think we'll both be as bad as each other,' Laura continues. 'I'd happily leave it all until after Christmas, but Conal is right – if we don't do it now, we'll just find it harder in the long run. It's just knowing where to start. All her things...'

Her voice cracks and the people pleaser in me, which is also exceptionally similar to the part of me feeling a bit lost without my immediate mammying responsibilities, speaks up. 'I can help you too, you know. I can come over if you want, and you don't mind Daniel coming too. You're not alone in this, Laura. That's why you have me... and Niamh.'

There's a pause and an intake of breath which is shaky, and then she sighs a 'thank you' and it's hard to ignore the crack in her voice. 'It would be brilliant if you could help. I don't want to impose, but I feel so lost,' she says.

'It's not an imposition,' I tell her firmly, and I mean it. Niamh helped me after Dad died and I'd have been for the funny farm had she not kept me on my feet – and on my antidepressants.

My lovely Niamh.

Which reminds me, she's the reason I'm calling Laura in the first place. 'Tell me this,' I say. 'Have you heard anything from Niamh since yesterday? She's been unusually quiet and I didn't think she was quite herself after the massage.'

'Well, she sent me a text last night just to check I was okay. Clearly she'd seen me self-medicating with whatever Prosecco I could get my hands on. I texted her back and said I was fine, if a little pished. I've not heard from her since, but I've not tried to get in touch with her either,' Laura says.

'And did you think she seemed a little out of sorts yesterday?' I ask.

'To be honest, I don't think I'm the person to ask. It's not like I've spent much time with her over the last ten years. I don't know that I could speak to what's usual for her any more. Are you worried?' There's a pause while I try and figure out what exactly it is I am feeling.

'I don't know,' I tell her. 'My spidey senses are tingling that something's up but I'm not sure how to ask her. She's normally so open with me.'

'What do you think could be wrong?' Laura asks, and I'm about to tell her about the lumpy boobs situation when it strikes me that she has only just lost her mother to breast cancer. Raising my, hopefully unfounded, fears with her would be insensitive at best, and downright distressing at worst.

'I just don't know,' I lie. 'But could you do me a favour and maybe just send her a little message. Just check in. And let me know if she replies to you. Maybe it's my phone that's on the blink or something.'

Yes, dear reader, there are straws in this room and here I am, grasping at them as if my life depends on it.

28

THE WAY WE WERE

Laura and I hug on the doorstep of the house that was like a second home to me during my teenage years. Of course, the intervening thirty years have seen lots of changes to the O'Hagan home. The walls are no longer rag-rolled and stencilled to death as was the style in the nineties. There isn't the faint smell of Regal cigarettes in the air – which were Kitty's poison of choice back in the day. She gave up smoking almost twenty-five years ago – which makes her death from cancer all the crueller to wrap my head around.

But even with the changes, I would know in a heartbeat this was the O'Hagan homestead. The same, if slightly dated and faded photos of Laura and Conal as children hang on the walls. Kitty loved a good family photo and she most certainly did not believe in hiding them away in albums or boxes. Her love for her two children was displayed, sometimes garishly, on her walls. It feels comforting now, somehow. Like it proves she lived and she created her own story and her own family – both of whom are now parents them-selves and standing in front of me as fully grown adults, as Daniel and Lazlo eye each other suspiciously from either side of the room.

It really doesn't feel like all that long ago that we were lounging in Kitty's living room, listening to the radio and telling Conal it was 'girls only' and he wasn't welcome. We made such a big deal of it, when the truth was that back then Conal didn't want to spend time with us. He was usually just popping his head around the door to tell us to turn the music down, or ask if any of us were heading up to the shop and if so, could we bring him back a Crunchie. I'm pretty sure that in 1992 Conal O'Hagan survived on Crunchies and hot buttered toast and nothing else.

A hundred versions of him, along with a hundred versions of his little sister, smile down from the walls now – in the hall, the living room, and the kitchen. Dressed like mini-adults for special occasions, Conal in a full three-piece suit for his First Holy Communion while Laura had the best of everything for hers. She had a long dress, gloves and even an umbrella. It's only when I got older that I realised how hard Kitty would've had to work to afford that on just one income – but she was a strong and fearless woman and she was determined no one would see her children as disadvantaged in any way by the absence of their father.

I spot a picture of both of them at the beach. At a guess I'd say Conal was maybe nine or ten in the photo, making Laura seven or eight. He's standing proud on what was clearly a windy day – his dirty fair hair blowing in the breeze – wearing a pair of what can only be described as budgie smugglers. While Laura is in a lemon-yellow swimsuit with a white waistband. Both look absolutely frozen and yet are grinning widely at the camera and it hits me square in the feels. Behind that camera Kitty would have been smiling back at them, encouraging them to grin and making them laugh in the way she always did. They might be fully grown now, but that sense of joy was something Kitty instilled in them every day of their lives.

'I think that particular picture can be safely stored in an album,'

Conal says, cringing. 'The eighties really were interesting times for fashion.'

'You telling me you don't still have a pair of those to wear when you go to the pool?' I grin.

'Dear God, no!' he says and there's a pause where both of us know we could make some sort of flirty comment in the way adults do, but are also aware of who the other is and how this might not be particularly appropriate in the current situation.

'Speaking of interesting times for fashion,' Laura says, 'look at this.' She points to another framed photo on the wall in the kitchen and there we are – three tragically uncool teenagers with bad perms, jeans that came from Dunnes Stores when anyone with any true fashion sense was wearing Levis, and brightly coloured T-shirts. We had scrunchies in our hair and braces on our teeth and we look not dissimilar to street urchins. Laura, Niamh and I are sitting side by side on Laura's bed – an open copy of *Smash Hits* in front of us. It is far from a remarkable photo – nothing more than a snap that if taken today would be instantly deleted but Kitty had put it in a frame and had hung it on her wall because I think she realised it isn't the quality of the photo that really matters at the end of the day. It's the people in it.

'There are worse atrocities in the living room,' Conal laughs. 'You may live to regret slagging off my fancy swimming trunks.'

'I already do,' I say, imagining what horrors await me.

'How about I put the kettle on and we decide how we're going to tackle this?' Laura says and Conal and I nod. Daniel just plonks himself down at my feet and promptly closes his eyes, having decided there is minimal craic to be had here.

'I sorted some of this paperwork into piles,' Conal says. 'Mum did a surprisingly good job of tying up loose ends and getting her affairs in order. I should've known she would.' He gestures to the kitchen table on which rests four stacks of letters and documents.

'She probably didn't trust us to get it right,' Conal adds with a smile that is clearly hiding his grief.

'I'm sure that's not the case,' I say as I sit down and start examining the pages in front of me. 'She just knew this would be hard and she wanted to make it slightly less so for you. That's all.'

'She shouldn't have been worrying about this in the last few months though,' Conal says and his voice cracks – at which I feel my own heart crack a little.

'You have to see it as an act of love,' I say, and swallow hard to keep my emotions in check. 'My boys are grown men now, but I know as long as I can, I'll do whatever possible to smooth their paths. That's what your mum was doing. She was just being the great mum she always was.'

As Laura sits mugs of tea down in front of us, I see Conal wipe away a tear as if he's embarrassed to have let his guard down. I can't help it – I reach out and give his hand a squeeze of reassurance which earns me a smile. I can still see traces of that Crunchie eating, smelly boy he used to be, but I also see the man he is – older and wiser – but with the same piercing blue eyes that used to make me feel as if he had X-ray vision, and the same full lips that...

I shudder. My libido has been absent without leave for the better part of a decade and it chooses now, in front of the grieving brother of one of my oldest friends, to walk back into the room, shaking her thang and hollering for attention. What the hell have Gabby and her magic healing stones done to me?

Suddenly I'm not sure if the rising heat in my body is a hot flush, a feeling of intense attraction or Satan opening the trap door to the fiery pits of hell to drag me in for being wholly inappropriate in front of a bereaved man.

I pull my hand away as if I have been burned, because I *do* feel as if I have been burned. But I have to play it cool and keep my shit together. I have to not think about his eyes or the warmth of his skin when I touched his hand.

'Did Niamh message you back yet?' I blurt, a little too loudly, turning to Laura, desperate to change the subject.

She shakes her head. 'She hasn't even read it yet. Maybe she lost her phone? Left it in Sonas or something?'

I momentarily get my hopes up.

'But no,' Laura adds. 'She messaged me last night, didn't she? I don't know, Becca. But I hope she's okay.'

I push the worry down, even though it feels a little overwhelming.

'Will we start with this bank information?' Conal asks, thankfully distracting me from my spiral by bringing us back on task. 'From what I can see she had everything up to date but obviously the bank needs to be informed she's gone and the account needs to be closed.'

'Where do we even start?' Laura asks.

'You have Kitty's death certificate?' I ask, knowing how surreal this sounds. I remember picking up a copy of my father's and really trying to wrap my head around the finality of it. Seeing his name printed on it, his life and death summed up in two words on one page. Subarachnoid haemorrhage. A bleed on the brain. So catastrophic that he never really stood a chance, the doctor had told us. He had looked so peaceful for someone who had undergone something the doctor described as 'catastrophic'. In time, I was grateful for that.

The worst bit about picking up his death certificate was having to hand it over to my mother. I felt as if I was breaking her heart all over again. There I was, confirming her worst nightmare had come true.

None of it felt real. I was not grown up enough to deal with it.

I'm not sure any of us are ever really old enough to deal with the death of a parent. I don't think it's possible.

Laura nods in response to my question. 'Conal registered her death.'

'And one of you is executor of her will?' I ask.

Conal nods in reply.

'It's relatively simple a task,' I say. 'On a practical level anyway. Emotionally it's tougher. But first go through your mum's accounts – see if there are ongoing payments which need to be transferred, cancelled or paid off. Then it's a matter of providing proof that your mum has passed away – so the death certificate – and the bank looks after the rest.'

'I don't feel ready,' Conal says in a small voice that reminds me we are still little more than the children of our parents, wanting to be loved and taken care of.

'I know,' I tell him. 'I'm not going to tell you it's easy. I cried in the bank when I was helping Mum sort out Dad's affairs. I cried in a lot of places. It was the worst time. Worse than my divorce by far. The staff were so kind though. That helped. I suppose they deal with this sort of thing all the time. And I tried to look at it as a way of taking care of Dad, like he used to take care of me.'

'I understand that,' Conal says. 'You're right.'

I'm looking at him when I hear the chair Laura has been sitting on scrape back loudly. This causes Daniel and Lazlo to launch into a volley of barks that would wake the dead while Laura shouts over them, 'I'm so sorry, Becca. I'm so, so sorry.'

'What?' I ask, genuinely confused. Why is she apologising to me?

'Here you are helping us, and I didn't... I wasn't... when your dad...'

Oh. *That's* why she's apologising.

Daniel and Lazlo are harmonising beautifully now and Conal

and I are trying to quiet them. I turn back to tell Laura this isn't about me. It's about helping her, but she is bolting from the room and even though Daniel is doing his best to drown out every other sound in the entire universe, I hear Laura sobbing loudly as she runs from the room.

'I'll go after her,' I tell Conal, as he manages to soothe both dogs into submission with a sneaky custard cream.

'Are you sure?'

'Yes,' I say, because I have realised that Nelly, the elephant in the room, is done with us ignoring her.

29

WITH A TRUMP, TRUMP, TRUMP

The bathroom door is locked and I can hear Laura sobbing inside.

'Laura,' I say while knocking gently on the door. 'Will you come out so we can talk?'

'In... a... minute...' she stutters between gasping sobs.

'Okay,' I say. 'But just so you know, I'm not going anywhere. And I wasn't trying to upset you. I wasn't trying to make you feel bad.' I hope she knows that there is no way, no matter what has happened between us, that I would be so cruel as to use her grief to make her feel guilty for not being there for me when my father died. I'm not that callous or cruel.

'I... know...' she says, her voice just a little calmer now. 'I know.'

I hear the loo flush followed by the sound of running water and then Laura opens the door, her eyes puffy and red-rimmed, her cheeks blotchy. She is twisting her hands together in the way she always did when she was nervous.

'We should talk about what happened,' she says. 'Shouldn't we?'

I nod, because as much as I don't really want to dig into that particular chapter of our lives we can't keep on with it hanging over our heads. I realise that Laura has been scared of that particular axe falling all this week, and on top of her raw grief, it must've felt like an unbearable burden. Maybe it was wrong of me to tell her we didn't need to talk about it when we first spoke. I'd thought it was the right thing to do to tell her it could wait. Looking at her now, however, I see it has been eating at her and it would be better if we pulled that old and horrible sticking plaster off once and for all.

'Let's sit down,' she says, leading the way into her old bedroom – which looks almost the same as I remember it. Of course, the posters are gone from the walls and the dressing table is no longer cluttered with Body Shop smells or stained with Heather Shimmer lipstick and the remnants of whatever dye Laura had put in her hair.

As I sit beside her on the bed, I wonder what it would be like if walls could talk. The things that this room saw and heard during those formative years would probably make us both cringe to the soles of our feet, but for the most part the hours we spent here were happy ones. They were of a time when we thought nothing would ever break our bond of friendship. We were so sure we'd be in each other's lives forever. Even more so when Laura's then boyfriend, Aidan, introduced me to his best friend Simon Cooke. The delirium we'd felt at being able to double date was next level. We had dreams and plans of holidaying together with our eventual families and growing up and growing old as besties.

And for the longest time, we stayed on that path.

'First of all,' she says, eyes cast downward, 'I need to tell you that I went to your dad's funeral. I'm sorry I didn't have the balls to come to the house for the wake, or to come up and give you a hug at the church. I was scared of making a scene or making the whole thing harder for you than it needed to be.'

My breath catches in my throat, the familiar pull of grief winding its way around my heart. 'You came?' I ask, my turn now to sound croaky and emotional. I'd be lying if I said I never wondered if Laura would show up at the funeral. It wasn't at the forefront of my mind, but it was there and I remember wishing she would. Even though it had been eight years since we'd last spoken. Even though I had Niamh to support me, and my boys to take care of. Even though my focus was on my own pain and on my mother's pain – I felt as if the final part of the puzzle was missing. I knew that with both Laura and Niamh by my side, it would be marginally more bearable.

'I couldn't not,' she says, blinking full tears, which fall freely down her cheeks. 'He was a great man,' she says. I nod in response because I don't trust myself to try and speak. I know if I do, I will merely disintegrate into a sobbing mess and the purpose of this visit is to help Laura with her grief, not come at my own full force. 'He was like a father figure to me, when I didn't have one of my own. You know that – how he watched out for us when we were teenagers and eejits without an ounce of sense in our heads. It was your daddy who would pick us up from town, or wait outside while we went to a disco or a concert or whatever we were at. I couldn't not go to pay my respects. But I sat at the back of the church and even though every part of me ached to run over to you and give you a hug when I saw you walking in behind his coffin, it wasn't about me. It would have drawn attention away from your daddy, and God knows he deserved all the attention and more.'

I'm drowning under the weight of conflicting feelings. I'm so touched, but there's also an old familiar feeling pushing its way into the light. It's the wee demon on my shoulder who has held on to all the hurt and pain that I'm supposed to have let go of in a bid to move on and who wants to scream that life can be brutally unfair.

So yes, Laura came to my dad's funeral but she didn't hug me. She didn't let me know. She wasn't there to support me. She was there to assuage her own guilt. She was putting her own comfort first. Just like she did when Simon started playing away from home.

She should've had my back. I trusted her to have my back. I needed her.

I can see Laura is crying, of course I can. And I know she is waiting for me to say something. She's probably waiting for me to do a 'Becca' and say it's all in the past and it doesn't matter. All that matters now is how we move on.

That's what I want to say. That's what I want to *feel*. But in this moment, I don't feel it. The person I feel sorry for in this moment is that teenage me who would sit with her best friends in this very room listening to music, experimenting with make-up and being utterly convinced that these girls were the best friends that anyone could ever wish for.

That girl who ended up, at the age of thirty-six, alone with two semi-feral nine-year-old boys trying to help them understand why their daddy had walked out. Trying to understand, herself, why he had. No, it hadn't been perfect. But it hadn't been awful either. At least I didn't think so. We were just busy parents raising demanding boys and working hard jobs.

Of course we didn't have the same time for each other that we once had. Of course we didn't get to go on romantic holidays, just the two of us, any more. Of course our weekends were spent running from swimming lessons, to football practice, to playdates instead of lounging in the house together reading the papers and drinking wine. Life wasn't as enjoyable as I thought it would be, but I didn't give up. Simon did.

And when he did, that woman who was once a hopeful teenage girl, and who is now the very cynical woman I've become, lost her best friend.

She had stood with Simon. 'He's Aidan's best friend,' she'd said, when she'd allowed Simon to move into their spare room. 'What am I supposed to do? I don't want to fuck up my own marriage by kicking him out,' she'd said, as she made a bed for him, cooked for him, drank wine with him in the evenings and washed his dirty socks and pants. 'I know he's hurt you. I know he's been a bastard but he has nowhere to go and Aidan wants to help his friend,' she'd say and I'd wanted to ask her why she didn't want to help *her* best friend with the same vigour.

'What am I supposed to do?' she'd asked time and time again, even though I'd told her that what she should do is pick me. Don't have the man who left me high and dry sleeping under her roof.

She never heard me. She just kept asking.

Until the day I'd told her exactly what she was 'supposed to do' and it involved going and fucking herself.

It had been the only, huge, stand-up row we'd ever had. There had been lots of little rows, of course, over the course of our friendship. Petty little fallings out over things that didn't matter. Like when she'd lost my favourite Mariah Carey tape. Or when we had battled over which of us would get to be which Spice Girl at Halloween. But there had never been a full-on, door-slamming, cursing fight. Not until that day.

We had been well into pretending we were coping with our new reality when Laura had invited me over for coffee. The men were at work. Robyn was at school. It was just going to be a coffee and chat, like we used to do. Niamh had urged caution when she'd messaged me from the staffroom. She'd told me to maybe wait until the weekend and she could come with me, but I'd been stubbornly determined to go anyway.

In the end it was something so small that proved to be the final straw. As I sat in her kitchen and we drank our coffees, she unloaded her dryer and started folding the clothes. I knew those clothes. Those were Simon's clothes and I don't know why but the sight of her balling his socks put me over the edge. How had he betrayed me and managed to end up having my best friend wash and dry, and roll into balls, his socks?

I remember staring at them and that shoulder demon was there whispering poison in my ear. 'If you were important to her, she'd let him roll his own damn socks,' it said. 'If you mattered, she'd take a pair of scissors and cut the big toe out of each one of them, followed by cutting the crotch out of all his boxers.'

Needless to say, I didn't drink the rest of my coffee. I'd asked her why she was looking after Simon and she had blinked back at me for a moment before replying, 'Oh for goodness' sake, Becca. I'm only taking his laundry out of the dryer.'

I'd proceeded to tell her she wasn't 'only fucking taking his fucking socks out of the fucking dryer'.

'You're shitting on thirty years of friendship,' I'd told her. 'You're choosing him. You're prioritising his needs and Aidan's needs and who the fuck is worrying about mine? Not you, anyway! You clearly couldn't give a flying fuck!'

My voice had been shrill and angry and I'd felt red hot rage bubbling up inside me because why was no one looking out for me? Simon had let me down when I needed him and now Laura was.

'That's not fair,' she snapped back. 'I get that you're hurt but all I'm doing is supporting my husband's best friend because it's important to him. It's not always about you. And balling his socks doesn't mean I'm okay with what he did. You know that. You're not stupid, Becks. There's no need to be so oversensitive about everything.'

She might as well have uttered the most unforgivable words that can ever be said to a woman in pain – 'calm down'. 'There's no need to be so oversensitive' was so painfully close to crossing that line. Needless to say, I did think there was a need to be what she described as 'oversensitive'.

So that was when I told her to go fuck herself. That was when I'd walked out.

And now, here we were, ten years later and that pain was resurfacing again because nobody had put me first. And my daddy had been added to the list of people who had left my life when I needed him most.

So here in Laura's bedroom, just over a week after she buried her own mother and while I am supposed to be helping her start to sort through the remains of a life now gone, I force my pain to stay silent. I want to tell her how hurt I was, but I know she is vulnerable and I don't actually want to hurt her. I just want her to know what it did to me. I want her to acknowledge it. I want her to see me. I'm so tired of being invisible. Becki never wanted to be invisible.

The anger that was building inside me suddenly, and maybe because it knows ultimately it has nowhere to go, transforms into the largest Unexpected Wave of Sadness to date.

'I love you,' I choke out, and I mean it. I love Laura. I wish it didn't still hurt to see her and relive what we went through but it does. 'And I don't want to hurt you.' I can hardly breathe while I force these words out of my mouth. 'But I don't think I should've come here today. I don't think it's the right time... for either of us. I thought I could put it behind me or work through these feelings but I can't. It hurts too much. It's too hard.'

'It's too hard?' she replies, her voice a mixture of grief and anger. '*You* find it too hard? My mother has just died but I'm supposed to feel sorry for *you*? Or invent a time machine and go back ten years and make different choices? Just so the perfect Miss Becca Burnside doesn't feel sad?'

Her words are slap in the face. 'I didn't say that,' I stutter.

'No, you didn't. But it's always about how you feel, isn't it? It was then, and it is now. It's always about how difficult your life is, as if the rest of us just sail along without a care in the world. I made mistakes, Becca. I'm big and ugly enough to admit that. But I can't keep beating myself with the same stick over and over again. And I absolutely don't have the strength to do it now.' Her voice is cracking as it stumbles over the words and I hear the demon on my shoulder screaming at me that it was just stupid to think we could ever, ever go back. There was no act of fate, or time capsule or letters from our younger selves that could fix this.

Tears blinding me, and my head buzzing with a million jumbled thoughts, I feel my way down the stairs and back to the kitchen where Conal looks at me, his face full of concern. He makes to speak but I raise my hand to stop him. I just can't.

As I pull my coat back on and clip Daniel's lead to his collar, I mutter a stuttering apology and then I leave. I'm sure I feel Laura walking down the stairs as I walk up the hall. I don't need to look up to know she is there. I can feel the weight of our collective sadness as I walk back out their front door and head for my car.

I drive away as soon as I can get my keys in the ignition, only to pull over at the side of the road as soon as I'm out of sight of the O'Hagan house. Daniel is whining, straining at his harness in the back seat, probably desperate to get back to his new BFF, Lazlo, as I cry like an absolute sad case, not caring if anyone walking by sees me.

So much for embracing life and finding my friends again. So much for moving on and being happy. Here I am, just a week later, and one of my best friends is MIA, and I've left the other hurt and angry in her dead mother's house. I feel as if my heart has been ripped out as the pain of both my divorce and losing my dad hit me afresh. One of my sons seems to be set on a path of self-annihilation and even the flutter of something remotely akin to attraction to a man has just been rendered futile after I've left his sister devastated.

And to top it all off, everyone in Asda in Strabane knows that I am now the proud owner of size-eighteen full briefs.

Fudge my actual life.

30

FLOWER IN THE ATTIC

Still sitting in my car, I dial Niamh's number once more. Again it goes to voicemail and I listen to her request that I leave a message, which I do, even though I know for a fact that Niamh Cassidy never listens to voice messages. Be it a voicemail or a voice note, it will be ignored because – in her words – 'God invented WhatsApp for a reason'.

'Niamh,' I say, my voice wobbly. 'I hope you're okay. You seemed out of sorts yesterday and I'm worried that I've not heard from you. If you're not okay, please phone me or WhatsApp me or something and let me know what I can to do help. Whatever it is we will get through it together, I promise. If you are okay – and by okay, I mean physically able to answer your phone – first of all let me ask you what in the name of all that is holy are you doing not answering your phone or your messages? Don't you know I worry? I need you, Niamh. I need you to be okay and I need to tell you what just happened with Laura because it was awful and I... I just need you to be okay.'

I end the call and allow Daniel to lick my hand a little in an attempt to reassure him that I've not completely lost it. The warmth of his breath on my skin and the softness of his fur are such a comfort. Turning round to look at him, I think about how important he is to me. He keeps me going on the days I just want to lie in bed and hibernate from the world. He might be a ginormous pain in the arse from time to time, but he is loyal and constant and he loves me unconditionally.

'You're a good boy,' I tell him. 'The best pupper in the whole world.' He gives me a look that screams 'tell me something I don't know' before resting the side of his face on my hand once more. With him beside me, his ridiculous floppy ears tickling my hand, I feel my breathing come back to normal and my tears stop falling. Dogs really should be available on the NHS to treat anxiety, depression and menopausal breakdowns. 'Shall we go home?' I ask and he jumps back to his usual spot on the back seat and lies down. I take that as a yes.

As we're just short of two weeks from the shortest day of the year, the light is already fading outside even though it's not yet three in the afternoon. The fact that it's bitterly cold and the clouds are heavy with rain waiting to be unleashed on the earth doesn't do much to brighten what is left of the day. Driving home, I try to find some tidings of comfort and joy in the twinkling Christmas lights in the windows of the houses we pass, but they just serve to remind me that when I get home, I will be walking into a festive-free abode, which will be dark, cold and empty. It's not so much an Unexpected Wave of Sadness that hits me but an Entirely Predictable Tsunami of Depression so large that I don't think even Daniel can fend it off entirely.

'Fudge this for a game of soldiers,' I say to no one but myself. I'm not going to lie down under this. I'm not going to do what I want to do most of all which is crawl under my duvet, pull it up over my head and hide from the world until the boys come home in two weeks. I will not fester in my own misery.

My father's voice rings in my ears. 'Just keep swimming,' I hear him say and although I know he totally borrowed that phrase from *Finding Nemo*, which he watched on loop with the boys, I decide to adopt it as his very own words of wisdom.

That said, it isn't so much that I need to keep swimming as need to go out to the spider-infested shed in the dark, get the old ladder and take it back into the house so I can conquer my worst fear and climb up into the attic to retrieve the decorations myself.

I can do this, I tell myself, slipping my phone into the pocket of my hoodie and starting my ascent to the one place in my own home that scares the ever-living Jesus out of me.

'It's only a space,' I remind myself. 'Just another room of sorts.' With wooden beams and a partially floored area on which a lifetime of family memories is balanced. I suppose I should be grateful to Simon who insisted on having a plywood floor laid in the loft shortly after we moved in. Death would be assured if I had to try and balance on the rafters instead.

As I reach my hand around just inside the hatch, terrified it will land on a spider, or a rat, or the bloodied hand of a serial killer, I'm also grateful to find the switch for the light Simon also installed. It may be just a simple bare bulb hanging on a wire, which adds to the kidnapper's lair feel of the place, but it at least blasts light into all but the darkest recesses of the loft. With the light on and my terrified heart relatively confident there are no murderers on the premises, I haul myself inelegantly through the hatch until I am sitting on plywood, legs dangling into the landing below.

It doesn't feel particularly secure but I refuse to allow myself the luxury of a panic attack. I'm up here now. If I fall, I fall. If God is good to me, I'll die quickly and not be left to starve to death in a crumpled mess on the carpet until the boys come home for Christmas and find my decaying corpse.

I wonder how long it will take for Daniel to start eating me.

'No point in worrying,' I tell myself as I twist my body around to survey the boxes of memories and long forgotten household gems such as the twins' cots. We'd never planned on having any more children. The boys were more than enough, but we couldn't bring ourselves to give their cots away either. Maybe I should do that now. Yes, they still haul at the old maternal heartstrings but I have to face facts. My babies are all grown up. Their cots are just gathering dust and quite possibly woodworm. I should probably go through the bags of their old baby clothes too. I can keep one or two of their favourite little baby-gros and donate what is still fashionable. Someone could be getting good use out of whatever isn't hideously out of fashion.

But I'm not here to lose myself down memory lane. God knows I've done enough of that this last week. I'm here to prove to myself that I am a bad ass who doesn't need anyone else to help her get the Christmas decorations down from the attic and who is perfectly capable of putting them up all by herself.

It doesn't take me long to locate them. The tree – which of course is the bulkiest item – turns out to be relatively easy to manoeuvre through the hatch and drop the short distance to the floor below. The boxes of breakable lights and baubles are a bit trickier. Of course, there's no one to hand them to, and while the top step of the ladder is wide enough to rest them on, that leaves me without the top step of the ladder to rest my feet on as I try and get down.

I refuse to be defeated, eventually deciding to put all the remaining boxes as close to the hatch as possible, reverse my way out in the hope of getting a good footing at the top of the ladder, and reaching up to grab a box. I'll have to make several trips up and down the ladder. My thighs are already crying at the thought of it, but I will be prouder than proud can be if I achieve this on my own, and while going through an exceptionally intense mental breakdown.

With shaking legs, I manage to get the first two boxes out of the attic and onto the landing floor relatively easily. The fear of climbing a ladder doesn't lessen though, I just start singing 'I Will Survive' to gee myself on. Before I know it, I'm on the last box and my singing has reached an ear-splitting crescendo when my phone suddenly vibrates in my hoodie pocket, scaring the living bejaysus out of me and sending me hurtling backwards. In the briefest of interludes when I am toppling down, tinsel flying into the air like fireworks being launched into the night sky, I swear I see my entire life flash before my eyes.

Dear Reader, sadly the montage of the life of Rebecca Louise Burnside, aged forty-six, is really quite unremarkable.

Let's just say if Clarence the angel came to visit me in this moment to show me all the joyous things I've experienced and the lives I've touched in a positive way, he would have to add some creative flair to his storytelling.

My ass hits the floor first, I think. It's all happening so fast I can't quite process it, but I do process the shock of pain that runs right from my bum to my lower back and I think I might have heard a crack – no pun intended. The noise could be from my head hitting the floor, or any one of the remaining baubles raining down on me like a hail of bullets while I cover my face to minimise the damage. My singing is no more. All that I can hear is a buzzing in my ears, and the frantic barking of a dog. It takes a moment for me to realise the buzzing sound is my phone which is still vibrating. At least that means I didn't drop it, or land on it, and it's not broken.

Gingerly, trying to assess my injuries, I pat my stomach and locate my phone still safely tucked away in the kangaroo pouch-like safety of my hoodie pocket. Ignoring how my arm feels achy and my head a bit spinny, I reach for it, hoping I'm able to answer before it rings off or I pass out. Not that I'm sure I'll get peace enough to pass out, not with Daniel barking up a storm at the living room door desperate to get up the stairs to perform his best *Paw Patrol* moves and rescue me.

My tumble, which of course I should've known was inevitable given my history of being accident prone, has, however, distracted me enough that I'm not even thinking about who might be on the other end. I'm so dazed I'm not sure I'd know my own name if I was asked, never mind remember if I was waiting for someone to call.

'Hello,' I answer, my mental assessment of my pain levels continuing. My arse hurts. Can you actually break your arse? If so, do you go to A & E and tell them you've a suspected broken bum or—

'Becca.' It's Niamh. And there is something in her voice I don't like at all one tiny bit. No longer thinking of my injuries, I pull myself up to sitting, something I immediately regret as a fresh wave of pain shoots up my spine.

'Sweet baby Jesus!' I call out, with a loud gasp. *Just keep breathing. Just breathe through the pain*, I tell myself. I've never heard of anyone ever dying from a broken bum so this is not life threatening it just hurts like a motherfu—

'Becca, are you okay?' Niamh asks.

'I think I'm supposed to ask you that?' I stutter through the pain.

'What's happened?' she asks.

'I feel off the ladder when the phone rang.'

'What in God's name were you doing up a ladder? You know better than that! We don't do ladders! *You* don't do ladders!'

'I was getting the Christmas decorations down from the attic because I'm a strong independent woman who doesn't need other people to help her,' I say, my words coming so fast they fall all over each other because I know that once I finish that sentence I am going to let out another yelp of pain as I try and make myself more comfortable. 'Aaaaaarrgggh,' I shout. So it seems that shifting my weight onto my right bum cheek is a mistake.

'Do I need to phone an ambulance? I'm on my way over anyway,' she says and her voice is shaky, which reminds me that she has been AWOL all day and I've actually been really worried about her.

'No. No. I don't think I need an ambulance, but if you're coming over can you use your spare key to get in because I'm not sure I can move yet.'

'Yes. Of course. I will,' she says, and almost immediately there is a rattle at my front door and I hear a key turn in the lock and the door open. I can't see downstairs, but I don't have to wait to find out that Niamh has just arrived.

'I was just outside,' she calls, as Daniel once again erupts into a volley of barks and whines. I hear the living room door open and there follows a stampede of feet as Daniel rockets up the stairs to perform emergency first aid in the form of jabbing me with his paw and his wet nose.

'I'm okay,' I grimace as I try to move again. 'It's okay, Daniel. Good boy.'

'Oh, Becca,' I hear as Niamh arrives at the top of the stairs looking miserable as sin, face pale, still wearing her coat and carrying a Superdrug bag.

'I'm okay,' I tell her. 'I mean my arse might be broken but I think I'm okay, I think I only fell a few steps...' The truth is I've no idea how many steps it was and I want to cry. I want to call my mum and get her to come over and make it all better, but looking at Niamh, there's no doubt in my mind that her need is greater.

The poor woman looks absolutely terrified.

She slumps onto the carpet beside me. 'Good. Good. I mean, obviously I'm sorry you're in pain. But I'm glad you don't think it's serious. Because I think I'm going to need you a lot over the next while.'

My heart plummets faster than my arse did out of the attic. 'I knew it,' I say, feeling the panic build inside but knowing I have to push it down because I have to be strong for Niamh. 'Did you find another lump? Is it cancer this time? We'll beat it, you know. I promise.'

I'm saying the words, but it doesn't feel real. Those don't feel like words people say in real life. They feel like words from a script of a medical drama or a soap and not what I have to say to my best friend, three weeks before Christmas.

'And if you lose your hair, I'll shave mine off too and everything. You won't be alone. I promise.'

'It's not cancer,' Niamh says, looking up at me, her eyes filling with tears. 'Shit, I don't know how to say this.'

What's worse than cancer? Oh God, I can't bear it. 'Niamh, what is it?' I ask although part of me wants to put my hands over my ears so that I don't have to hear whatever it is she is going to say next.

'Just say it,' I plead.

She looks at me, her face etched with worry. 'Becca, I'm pregnant.'

31

PAPA DON'T PREACH

'You're pregnant?' I ask, forgetting about my own injuries while I take in the look of terror on Niamh's face.

'I'm so... so... embarrassed,' she says. 'I'm forty-six. I have four children. It was bad enough that Fiadh was a surprise when I was planning my fortieth birthday – not that I'd change her for the world – but to do it again? At my age? Jodie and the boys are going to absolutely lose their shit.'

The same Jodie who is currently in Manchester with my boys and who might be starting a relationship with one of them. I don't have time to think about that now, though. Not when we have real drama.

'But how? Why? When did you find out?' I ask.

'Remember when we were talking on Friday? And you made that crack about "unexpected baby in the uterus area"? I thought it was really funny, until I really thought about it and realised that I'm late,' Niamh says, rubbing her temples with her fingers. 'And I've been feeling out of sorts, you know. Tired. A bit queasy. Definitely a bit gassy. And my boobs' – she gestures to her chest – 'are swollen and heavy and so incredibly sensitive. I almost decked Paul when he tried to cop a feel in the kitchen on Friday night.'

Amid the clear distress of the situation I can't help but feel a pang of jealousy that Niamh has a husband who still wants to cop a feel. Although, I suppose that's not all he wants to do if she has found herself up the duff again.

'And you've had sex?' I ask.

'Well it's not likely to be the second coming of Christ, is it?' Niamh says. 'God in all his infinite wisdom would not entrust his only son to me – an ageing heathen who believes in the theory of evolution. Yes. I've had sex. With my husband.'

'And you didn't use protection?' I ask.

She blushes. 'We used a condom. Like we always do. Ever since Fiadh was born and I refused to go back on the pill. I thought it would eventually drive Paul to get the snip but he's a big fucking coward who's terrified of anyone coming near his balls with a scalpel. Funnily enough, he doesn't mind my perineum being ripped from hither to thither for the fifth time by one of his ginormous headed offspring. You'd think by this stage they'd have invented a perineal zip or something for women of childbearing years. But anyway, the bloody condom must have split or something. Because I'm late. Two whole weeks late. How the hell did I not pick up on this before now?'

I don't know what to say so I just take her hand.

'Like, the age of me now and I fall pregnant? Like some stupid wee schoolgirl who doesn't know better. Oh God, Becca, by the time the child turns thirteen, I'll be sixty! It was bad enough when I had Fiadh and I was the oldest by far on the maternity ward. The looks I got from some of the young ones, as if I was encroaching on their rich and fertile lands. I'm old enough to be a granny, for the love of God. I can't do sleepless nights and breastfeeding and all that potty training shite again. I just can't.' She dissolves into a flurry of tears.

'What does Paul say?' I ask.

She shakes her head and I swear if Paul Cassidy has made my friend feel worse than she already did I will perform a vasectomy on him myself, with a pair of pliers and my kitchen scissors.

'I haven't told him,' she sniffs. 'I don't know how. He's started talking about how he's looking forward to retiring. How the both of us could maybe look at going early. We'd have our teachers' pensions to back us up and we could get wee part-time, stress-free jobs if we needed. Or we could just, you know, start living a wee bit. He says the boys are nearly old and wise enough to be trusted with Fiadh so we could even go away the odd weekend. If I tell him that's not going to happen, I'm actually afraid it might break him. His blood pressure is on the high side anyway.'

'But you have to tell him,' I say. 'I mean, it's his baby too and he's bound to find out sooner or later.'

'I know, I know,' she says. 'I'm just so ashamed. And I'm scared too. Things go wrong with older mothers. There's a higher chance the baby could have problems too.'

'Do you think you might not want to go through with it?' I ask, my voice soft and low. I know that Niamh, like me, is pro-choice. We campaigned for abortion to be decriminalised in the North of Ireland and were delighted when it finally was in 2019. But we also grew up in the eighties and nineties and went to Catholic schools where there were entire RE lessons on the evil of abortion and where we were encouraged to wear badges of tiny little silver feet to represent the size of a foetus. It was drummed into us that it was a sin to end a life and that life begins at conception. We were taught this with religious fervour and like most girls then, we bought into it. While our views may have changed in the intervening years, the guilt and the fear of judgement still lives in our psyche.

Niamh just bursts into tears again. 'I don't know. Is that awful? I don't know. I don't know if I *can* go through with it. Physically or mentally. You remember how tough I found pregnancy with Fiadh – how I thought I was losing my mind? She was worth it, of course she was, but I don't know if I could go through it all again and still come out the other end smiling.'

I pull her close to me, using all my strength not to yelp in pain as my body reminds me of my tumble. 'Sweetheart, we'll get through this. You'll get through this. You don't have to have all the answers today. We'll get through it one step at a time,' I soothe. On her other side, Daniel has noted her distress and is nudging her with his nose to indicate that she may hug him if she wishes. He can be very generous with his affections like that. Of course, Niamh finds him irresistible and messes with his fur, pulling his soft, warm body close to hers. She allows him to lick the tears from her face even though she normally says letting animals lick you anywhere is 'rancid'. 'They lick their arses then want to give you a kiss! No thank you, Rebecca! They can keep their bum slabbers to themselves,' she would say.

I use Daniel's affection towards Niamh as a distraction to allow me the chance to try and get to my feet. It's not something I'm looking forward to. I know it's going to hurt but at the same time I know it has to be done. I take a deep breath and slowly pull myself to standing, a burning pain coursing from my tailbone both up my spine and down my legs. I half expect my legs to buckle under me if the truth be told.

Letting out a howl so loud it sets Daniel off into another barking frenzy – right in Niamh's face – I wonder how a weekend that started so nicely for all of us has ended so absolutely awfully.

'I need to lie down somewhere soft,' I say and Niamh lets me lean on her as I step over the scattered tinsel and baubles and into my bedroom.

'Thank you,' I say, my voice just a little hoarse with emotion.

'No need to thank me, now what else can I do to help?' she asks, sniffing and lifting the packet of make-up wipes from my dressing table to clean her face of dog slobber.

'I'm supposed to be helping *you*,' I mutter as I gingerly lie down on the bed, no longer feeling as if my body fits in the well-worn dips and grooves. I try to roll onto my side.

'Yes, but I'm not the one in pain right now. What can I get you to help?'

'Hot water bottle,' I stammer. 'In the cupboard on the left in the utility room. Beside the medicine box. There's Deep Heat. And ibuprofen. And a glass of water. Then I promise we can talk more about you.'

'Okay,' she says, and I can see her slip into helper mode. The can-do attitude is back now that she has something to focus on other than being pregnant. I wonder why she didn't mention anything yesterday. Maybe she hadn't tested yet. Or maybe she was just trying to wrap her head around it. I feel awful, and a little put out if the truth be told, that she didn't talk to me about it. I have been by her side through every pregnancy and pregnancy scare of her life before now. I have sat on the edge of her bath while she peed on a stick to find out she was pregnant with Cal. She was the first person I told when I found out I was pregnant with the twins. Simon still doesn't know that to this very day, but it was always going to be Niamh who knew first because we are so completely immersed in each other's lives, it just felt natural.

My back twinges as I stretch again, and I let out another howl. That only attracts Daniel once more who springs onto the bed with no consideration whatsoever of the pain he might cause with all his jigging about. He's too busy being absolutely delighted with himself at having found a new toy, in the shape of Niamh's Superdrug bag, to play with.

'Daniel! Let go!' I say, reaching out to retrieve it from his clamped jaws. 'That's not yours. It's not a toy!' Daniel, however, thinks I'm very much mistaken and it is a toy – one that he can enjoy a lovely game of tug of war with.

Who would've thought that a bruised arse would make a simple game of tug of war with a plastic carrier bag so intensely painful. It takes considerable effort, and a smattering of my foulest but most effective swear words before I pull the bag so hard it shreds through this teeth and the contents are flung all over the bed.

As if I've not been injured enough, I am hit square in the face by a rectangular cardboard box. As I bat away it, grateful it hasn't taken my eye out, I'm surprised to see it's a pregnancy test.

An unopened pregnancy test. This seems very strange.

'Niamh,' I call out.

'Hang on, I'm on my way,' I hear her shout as I try and gather the remaining items from her now well and truly murdered shopping bag. There's a second, also unopened, pregnancy test. One of the fancy digital ones this time. There's also some haemorrhoid cream and I don't know if it's for her or for Paul but I make the decision that some things are best left unknown. For now, I just need to focus on the big issue at hand – the case of the mysterious pregnancy testing kits.

My best friend appears at my door with a glass of water in one hand and a hot water bottle in the other. 'I have some co-codamol in my bag if you want to take that instead of ibuprofen,' she says. 'Maybe you need the hard stuff today?'

I am, in this moment, intensely grateful for my friend's drug stashing habit. 'Yes please.' I nod. 'Give me the strongest you have.'

She helps me get nice and comfy to take my painkillers before she lies on the bed beside me – on the side usually reserved for Daniel or, many moons ago, Simon.

When she is settled, I speak again. 'Niamh,' I say. 'I'm very sorry – Daniel decided your shopping bag made for a great toy.'

'It's okay. I forgive him,' she says. 'Did you know I was going to pour myself a gin and tonic when I was downstairs and then I remembered that I can't drink and it has disproportionately upset me.'

'There were a couple of pregnancy tests in the bag,' I continue, not allowing the talk of gin and tonics to derail me.

'Yeah, I stopped at Superdrug on the way over,' she says. 'I want to be sure and I didn't want to have them in the house. God forbid the boys or Fiadh find them. Or Paul. Like I told you before, I need to be ready to have that conversation.'

'You wanted to be sure? How many tests have you done already? How many will it take for you to be sure?' I ask. 'Because, darling, you do know that it's next to impossible to get a false positive. You don't need to keep doing more tests.'

It seems that I am not the only person employing the old clutching at straws approach to life at the moment.

Niamh turns her head to look at me. I can't quite read her expression. It's entirely possible I'm hallucinating with pain at this stage. 'The thing is, Becks, I haven't tested yet. I just know.'

'You haven't tested yet? Not at all?' I ask, incredulous. Dear God, give me strength. She hasn't even peed on a stick yet?

'I've been pregnant four times before,' she says. 'I know what it feels like. I know what my body feels like. This is the same. Exactly the same. And my missing period is a pretty big clue.'

Niamh Cassidy is one of the smartest women I know. She is fierce. She is brave. She is determined and feisty and often appears to know everything there is to know about everything. And yet...

'Oh love,' I say. 'You're forty-six, Niamh. You're a science teacher. You know your biology. Surely you know there's another, perfectly normal, explanation for the absence of periods for women of our age?'

32

A PAIR OF JEANS AND A NICE TOP

'It's not the menopause,' Niamh says.

'How do you know that for certain?' I ask.

'Because I know what being pregnant feels like. And I know I'm ridiculously fertile. *And* I know that certain risky behaviour was carried out.'

'You know that menopause can mimic the symptoms of pregnancy, Niamh,' I say, feeling increasingly exasperated.

'It's not the menopause,' she says and there's a borderline aggressive tone to her voice. I raise my hands in mock surrender. If she wants to die on this hill I shall let her – although she might regret her passing if the pregnancy test comes back negative.

'Maybe,' I say with a shrug. 'Who am I to judge? It's so long ago since I was pregnant I can barely remember what it felt like. And I only did it once, but with two babies, so my experience maybe wasn't typical.'

'Well it's only seven years since I did it,' Niamh says. 'And I remember every last detail. I'm not a stupid woman. I know my body and I'll prove it.' She grabs the two pregnancy testing kits from on top of my bed and informs me she's going to do the tests right here and right now. 'I want to do two tests so do you have a cup or something I can pee in so I can dip both sticks in?'

'You want to pee in one of my good cups?' I ask.

'Good cup. Bad cup. I don't care. As long as it can hold a fairly decent amount of wee, we're good. I drank half a litre of Fanta on the way over. Which, you know, is also a sign because when I was expecting Cal I was obsessed with Fanta,' she says.

'You're always obsessed with Fanta,' I remind her. It was her go-to hangover cure throughout our teen years and early twenties. A can of full fat Fanta, a Mars Bar and a bag of beef flavoured McCoy crisps. Even now she's often seen swigging from a bottle.

She rolls her eyes. 'Cup, Becca? Or I'll grab your favourite Michael Bublé mug and sully it forever!'

'You wouldn't dare!' I say, but not really trusting that she wouldn't, in fact, dare. 'Look in the tall cupboard by the fridge. There are some of those red disposable cups the boys used at their birthday party. You know, like the ones you see in movies.'

'Those are a bit *too* big. I don't think all that Fanta has gone through me that fast,' Niamh says. 'But thanks. You're a life-saver.' With that she disappears off down the stairs and I'm left trying to assess just how much pain I'm in. I lift my phone and google 'Can you break your arse?' Visions of some sort of full body cast contraption fill my head. I wonder momentarily whether this is where the expression 'handing your arse to you in a sling' came from. I also wonder whether they will bandage me up in some intricate way or make me lie face down in a bed in some sort of arse-repairing traction if I go to hospital. Like Tom Cruise in *Born on the Fourth of July*. Not that his problem was a broken arse. It was a bit more serious than that, but...

I hear the toilet flush. It's been a good five minutes and there has been not one peep from the bathroom. The flushing of the toilet would seem to indicate the deed has been done, and the recycled Fanta disposed of.

The bathroom door creaks open and I hear footsteps across the landing. My heart quickens. What result do I want for Niamh? Surely as she doesn't want any more children and we are both hoping to start living the lives we once dreamt of, I should hope it's a negative. But the part of me that feels a little dried up and less womanly really wants to convince myself we're still in our fertile years. And a baby... I do love babies.

I read somewhere that you never know when the last time will be. That there will be a last time you lift your child into your arms. A last time you tie their shoelaces. A last time you rock them to sleep. And you don't tend to know when that will be. Time moves on until you realise one day that something has changed. Your baby doesn't reach for a dummy any more. They start pronouncing their words correctly instead of in the endearing way you've grown to love. Saul used to confuse his v and f sounds with bs. I miss him asking if he got an 'inbitation' to the party. Adam called grated cheese 'spiky cheese' – something I still do but they have long forgotten.

If I sit very still in a very quiet room, I can close my eyes and in those moments conjure the sights, sounds and smells of them when they were young and they needed me in that all-encompassing way small children need their mothers. I can imagine the imprint they used to leave as they lay on my chest and yes, I wish I could feel it for real. Just for five minutes. Being a mother was such a huge part of my full-time identity for so long, I'm not sure who I am without it. So yes, a part of me would love it if she walks into the room and waves a positive test in my direction. Sure, it won't be my baby, but it will be a baby for me to cuddle and coo at, to smell and care for.

And yeah, hand back at the end of the day.

Because, I also realise, I am ready to move on from that stage of life. I'm ready to live a little for me, even if I don't know how to do that just yet. Even if I have no idea what that looks like or feels like, because there's a whole other set of last times no one warns you about either.

Just like I never knew when it was the last time I'd walk down the street with my child's hand in my own, I also never knew when it was the last time I'd dance to 'Boom! Shake the Room' in Squires, or the last time I'd hold Niamh's hair back as she puked neon alcopop everywhere. I didn't know when it was last time I'd have a chips and Mexican beef special in Abrakebabra on the way home, or suffer severe chipulary burns. I didn't acknowledge what would be my last after-work drinks with the girls, or the last Saturday afternoon I'd spend trailing the shops for a nice top to wear with jeans that night. I had no power to stop any of it, of course. Time cha cha slides on, whether we like it or not. But what I do have the power to do, two decades later, is claim a little bit of it back.

Another column idea comes to mind. Ten Ways to Figure Out Who You Are in Your Forties.

Niamh's face gives nothing away as she walks back into the room. Her expression is completely blank. This could mean she's in shock at what she has just discovered and is processing the news. I just don't know if that news is good or bad, or what even constitutes good or bad. She doesn't want another baby – she says – but she refused to consider all probable explanations for her missed period. Was that just a case of the lady protesting too much?

'Well?' I say, starting to feel a little woozy thanks to the extra strength co-codamol now weaving its way through my blood stream. She hands me the sticks and I try to not think about the fact she has just dipped them in her pee. The first has just one blue line – a negative result. The second – the fancy digital one – says 'Not Pregnant'.

I look up at her. 'So you're not pregnant. This is good, isn't it?'

'Just because it's negative doesn't mean it's actually negative,' she says, sitting down on the bed beside me and taking the two tests from my hand. She holds them to the light and squints at them. 'I think there might be a very, very faint line on this one,' she says, handing the non-digital stick back to me. There is very clearly no line – faint or otherwise.

'It's a negative, pet,' I say. 'You're home free!'

'But maybe it's just too early?' she says and by the look on her face I'm starting to wonder if she's upset there isn't a screaming positive line in front of her.

'Niamh,' I say gently, 'you said you were two weeks late. If you were two weeks late, a bun in the oven would show up on a pregnancy test.' I have to play this one carefully. Yes, there might be a part of me that wants to shout, 'I told you so!' or 'IT'S THE FECKING MENOPAUSE, WOMAN!', but I can see that Niamh is not in the place for ribbing or teasing or even being given a stern talking to.

'So I'm probably not pregnant,' she says, blinking tears up at me.

I shake my head, which makes me more than a little dizzy due to the co-codamol. 'Probably not,' I say.

'That's a good thing,' she says with a nod and an uneven smile. 'Having a baby at my age would be ridiculous and disastrous.'

'It wouldn't be easy,' I say as softly as I can.

'It's probably the menopause,' she says, as if this thought is really just registering with her for the first time.

'It probably is. We can go and get you a hormone test done. I could do with one myself so why don't we both make appointments?' I say.

'When we said we wanted to start living more adventurous lives I didn't think we meant chasing HRT together,' she says with a weak laugh.

'We sure didn't,' I tell her. 'The sixteen-year-old us never really took that into consideration, did they?'

'Nope. Can't say it was on my list of hopes and dreams for life,' she says.

'At least we have each other to do it with. I've been kind of in denial that I need HRT but I really think it could help. Between the hot flushes and the mood swings, my dry skin and sudden almost overnight aged appearance, I think it's pretty obvious my oestrogen levels are through the floor.'

Niamh nods. 'I'm not sure I'm ready to be old enough for the menopause yet.'

'Perimenopause can start in your thirties,' I tell her. 'We've done well to get this far.'

'No, I know I'm *biologically* old enough for it. I don't think I'm emotionally ready for it.' She doesn't look at me while she speaks, instead keeping her head cast down as if she's embarrassed to be voicing these altogether understandable feelings. 'I didn't... don't... want another baby but there's something different about it being my decision not to have more babies than Mother Nature taking that decision out of my hands. I don't feel in control of my life right now. And God, we're ageing, Becca. I looked through the Facebook pages of our school friends and I wondered who all those proper adults were staring back at me. Did you know that Marie Barr is a granny now? Twice over? And she *looks* like a granny. She looks how I remember my granny looking, except with less dootsy hair and she doesn't wear a pinny all the time. I can't help but wonder, do I look that old? I mean, I know we're heading towards fifty but...'

She seems genuinely quite upset and I understand it. The cognitive dissonance between knowing I'm forty-six and realising I look forty-six is quite big, but there's not a lot I can do about it apart from sticking to the new skincare routine Gabby designed for me at Sonas, and drinking more water. Even then there are definite limits to what that can achieve. I'm never going to be mistaken for being in my twenties again.

'I feel as if I'm staring my mortality in the face, you know. Bits of me aren't working as well as they used to. My eyesight has gone to shit for one. If I want to drop a couple of pounds I have to literally starve myself. I wake up stiff and sore now and can't get out of bed without making some inhuman noise. I know people joke about that kind of thing, but honestly, there are times I feel as if my body is already starting to decay and I just wonder what the point of it all is.'

That's when Niamh – bouncy, funny, takes-no-shit Niamh bursts into tears.

Today is proving to be the gift that keeps on giving.

33

AN ELASTICATED WAIST IS A GOOD THING

It's entirely possible that I am too stoned on painkillers to be any sort of a useful comfort to Niamh. Everything feels a little hazy, except for the loud sobs coming from my friend.

'Forty-six isn't old,' I tell her, even though I complain frequently about feeling old. 'It's certainly not body-decaying-what's-the-point-in-life old,' I tell her, trying to gauge just how serious she is about feeling this way. Is it hyperbole, or is my friend really feeling that hopeless about life? If so, how have I not noticed before now?

'It feels that way,' she says. 'The world isn't designed for middle-aged women. Try going clothes shopping and it's either the option of dressing like a young one with a bare midriff and arms fully on show – as if we don't all struggle with our bingo wings – or dressing like an auld doll – all knee-length skirts and twin sets, or jeans with elasticated waists.'

'I love an elasticated waist,' I say quietly.

'Yes, well, so do I, but they make me feel old. Everything makes me feel old and I worry about what there is to look forward to. The best days are behind me. The kids being small, Paul and me being in that can't-keep-our-hands-off-each-other stage – that's a dim and distant memory.'

'It's not that distant a memory considering you just thought you were preggers,' I tell her.

'Well, maybe. But it's not the same. And my career has reached the stage where I'm starting to look forward to retirement. I don't want to continue to climb the career ladder. I'd rather stick needles in my eyes than become a head teacher. Paul wants to take up golf. He wants me to come with him. Me! Playing golf? I'll have to start wearing slacks and pastel-coloured jumpers!' Niamh pulls a face which lets me know just how disgusted with that particular idea she is. 'When did we go from being the first on the dance floor to being afraid of putting our backs out, or thinking that slut drops are a recipe for a trip to A & E? I feel as if I'm drying up, Becca. As if I'm already in the "and unto dust you shall return" stage of life.'

I'm so used to Niamh joking about just about everything that I hardly recognise this emotional woman in front of me – this person so lacking in confidence.

'You are one of the most full-of-life people I know,' I tell her. 'Menopause isn't going to change that. You could live for another forty years. That's almost the same as you've already lived. So don't give up on it all now. You've ages yet to turn into dust, and I'm not planning on letting you any time soon. Sure, aren't we going to have some grand big adventures? You, me, and Laura?'

It strikes me that Laura may not actually be a part of our plans after our set-to at her mum's house earlier. I've not even had a chance to tell Niamh that yet and I don't think now is the right time to start. I feel that familiar lead weight in the pit of my stomach.

'We might have forty years, but what if we're like Kitty and only have twenty? Or what if we get ill or infirm, or lose our marbles? What if I get Alzheimer's or something? You can't compare the later years of your life with the first half. Why do you think I've not read that damn letter? It's because I don't want to look back at the young woman I was, with my whole life ahead of me, and realise that where I am now is on a downward spiral.'

I take her hand. I'm beyond feeling a bit woozy and am feeling remarkably chilled out in spite of her highly emotional state.

Maybe this is what it feels like to smoke weed? Maybe we should add a trip to Amsterdam to our to-do list and go and get legally wasted on some weed brownies?

I become aware that Niamh is still talking, while I'm now sitting with a vaguely cheesy smile on my face imagining getting stoned in some cool Amsterdam cafe with my friends – doing the kind of thing young Becki would never have dreamt of. I was terrified to drink before I turned eighteen, never mind consume drugs. I'm still terrified of drugs to be honest. My generation had the 'bad batch' warnings drummed into us. But can you get a bad batch of weed? If a cafe is openly selling it, surely there must be some form of quality control?

'We should get stoned,' I tell her and that seems to jolt her from her misery monologue.

'We should do *what*?' she asks, her face a picture of incredulity.

'We should get stoned. We should go to Amsterdam and enjoy the full Amsterdam experience. Without the hookers, obviously. Unless you're into that kind of thing. I wanted to go to the Yorkshire moors and pretend to be Cathy from *Wuthering Heights* but I'm skint. I mean I'm too skint for Amsterdam too, probably, but maybe we could get a bargain? Don't you think that would be fun?' I rattle these words off at the speed of light.

'Are you stoned right now?' Niamh asks, one eyebrow raised. 'Because this is very un-Rebecca type behaviour.'

'I think that maybe I am a little stoned on those pain pills for my broken arse,' I say with a hint of a slur. I try to turn over to point to my tailbone and Niamh stops me. 'I don't need to see it to know it's sore,' she says.

'I wasn't going to show you,' I say. 'I was just going to point to it.'

'I know where your arse is,' Niamh says, but I'm not that stoned that I can't sense she is amused. I'm glad of that. Even in my hazy state. I'm glad she's smiling because I really don't like sad Niamh. When she is sad it makes me feel as if my entire world is off-kilter. It's very disorientating.

'I know you do,' I tell her. 'I'm trying to make you smile, although I am really serious about Amsterdam. We need to go. It would be a laugh. If you want something to prove that you're not hurtling towards death then going to Holland and getting off your baps on weed is a good start. I'd think. My boys would be scandalised. That's almost a good enough reason in itself.'

'And I suppose since I'm not pregnant I can go all out on booze and narcotics anyway,' Niamh says with a sad smile.

'Exactly,' I tell her. 'It's all going to be okay, you know. We've got this. This getting older thing. We're knocking it out of the park and we're going to pack a lot in to this second half. I promise. And, I'm going to pitch some columns to *Northern People*. You know, about being our age and also being amazing. There's a thought – I could write Ten Ways to Be Amazing With a Broken Arse in Your Forties! What did you call that girl we went to school with who edits that magazine now?'

'Grace Duddy? Although she's married now. Adams I think is her surname,' Niamh says. 'And you absolutely should pitch a column. Maybe not about your arse, but I'm sure you've loads of ideas.'

'I do!' I tell her. 'I really do. See, we're going to be okay, you and me. We've a lot left to do.'

She lies back on the bed and rolls towards me to give me a big hug. 'I hope you're right,' she says, as I stiffly roll onto my side and she spoons me.

'Sure, I'm always right,' I tell her, my eyes growing heavy as I enjoy someone who isn't a hairy, slobbery dog, lying beside me.

'And we'll go to the doctors *and* to Amsterdam,' Niamh says, but her voice already feels a little distant. Whether or not I want to, I'm going to have a nap. I can fill Niamh in on what happened with Laura, and ask her about Jodie being over in England with my boys and... and...

* * *

It's dark when I wake up, and I'm immediately aware that I am not alone in my bed. And that whoever else is here is not Daniel, because he is currently standing on the floor beside my bed, licking my face to wake me. My eyelids feel so heavy that even with the threat of imminent murder by a stranger, I contemplate just going back to sleep anyway. Let's face it, if someone has come into my house to murder me, I'm not really fit to put up any kind of meaningful fight, so if they can kill me while I'm sleeping, that seems preferable all round.

As I move a little, trying to get comfortable, I feel a shock of pain in my lower back, which hauls me from my drowsy state and makes me swear loudly. My shouting startles poor Daniel who erupts into a volley of barks, which in turn wakes the murderer behind me. Who just so happens to be Niamh.

'Holy mother of God,' she says, sitting bolt upright ready to fend off whatever threat has scared the heart from her. Daniel, delighted to lay eyes on her, jumps onto the bed, running full force in her direction while I try and ease myself out of the bed – now aware I need to pee very urgently.

'I can't believe I fell asleep,' Niamh says, showering Daniel in kisses until he calms down and curls up at her side. Glancing at my phone I see it's gone nine. We've been asleep for hours. It's no wonder my bladder is threatening to burst.

Still drowsy and quite stiff, I shuffle to the bathroom as memories of the last two days come into focus.

First of all, the positives. We had a lovely afternoon being pampered at Sonas which had awoken some long-hidden desires in me. I'd had an unexpected frisson of something that felt really quite nice with Conal while I was helping Laura. I'd conquered my life-long fear of my attic – not entirely successfully but it hadn't been a complete disaster either. I am still alive, after all. And the Christmas tree and decorations have made it onto the landing. Oh, and I've decided to go to Amsterdam and get high. Becki would be in awe at that one. How rebellious! Becki Burnside contemplating drugs! The scandal!

But there have also been disasters. Biggest of all is that Laura and I have clashed. We have torn off the sticking plaster that our reunion had been and we're both going to have to face all the messy, painful feelings that brings up. Whatever way this is going to go – whether we are able to rebuild our friendship or just accept that too much has been said and done in the past – I do know we need to talk it out.

To add to my worries, I've also learned that my beautiful, crazy, hilarious best friend is experiencing her very own, very real mid-life crisis. She's normally so adept at making sure we all stay happy and buoyant that I've just assumed everything is great on Planet Niamh. I've clearly overlooked the signs that she might need a little help herself. I'll be there for her now, though. I will. God knows she has hauled me from the horrors more than enough to times to be owed that much.

These are our realities just now. Niamh can't run from her

mental health worries, or the fact she's ageing like the rest of us. And I can't run from the fact I'm still angry at and upset with Laura. I was stupid to think I could.

Most of all, I'm learning that just like standing up now I'm finishing having a wee is going to hurt like the bejaysus, so will digging up some very painful memories.

34

INSTAGRAM OFFICIAL

Niamh is still cuddling Daniel as I half walk/half stumble back to the bedroom.

'Do you think you need to go to A & E about that?' she asks, her face wide with concern.

I shake my head. It hurts, yes, but a quick google while I was trying to build up the courage to stand up in the bathroom revealed it is more than likely just a bruised coccyx and pain relief, combined with cold and heat therapies should ease it. Apart from that I'm just going to have to ride it out for a few days. Only then, if it still hurts, will I consider going to A & E just in case it is actually broken.

'I'm pretty sure I've just bruised it,' I say, as I shuffle back onto the bed beside her.

'Do you want me to look?' Niamh asks.

'That would be a no,' I say. I have no desire to flash my arse at my best friend. We have shared a lot in our many years of friendship but there are certain lines I don't ever want to cross with her. My arse falls very firmly across one of those lines.

'Thank the Lord for that,' Niamh says with a grin. 'I love you and all but there are some things I'm happy to never see.' She seems a little brighter for having had a big cry and a big nap. Maybe at heart we're all just like big children and every now and again we need to blow off steam and then sleep off the aftermath. Whatever the reason, I'm happy to see her more like the Niamh I know and love. It's just going to be my job to keep a watchful eye on her in future and do all there is in my power to do to support the times when her low mood comes calling.

She stretches and makes to get up, much to Daniel's disgust.

'I know Dan the Man,' she says. 'I'd love to stay and cuddle with you all night, but I have men folk at home who are basically useless and a semi-feral seven-year-old so I need to go home.'

'You know you're always welcome to stay any time you want,' I tell her. 'If you need to take the pressure off a little bit, or just escape, or just hug a dog or whatever.'

'I know,' she says with a small, warm smile that says everything that needs to be said about our friendship. 'I think I need to go home tonight though. I want to talk to Paul about how I'm feeling while I'm in the moment. He's the one living with my mood swings after all. And I want to hug to my children – even the annoying ones.'

'I totally understand that,' I tell her, as I feel a pang for my own boys. 'And that reminds me. Did you know Jodie is in Manchester?'

Niamh is standing up and straightening her clothes. 'Jodie who?'

'Your Jodie!' I tell her, shimmying my way to the edge of the bed to prepare myself for the inevitable pain that will come with standing up.

'My Jodie? My daughter Jodie?'

'Yes!' I tell her. 'I'm going to assume by your response that you were very much not aware she is in Manchester. Although to be fair, she might've come home by now.'

'Are you sure? As far as I'm aware she's still in Belfast.' Niamh says, pulling her phone from her bag and scrolling through it.

'Adam told me,' I say. 'She's over visiting him and Saul. He hinted at a romance.'

With that, her eyes fly from her phone to look me directly in the eye. 'A romance? Who with? No, she would've said.' Her eyes dart back to her phone where she is scrolling some more.

'With Adam,' I say, adding, 'My Adam,' before she asks the inevitable, 'Adam who?'

'Get. To. France!' she declares and I admire her restraint in using France instead of the swear word that is very clearly on her mind.

'It's true,' I say. 'He sounds sort of smitten.'

'I know it's true,' she says, turning her phone screen to face me. 'That's her location. I have her on Find My Phone and that is definitely not Belfast on the map – it appears to be some sort of student digs in Manchester.'

I blink and squint at the screen, thinking I very much need to book in for an eye test. And yes, it is student digs, and it is the student digs where my boys are staying. Not that I needed convincing. If Adam tells me something, then it is guaranteed to be the absolute truth. Saul is another story... but not Adam.

She pulls her phone away again and taps furiously at the screen. I'm trying to read her face. Is she annoyed? If so, is she annoyed at Jodie for not telling her? Or Jodie for hooking up with my son? Because if it's the latter, my mama bear instincts are getting primed to tear her to shreds. Any mother should be delighted to have Adam dating their daughter. Of course, again, Saul is another story. But Adam – sweet, gentle, responsible Adam – he's a catch. If that doesn't sound too weird coming from his mum.

'Well, ride me sideways!' she declares and turns her phone to my face and once again I have to try and focus on the screen in front of me.

'What am I looking at?' I ask her as the phone is waved in front of me, but then, slowly at first, the image on the screen comes into focus. It's a picture of Adam – his very handsome face dominated by the widest of smiles – with his arms wrapped around Jodie. Jodie who happens to be wearing a matching grin. The kind of grin that only comes with that all-encompassing rush of dopamine and endorphins and all sorts of happy hormones that flood our system when we are falling in love for the very first time. Their happiness exudes from the screen so much that it takes me a moment to notice Saul pulling a very confused, ridiculous face in the background in one of his trademark photobombs. Somehow this picture sums up absolutely everything about my children.

Below the picture is a three-word caption. 'Insta official now!'

I look at Niamh, who is staring directly at me as if trying to read my reaction. We used to joke about this, of course. When the children were born. We did that really awful thing that parents do and referred to our babies as each other's boyfriend and girlfriend and talked about who would get to wear the biggest hat at the wedding. Niamh always called that particular one because she, of course, would be the mother of the bride which overruled any sort of mother of the groom nonsense.

'So,' I say. 'I'm assuming she didn't tell you this.'

'She did not,' Niamh says, her face falling.

'I only found out by accident last night,' I soothe. 'Seems we were both being kept in the dark.'

'Sure, as long as Instagram knows, what do we matter?' she says, her voice bitter and her expression sad. Damn it. We had got back happy Niamh for a bit and now she is back in the feeling pointless and unloved space.

'They're young and selfish, just like we were young and selfish,'

I tell her. 'It's a privilege only the under twenty-fives really get to enjoy. I'm sure they didn't mean to exclude us.' But as I speak, I start to feel a little sad too. Maybe I need to take more co-codamol and sail off on another opioid induced cloud of bliss.

'Maybe,' she says. 'But it would've been nice to be told before the world and his mother. God, I'm even sounding like my own ma now – giving out about social media and people sharing their lives.'

I haul myself to standing and walk around the bed and open my arms wide. 'Here, give me a hug. It will make you feel better. But don't squeeze too tight. My arse won't like it.'

She lets out a loud, heartfelt laugh and walks towards me so I can hug her. 'It's a good thing though, isn't it? That our children have found each other?'

'I suppose it is,' she says.

'And at least she's with Adam and not Saul.'

'That is a very fair point,' she says with a laugh. 'Not that I don't love the very bones of my godsons the same.'

'Oh, I know that,' I say. 'But Saul's an eejit.'

'He is,' she says, and she is the only person in the entire world who I would allow to speak about my son in that way. 'But a nice eejit,' she clarifies.

We hug a little more before she pulls away. 'I really better get home. It's only a matter of time before Ethan or Cal see that Insta update, and say something to Paul and all hell breaks loose because there's no way he'll believe I knew nothing about it.'

'I am always here to be your character witness,' I say as I hobble down the stairs, ouching and oohing as I go.

'Are you sure you don't want me to look at that before I go?' Niamh asks as she gets ready to leave.

'I think you've had a tough enough day without me forcing my bum on you,' I say. 'Honestly, I'll be fine. I'd like to say my ego is more bruised than anything but I don't think that's true.'

'I'll check in on you tomorrow morning, okay?' Niamh says, opening the door and letting an icy blast of wind and rain in.

'Not if I check on you first!'

'And we definitely need to go to Amsterdam. Let's get that in the diary. See when suits Laura and let's make it so,' she says, kissing me on the cheek and walking down the drive towards her car singing the only two lines from 'Tulips from Amsterdam' that she knows.

Balls. I realise that between my fall, her pregnancy scare, Adam and Jodie getting it on, and the high-strength painkillers, I haven't even told her about Laura. Maybe because I'm terrified that this time she'll take Laura's side.

35

THE RECKONING: PART ONE

My to-do list is now as follows. In no particular order:

1) Speak to Ruairi about a Donegal trip with Mum.

2) Book a Donegal trip with Mum.

3) Clear up the scattered and shattered baubles from the landing. Use what is salvageable to decorate the Christmas tree.

4) Research a trip to Amsterdam and whether or not pot brownies interfere with HRT.

5) Arrange doctors' appointments for both Niamh and me, preferably on the same day, to get hooked up with some of the good stuff.

6) Warn Adam that Niamh is raging that Instagram knew her daughter had a boyfriend before she did.

7) Get worming tablets for Daniel. I do not want to have to deal with bum crawlers on top of everything else.

8) Take Daniel for his Christmas haircut, with added photoshoot with Santa Paws – because it's cute, okay? I don't have to explain myself to anyone!

9) Put the Christmas duvet covers on the boys' beds in preparation for the return of the prodigal twins.

10) *Order the god damn turkey* or it will be potato waffles and turkey dinosaurs for Christmas dinner. And not for the first time.

11) Work on these column pitches for Grace at *Northern People*. If I can offer her a selection to show my diversity, I might be in with a better chance.

12) Get in touch with Laura and try to sort this mess out once and for all, even if it means amicably deciding to cut all ties.

It doesn't look like much when you say it out loud, I think. Except it really does look like there's quite a lot to do and only me to do it. And some of it is just an absolute land mine of emotional trauma.

Some things on the list are easier to deal with than others. I pop Ruairi a WhatsApp voice note because he never answers his calls, and it's just easier than trying to type out a lengthy message. I also know he hates WhatsApp voice notes and if it's not a little sister's job to annoy her brother's very existence then whose is it?

I get up before eight so that I'm poised and ready to participate in the GP appointment *Hunger Games* as soon as the surgery opens. My finger hovers over the dial button as I watch the clock face change from minute to minute in the countdown to eight thirty, the theme from *Countdown* playing in my head as it does. Once it reaches the magic hour, all I have to do is hit the call button approximately ninety-four times before I get through, only to be told all the appointments are booked up and I need to call back tomorrow. It's now almost nine thirty and as Ruairi has yet to listen to my message or reply, not a single thing can be ticked off my list, which I now need to put on hold while I get on with some work. God knows I do not want to add 'search for a new job' to the bottom of my list.

By lunch time, I'm getting a bit antsy that Ruairi *still* hasn't listened to my voice message so I type a shorter version of it and hit send. In the war of attrition between siblings, I should've known he would win. He usually does.

No messages have landed in my phone from Laura, which is entirely understandable and expected, but yet it has me on edge. I want to get in touch with her, but I don't know the best way to do it. It seems so impersonal to deal with something so big via text – and the written word is so open to misinterpretation that I'd risk making things even worse than they already are.

I'd perhaps contact Conal if I wasn't worried that by now, I look like a complete psycho who loses dogs, runs out of houses and makes his sister cry. Plus, I don't have his number – which is probably a good thing.

I use the nervous energy that is coursing through my body to clear up the baubles from the landing floor and I brave the pain which still exists in my rear to carry the tree down the stairs. This earns me a tilt of the head from Daniel who is clearly unimpressed that I've not taken him out for a walk or set off on a quest to reunite him with Lazlo. Guilt nips at me, but it's icy outside and I simply can't risk slipping and doing further damage to my already battered bum. Every gluteal muscle I own cringes at the very thought of another impact with the ground as if begging me to be gentle.

'I'm sorry, Daniel,' I tell the floppy-eared mournful beast on the rug and promise him a breast of chicken with rice later as an apology.

By teatime – when Daniel eats the meal I've lovingly prepared for him in approximately two and a half seconds – I feel a little more in control of the day. I've done a sneaky little bit of internet research into Amsterdam and found a gorgeous houseboat on the canal which is rented out as an Airbnb, which doesn't seem to cost the world but is a little different from the norm.

Ruairi has finally replied and told me of course he'd be up for a

weekend away with Mum, but he's up to his eyes in his very important job so if I could just make the arrangements and send him the
deets and the bill that would super. I don't have the energy to be
annoyed at his presumption that I have the time to make the
arrangements single-handedly. This is Ruairi. This is what he has
always been like. There's little point in me trying to change him now.
And besides, Ruairi would book something outrageously expensive,
or in the middle of nowhere, or which has a strict no-dogs-allowed
policy. Wherever we book, there must be room for Daniel. He is,
after all, the closest thing I have to a partner at the moment.

I've even channelled my anxiety-induced hyperactivity into
completing the first of the 'Ten Ways to...' columns. And coming up
with an idea for another. 'Ten Ways to F*ck Up Your Life in Your
Forties'. I accept that while I seem to have direct experience of this
with the implosion of my newly resurrected friendship, it might be
a hard sell to the magazine. Still, it should be cathartic to write.

But perhaps most importantly, by teatime I've decided to put on
my very brave big girl pants and go and visit Laura. Just the thought
of it makes me want to boke my insides out, but I can't live with the
weight of my hurt, and the guilt I feel at hurting Laura just after her
mother died. Maybe she's right. Maybe I do always make it about
me, but surely sometimes it is? Surely it was when Simon left?

I've realised the best way to tackle all this horrible tension is to
face it head on, in person. Even if it's hard. Even if we both cry. Even
if we both come to accept that the Laura and Becki who wanted to
be friends forever all those years ago are not going to get their wish.

I feel so sick worrying about it that I can't eat my dinner, which
Daniel is delighted about. He's not a dog that would ever turn his
nose up at a second chicken breast, which is a good thing as it acts
as a distraction to get me out of the house without him spotting me
heading for the door. I'm not sure I could handle the look of 'but
you said it was too cold to go out' judgement on his face. I am

already riddled with guilt and fear. So much so that my hands are shaking as I get into my car, and it's not just from the cold.

I'm nervous. I'm more nervous than I've been in a long, long time and given that the menopause has reduced me to a ball of anxiety where I can risk a panic attack just leaving the bins out, that really is saying something.

When I get to Laura's I sit outside for ten minutes, willing myself to just get out of the bloody car and walk up to her door. *You're not walking into Mordor*, I tell myself. *You're visiting a friend. Or someone who was a friend. There is no need for you to feel as if you're about to walk the Green Mile. The hardest part of this will be getting out of the car given your bruises. You're a big girl and you need to act like one.*

As I walk up the drive, reach for the doorbell and press it, I'm rehearsing over and over what I will say, trying to pre-empt what her reaction might be. If she's angry, I'll let her rant. If she's sad, I'll let her cry. If she looks like she could cut a bitch, I'll turn and run/hobble down the icy path as quick as I can.

But it's not Laura who answers the door. It's Aidan. Aidan who looks tired and middle-aged and has a bit of a paunch which certainly wasn't there ten years ago. Not that I can judge anyone on excess padding gained in the last decade.

Although I saw him at Kitty's funeral, it still feels odd to see him now. My brain still expects him to be how he was ten years ago. Just as it expects this house – Laura's house – to look just as it did. This place was once so familiar to me but now I'd be hard pushed to recognise it. There's a new front door for a start. One of those fancy black composite jobs which cost a fortune. It's decorated with a holly-laden Christmas wreath, faux frost glistening on the forest-green leaves.

The laminate flooring Laura once had in her hall has been replaced with high polished tiles. The walls are no longer sage green, but now a subtle greige, with accents of gold in the artwork on the walls. It looks well, but then again, Laura always has had good taste.

'Becca,' Aidan says from behind his fine rimmed glasses. Those too are a new addition. None of us can hold back the ageing process.

'Aidan,' I say feeling exceptionally awkward. 'I've come to see Laura. Is she in?' I peek over his shoulder as if expecting her to materialise behind him. There's a pause and I realise she may not actually be in. I may have come all this way for nothing.

'Actually, she's at her mum's house,' Aidan says, his tone unreadable. 'She went back to work today so clearing the house is going to be an evenings-only job. I offered to go with her, but she wanted to go alone. Today has been a tough one, you know.'

The way he says it is so pointed I can tell he's pissed off at me for upsetting his wife. Of course that's completely understandable, and I'm certainly not going to try and talk him round – not here, and not now. Laura's not in. It's freezing cold and starting to rain the kind of icy cold rain that jabs at your skin like needles. Right now, I just want to go back to my car.

'It meant a lot to her,' he says. 'That you girls came to the funeral. That you've been there for her. It's been a tough time, but finding you girls again added a spring to her step that I haven't seen in... well...'

He doesn't finish the sentence and I fight the urge to reply with a snarky 'ten years'? I know that demon on my shoulder is clawing to be set free and, similarly, I know I have to keep her under control. Nothing good ever happens when she gets out to play.

'I understand,' I say instead. There's a pause that is just bordering on uncomfortable. 'Well, if you could let her know I called by anyway. I'd best get on home before this weather gets any worse. It's not a night to be driving.'

As I turn to leave, I hear him say my name again, calling me back. I stop and turn to face him once more.

'It was a horrible situation, you know. When you and Simon split up,' Aidan says.

'When he left me, with two boys who were broken-hearted that their daddy walked out?' that pesky demon snaps, and I hate myself for letting her. But more than that I hate myself for still feeling abandoned, and feeling it so deeply at that. If anyone had asked me before this moment if I was over the break-up I'd have laughed and told them I was so very, very over it that I didn't even think about it any more. But this last week has brought a lot of long buried feelings to the surface. Seems I wasn't wrong when I called the time capsule Pandora's Shoebox. It has spilled out its messy contents in style and forced us to confront more than we wanted to.

'Yes,' Aidan replies. 'When Simon walked out on you and the boys. I'm not going to defend him, Becca. He may well be my best friend but he really fucked up back then. Yes, your marriage was over and I think even you probably agree that him leaving was ultimately for the best. But he was wrong to cheat on you. I told him that at the time. *Laura* told him that at the time and many times since.'

His words stop me in my tracks. Laura had told him he was wrong. She had stood up for me. I've needed to hear that so much over the last ten years and here it is, being said to me right at the time I might have carpet-bombed what little chance there was left for a lasting reconciliation between us.

Aidan is still speaking. 'We *were* angry at him – Laura especially,' he says, 'but I wasn't going to abandon my friend. He might have been an arsehole, but he was my friend and even if you don't think so, the break-up hurt him too. He lost the family he thought he'd have. He lost the chance to live with his boys as they grew up and yes, he might've been to blame for that but it still hurt him. I wasn't going to let him go through that alone. But I'm sorry it hurt you so badly.' He pauses, shakes his head wearily. 'We all could've handled it so much better.'

The 'all' in that sentence lands heavily because I know that it's true. Others handled it badly, but so did I. I knew my marriage was past the point of rescue when Simon told me he was leaving. If I'm being honest with myself, it was over for a long time before that day. I didn't want him to stay. I didn't fall to pieces and beg him not to go. I knew in my heart we had nothing left worth fighting for. I knew deep down that the boys would benefit more from being in a happy single-parent home than with a mum and dad who had stopped loving each other. If we'd stayed together any longer the apathy with which we now viewed each other would've turned to resentment and anger.

I knew it was the right thing to do, even if I couldn't admit it to myself. I buried the inner voice that was, perhaps, relieved he had made the decision for us, and I didn't have to ask him to leave. Yes, I was bruised and blindsided by his infidelity, but that same inner voice, if I was being really honest with myself, told me she felt relieved to be single again. I did my best to ignore her and push her down because even with all those thoughts in my head, it was still sad. I was still sad.

I still grieved the life I thought Simon and I would have. We had, after all, loved each other once. We'd loved each other enough to get married and start a family. When we stood at the altar and made our wedding vows we had meant them with every part of our bodies. I dreamt of having a marriage just like the one my mum and dad had, where love was a daily declaration. We thought we would have the perfect, life-long bond and it was going to be sweeter because our joint best friends, Laura and Aidan, would be coming along for the ride with us. Our friendship group was as solid as any could be. Until it wasn't.

So even though breaking up was the right thing to do, and would've been the right thing to do whether or not he had been seeing someone else, it still hurt. And my reactions to everything that happened then came from a place of hurt. Including, I realise with a thud, trying to force Laura to choose between her husband and her best friend. I was wrong to assume she wasn't calling him out on his behaviour. I had no right to enact the Girl Code Manifesto and tell Laura she couldn't be friends with my ex-husband and still be friends me, not when Aidan was still very much a part of his life. Standing in the rain, icy rivulets now running down my face and neck and under my scarf – making me shiver – I realise it all now.

Just as I realise, with another sickening thud, that it wasn't so much that I didn't want Laura to be friends with Simon any more, it was more that I hated that I wasn't going to be a part of that precious friendship bubble that had meant so much to me any more. I hated that so much.

36

THE RECKONING: PART TWO

I don't go home when I leave Aidan and Laura's house. I know that if I did, I would only be consumed with a restlessness that would keep me awake and anxious all night.

So I have arrived at Kitty's house, ready to sort this all out once and for all and wondering if there is a human equivalent for 'tail between my legs'?

All the fight has gone out of me. But not in a bad way. The hurt I have carried on my shoulders for the last decade, in the form of the demon troll, has melted away – like the Wicked Witch in *The Wizard of Oz* when she gets a bucket of water thrown over her. It's a relief, of course, in many ways. But it would be more of one if it hadn't been replaced by a sizeable wedge of guilt and shame.

Aidan had said that we *all* handled it badly, and I can see that now. Ultimately though, it was me who threw the mother of all tantrums and walked away from one of the most important friendships of my life.

Be it through pride, or pain, or just because I was ridiculously immature about the whole thing, I pushed away one of the two friends I really needed. I didn't acknowledge the awful position

Laura was in. I don't think I allowed – or could allow – myself to consider how awful it was for her.

Simon hadn't wronged Laura. He hadn't wronged Aidan – his best friend since school. When I think of the bigger picture, Simon hadn't actually wronged me all that much either. In the end, his cheating was just a symptom of a much bigger problem and without it, maybe we'd have rumbled on unhappily for another few years. The truth is, though, we just weren't meant to go the distance and I don't think there is anything either of us could've done to change that.

We'd married too young and without knowing each other as well as we should've before agreeing to a 'til-death-do-us-part deal. With each year that passes I think more and more that people should be actively dissuaded from getting married in their twenties. Who the hell knows anything about life in their twenties? We all think we do, of course. But we don't. Then again... I'm not sure I know anything about life even now.

But when Simon and I were dating, we had such a naïve, short-sighted approach to life. We'd fitted into each other's lives and social circles so perfectly, that initially it had been easy to ignore the niggling doubts and red flags. We were both on our best trying-to-impress-each-other behaviour then too. We allowed ourselves to be malleable. We made the sort of compromises that only really happen at the start of relationships when you do all you can to make yourself a desirable prospect.

The harsh reality is we all pretend, in a benign way, to be much more perfect for each other than we really are. Sooner or later the truth slips out. For some people there are annoying, but surmountable, little foibles. For others, those foibles become like a dripping tap. The more they happen, the longer they go on, the louder they get, until it's just about all you can hear or think about.

For Simon and me, it was only after we were locked in to life together that the dripping tap got louder.

We found we didn't have as much to talk about as we once did. We didn't like watching the same programmes on TV. We didn't have the same ideas of what made for a good holiday. Simon was not a man who took life particularly seriously – which was refreshing to begin with. I had loved how he made me laugh.

But a few years and twin boys in, I needed him to wise up and take on more responsibility. I needed him to be a parent and a partner and a functioning human being. He just didn't see the appeal of being organised and structured about life, or in disciplining the children or helping with the housework. 'The boys are just being boys,' he'd say, or, 'You're so fussy. A house should look lived in.'

And yes, a house should look lived in, but it also needed to meet certain basic levels of cleanliness, for the love of God. I felt like I had three boys to mind and I resented him for it.

I'm sure his version of events won't paint me in the best light either. I was, according to his angrier days, a nag and a 'craic vacuum'. He reacted to my criticisms by doubling down on being the fun parent, which left me to be play the bad cop role in our dynamic.

Unsurprisingly, resentment started to fester. Fester is not a good word, people. Festering is not pleasant. It doesn't have positive connotations or outcomes. It's rot. And our marriage was rotting.

We tried to fix it. There were many long nights and big talks – at least in the earlier years – where we promised to compromise and listen and try.

The new order would last a while then the tap would start dripping again. After a few years, we just sort of slipped into apathy for a while. We knew the tap was dripping, we just didn't try to fix it.

Maybe we realised that it couldn't be fixed but we just weren't ready to admit it yet.

Then he left. It came out of the blue. There were no big arguments. No tortured discussions. He just packed his bags and said we both deserved to be happier than we were. It was fairly straightforward and matter of fact and it was the calmness of it that made it sting so sharply. I knew, instantly, that there was no point in trying to fight it. He was right. He had hit the nail on the head. The me who had felt the disconnect between us for a long time knew that instantly.

But the me who was going to be left with two nine-year-old boys who had to watch their fun parent pack up and go, leaving them with Mama Bad Cop, was hurt, and scared. I'd felt overwhelmed with responsibility even when I had another parent in the house helping me. I was terrified that without him – even though things had been far from perfect – I would fall to pieces.

And yes, I was angry. He was swanning off into the sunset – with his reduced responsibilities and I was not. If I'm honest with myself, I was a little jealous. Who wouldn't want a chance for a do-over? A chance to wipe the slate the clean and start again, with extra fun?

When he told me, just before he left, that he had been seeing someone, the bitterness kicked in too. My ego wasn't just bruised. It was pulverised. My feelings about the break-up had been manageable when I could put it down to us just not working. But to know he had already moved on before he had moved out, that stung. I'd sat on our sofa in what had been our joint home and listened to him tell me that he was sorry. He wanted to tell me in case the news reached me via Facebook or Instagram, or the good old Derry grapevine. I don't know if he expected me to be grateful on that score, but I wasn't.

So when Laura and Aidan had still put Simon up in their spare room – taking pity on the poor single man who had won his get-out-of-jail card, I had – to put it mildly – lost my shit.

And that was unfair of me, I realise. I think, truth be told, I realised it a long time ago, but I just couldn't admit it to myself.

But now, as the rain has turned to sleet and the neighbouring houses are illuminated with Christmas lights, I'm looking up at Kitty's house, which was once the brightest and most colourful on the street, and I know it's time for me to not only admit all this to myself, but to Laura as well.

For ten minutes I sit in the rain trying to think of the right thing to say. Everything sounds trite or like I'm trying too hard. I feel as if I'm sixteen again and practising a monologue for drama class and every which way I put the words together in my head I sound like some sort of wanky after-school special. All that's missing is Tiny Tim jumping up from the back seat and declaring, 'And God bless us, everyone,' in a cockney accent.

Fuck it, I think eventually when the cold from outside starts to seep into my bones. I'm just going to have to wing it.

That doesn't stop my hand from shaking as I reach out to press the doorbell, or my legs from shaking when the hall light switches on and I can hear approaching footsteps.

I'm even more flustered when the door opens and once again, it's not Laura standing in the hallway but Conal. I don't know why but seeing him and seeing that his expression is one of concern and not anger at me breaks something deep inside me.

I want to handle this like the mature, capable woman that I am but seeing him look at me with such warmth and care makes it impossible for me not to break down. It's a mixture of shame and grief, embarrassment and yet hope that makes me crumple like a soggy rag on the doorstep of his dead mother.

Before I know it, he is guiding me inside and I feel the warmth of his hand on mine, and then the warmth of his body against me as he pulls me into a hug while I sob like a fucking eejit and mutter that I'm sorry and I need to talk to Laura, and that I had felt so lonely and I still feel lonely, and I was a bitch walking out on Laura yesterday while she's grieving and... and... and...

He just holds me and I feel his hand stroke my hair as he comforts me and tells me it's okay and we're all just very stressed and tired and emotional, and sure, it's Christmas and everyone loses their shit at Christmas. 'Even if Mum hadn't just died, and you guys hadn't just tried to build bridges, there would still be something that would reduce us all to a wreck. I had a good old sob at *Strictly* on Saturday night,' he says and I laugh. It would be cute, and maybe even a bit flirty if my laugh didn't also launch a snot bubble all over his jumper. He has the manners not to comment on it, and instead just continues gently rocking me while I work my way through that weird stage at the end of a crying fit where the tears come in occasional bursts and hiccups and sighs.

I swear I feel his lips gently brush the top of my head, but I'm willing to concede that could be wishful thinking and he might just be wiping his nose on my hair in an act of revenge. The Conal of 1994 would have totally done that.

'Jeez, not my friend, Conal!' I hear Laura call from the top of the stairs, but her voice isn't angry. It's a little shaky, but it's clear she's trying to be light-hearted. Blinking, I pull back, somewhat reluctantly, from Conal's embrace and look up at her. Her expression says it all. At once she looks scared, but hopeful. She looks open to seeing me and talking with me and she referred to me as her friend. It's as much as I could hope for.

As soon as she sees me she must notice that I've been crying. I dread to think what state I'm in. Half my make-up is now streaked across Conal's jumper. I imagine the other half of it is sliding down my face. I probably look like a sad, middle-aged version of the lead singer from Kiss, all panda eyes and pale face.

She pads down the stairs and without speaking pulls me into a hug that is genuine. I mutter that I'm sorry, that I know I should not have walked out yesterday. That I should not have walked away ten years ago. That the things I'd said to her were cruel and from a place of anger and I'm just so sorry.

'I'm sorry too,' she says. 'For how I reacted. For the things I said.'

'We were both dicks, weren't we?' I ask, trying to lighten the mood but failing miserably when my voice cracks and yet more tears fall.

'Absolute dicks,' Laura says and pulls me back into a hug. What Conal thinks of this is anyone's guess but I can't think about that. Not now and not even when he says he's going to put the kettle on and make us some tea, even though I'm pretty sure it's just a ruse to get away from us.

'Tea would be lovely,' Laura tells him. 'Milk, no sugar for both of us,' she adds. 'Assuming you still take your tea that way?'

I nod. 'A creature of habit,' I say.

'Let's go and sit in the living room,' Laura says. 'We can put the gas fire on and get a bit of heat going.'

'That sounds good,' I say, glad to have someone else take the lead.

'I suppose we knew it was never going to be easy,' Laura says, as she takes a seat by the fire. By the well-worn appearance of the chair, the slight sag in the seat, I imagine this was Kitty's preferred spot. A crocheted blanket hangs over the back of the chair, which Laura pulls around her knees.

'I made this for Mum,' she says, as the gas flames start to heat the room. 'Can you imagine it? Me crocheting? Took me much too long and you wouldn't want to look too closely at it.'

'It looks perfect,' I say and mean it. And I know that Kitty would've adored it. Kitty was the kind of woman who kept every drawing and wonky Mother's Day present her children brought her home from school. 'The flaws are what make it perfect,' she'd say. 'They make it unique.'

'It's far from perfect,' Laura laughs. 'You do remember that my skills do not lie with any sort of crafts. Remember that time I tried to knit a scarf and it ended up looking like a string bag instead, but with holes too big to be of any use to anyone.'

I can't help but smile. I remember it all too well. Laura's face had flushed crimson as Mrs McCay, our Home Economics teacher, had actually laughed at her efforts, but Kitty had made a point of wearing it anyway – to the parent-teacher meeting where she had let Mrs McCay know exactly how she felt about teachers laughing at pupils.

'Your mum loved it anyway,' I say and laugh. 'Do you remember she used to say it was a real one of a kind?'

'I found it in the back of her wardrobe yesterday. I threatened Robyn that I was going to wear it, expecting her to be horrified, but she said it was actually really cool and gothic and she asked if she could have it.'

I have to admit, I'm impressed. 'Maybe it's time to start building the dodgy scarf empire you always dreamt of?' I joke.

'Maybe,' Laura says. 'But I think I'd like to rebuild our friendship first.'

'I'd like that too,' I say as Conal carries two mugs into the room and hands one to each of us. Lazlo runs in, does a quick scan of the room, lets out a disappointed bark and leaves. 'He's such a diva,' Conal says as he hands over the mugs. 'Is that enough milk for you?' he asks. 'I can get some more.'

'It's fine, Conal. Thanks a million,' I tell him, feeling something I can't quite put my finger on in the way he looks at me. He gives me a slow smile – the kind that makes your heart beat a little faster and gives you those delicious curls right in the very pit of your stomach.

I watch as he leaves the room, before turning my attention back to Laura and rebuilding what was lost between us.

'You know he always fancied you,' Laura says, as she raises her eyebrows and sips from her mug of tea.

37

MISSION IMPOSSIBLE

Conal O'Hagan used to fancy me? It seems absurd. Back then he was the cool big brother who would tell us to stop screeching along to Madonna, or roll his eyes if we spent more than five minutes in his company. It always felt as if we were an irritation to him. I certainly didn't get any 'I fancy you' vibes.

I'm sure I'd have remembered if I did, given that, as Niamh reminded me, I did kind of fancy him too. But back then I also saw him as totally and utterly unattainable – like Fox Mulder was unattainable, and Robbie Williams was unattainable – mostly because it felt like we annoyed his very existence.

'Wise up!' I tell her, even though I secretly hope it's true. 'I was just his wee sister's geeky friend.'

'It seems you were more than that,' she says in an almost whisper. 'Not that I knew it at the time. But Mum told me, during one of our long chats near the end.'

The hairs on the back of my neck stand up and I have to suppress a little shiver. If I believed in ghostly matters I would swear Kitty O'Hagan was in this room now weaving all of this together in that unique way she had of making things right.

'I made sure we talked about everything in those last weeks,' Laura says. 'And as you know, my mammy liked to talk. I was supposed to be comforting and nursing her, but I think she was giving me a lifetime of mammy advice and experience to carry me forward. I think she always knew that you and I, and Niamh, would talk again one day. She would tell me that I would have people – friends – around me to hold me up when she was gone and so I wasn't to be scared.'

I'm filled with a sense of love and admiration for Kitty and immense gratitude for her faith in our friendship. But there is also a heavy feeling of sadness and guilt that it took her passing for Laura and me to finally talk again – that she never got to see us reconcile and know for definite that Laura would be okay. And that it took her passing and the reconnection with Laura for me to finally sit down and really examine my life and the decisions I've made along the way.

'I was hurting back then,' I tell her, and Laura looks genuinely confused.

'When Mammy was dying?' she asks with a raised eyebrow.

'No, sorry,' I mumble. 'My brain is just jumping all over the place.'

'I think we know where your brain is jumping and it involves my big brother,' Laura says. 'Which is sort of quite weird, if I'm being honest.' She smiles to let me know it's not really all that weird – that this a safe space and even though things have been tough, there is still the potential to mend this friendship once and for all. That we still understand each other. That we can still joke together and know each other's sense of humour and each other's boundaries.

'Very funny,' I tell her. 'But no, I meant then. The big "then". When Simon left. I felt like such a failure. I was embarrassed we couldn't make it work, and ashamed to be heading for divorce and I,

I don't know, I was unreasonable and I wanted someone to choose me and...'

'You were in an impossible position,' Laura says and I freeze.

'I'm pretty sure that's what I'm supposed to say to you,' I tell her but her words settle in my bones. I *had* been in an impossible situation. Simon and I had to break up – for our joint benefit and for our boys' benefit. It would have been unfair to keep limping along in something that was dead and rotting. If we hadn't split, the things that were wrong between us would have started to eat away at what positives we had created. They would have eaten away at the people we were. But that didn't make breaking up an easy decision. We both knew it would throw a bomb into the lives and dreams we had. There was no way around that. No escape from it. That's why I'd never had the courage to make that decision. It was why Simon had to make that decision for me. For us.

I knew that breaking up was the right thing to do but wished it didn't have to change absolutely everything.

'I wish I'd handled it differently,' she tells me. 'I've no idea what I would've or could've done differently, but I wish I knew, and I wish I did it. It was just a horrible situation and I'm so sorry that you were hurt.'

'Well, *I'm* sorry *you* were hurt,' I tell her. 'It must've been awful losing Niamh and me like that too. That was brutal. It was awful of me. I was so selfish and cruel and childish.'

She gives a small smile to show we're still friends, but she can't hide the tears that snake their way down her cheeks, and which she tries to wipe away discreetly.

'I think we all went through a lot,' she says with a tremor in her voice. 'And we've all missed a lot. It's been quite the eventful ten years.'

'I've missed you,' I say and mean it – from the bottom of my heart, I mean it. 'I don't want to do another ten years like that.'

'Me neither,' she says. 'I want to have fun again, you know. If it doesn't sound too cringey I want to make memories again. Good ones. With stupid dance routines, and embarrassing celebrity crushes. I want to go on a girls-only holiday. I want to take up new hobbies – trendy ones. Not just crochet.'

'But the crochet could come in handy for your dodgy scarf empire,' I tease and she laughs.

'True,' she says. 'Okay then, I want to take up new hobbies, as well as crochet.'

'Atta girl,' I say, and take a sip from my mug of tea. Dear me, but Conal makes the perfect cuppa. This could be the start of something beautiful.

'So we'll be friends again?' she asks.

'Yes please,' I tell her. 'Wait until I tell you what Niamh and I are getting up to next. You can join in if you want?'

'Ooh,' Laura says as she sits forward in her chair. 'What is it?'

'Well, we're going to the doctors and we're going to get us some of the best HRT the NHS can provide. Patches, pills, tablets, pessaries – whatever's on offer.'

She smiles. 'I'm going to have to sit this one out,' she says, a little sadly. 'With mum's history, you know, I've decided to swerve HRT and try some natural options. I am more than willing to be our group hippy and fill you in on complementary methods of supporting menopausal women. I've done a lot of research these past few years.'

'God, I'm sorry. I didn't even think about your mum and the breast cancer risk,' I say, my face blazing.

'It's fine,' she says, reassuring me. 'I don't have the BRCA gene so I'm really just being extra cautious. And you know, it's quite fascinating to learn about natural remedies and how other cultures approach it. So I'm good.'

'I'm glad,' I say. 'I'm embarrassed to say I'm pretty ignorant about it – except that I know it is messing with my head a bit. You know, all this getting older carry on. And Niamh, she's finding it very tough.'

'It is tough,' Laura says. 'But do you know what helps?'

'Gin?' I offer.

She laughs. 'I hear that can help, for sure. But what has helped me is reading about the Mayan culture and how they view it. Mayan women believe menstrual blood is imbued with a certain power and wisdom. Because it's so closely connected with the creation of life, they believe that having their period allows them to tap into their shamanic and healing powers. So when a woman reaches menopause, her body holds on to that powerful and life-giving blood which ushers her into her wise woman years.'

'So the menopause makes us extra witchy and powerful?' I ask, one eyebrow raised.

'Exactly!' Laura says. 'So bring on the wise woman years.'

'Witches assemble!' I cheer.

'Would you two ever stop your screeching and carrying on?' I hear Conal say, before he pops his head around the door and I see he is smiling.

Why have I never noticed before now just how sexy his smile is?

* * *

By the time I get home I am exhausted, and sore, and most likely dehydrated from all the crying. The cup of tea Conal made was good, but it wasn't that good. I have cried more today than I have since the weeks after my dad died.

As Daniel snakes his way around my legs, doing his very best to make sure his body is touching mine at all times, I run a tall glass of water at the sink and drink it all in one go before filling it again. Daniel looks up at me as if to say I'll regret this when I have to get up seventeen times in the night for a wee, but I'm confident that my haggard husk of a body will hold on to what moisture it can so that it's able to continue doing all the things a body should do.

My house is quiet. The kind of quiet I used to long for. There's just the gentle hum of the fridge, the ticking of the kitchen clock and the occasional 'boof' of disgust from the dog who is raging that I'm not feeding him chicken or ham from the fridge. He's definitely starting to get a little demanding – then again I have perhaps been lavishing too many treats on him since Adam and Saul left for university.

'There are no more treats tonight,' I tell him. 'But I promise I'll get you a Jumbone tomorrow if you're good.' I swear he shrugs in a kind of 'it's a deal' gesture and pads away from me towards the bottom of the stairs. Clearly, he has decided he wants tomorrow to come as quickly as possible so a good sleep will make that happen.

As I'm finishing my water, I look to where the time capsule is still resting on the worktop, the lid sitting loosely on the top.

I can't help but go and have another nosey through it. Those were such innocent times, and no, things hadn't worked out the way we thought they would, but we are still here. We are all speaking again. Life has kept us weaving in and out of each other's stories. Maybe that's as much as any of us can hope for.

Finishing my drink, I rinse the glass and sit it on the drainer before making my way upstairs, much to Daniel's delight. Of all the things that were on my to-do list at the start of the day, I appear to have ticked off some of the bigger items. For now, I'm going to climb under my duvet and get a good rest before round two with the GP appointment *Hunger Games* in the morning.

I'm plugging my phone in to charge when it beeps to life with a message from an unknown number. I click to open it, half expecting it to be some dodgy scam about a parcel that couldn't be delivered or the like but it isn't. It's something altogether more pleasant.

> Becca, it's Conal. I hope you don't mind that Laura gave me your number. I just wanted to check you were okay after earlier? You were so upset. Look, I'm fifty years old and that means I'm beyond playing games. That's even more the case after Mum passing. Life is too short to drag the arse out of things. So I'm just going to say this. I'd very much like it if I could take you out for a drink sometime. If that's something you would like, just say the word.

It's a long time since I squealed with excitement. But that's what I do. I can't hold it in. I let out a little, high-pitched yelp as I feel my nerve endings fizz. My body floods with endorphins and dopamine and, yes, a little desire too. I think of Conal and how he hugged me. It wasn't just the warmth of his body that felt so good. He offered the full sensory experience. He knew just how tight to hold me. He knew just how to soothe me with his words. He knew that I needed that soft brush of his lips on the top of my head. He looked, and felt, and smelled delicious and manly and yes, I want to learn what it's like to kiss him. I want to know what he tastes like too. I shiver with pleasure at the thought then squeal again when I realise that I don't feel scared of it. I don't feel like I want to run from him. I want this. I want him. I reply:

> I would like that very much indeed

My cheeks are already hurting from smiling so widely. I feel like getting up and dancing around the room when my phone pings to life again with a smiley faced emoji and a message asking if I am free on Friday night.

While my internal soundtrack starts blasting 'I'm Free' by the

Soup Dragons, I reply with a smiley face *and* a winking smiling face to show that I too have no interest in playing games and that I am, indeed, free.

Grinning, I hug my arms around myself. I did not have scoring a date with Conal O'Hagan on my to-do list but here I am, having done it. And I already know he likes me. I'd call that a win of epic proportions.

38

LIFE IN THE OLD GIRL YET

I am in incredibly good form this morning. Even though my arse still feels as if it has been battered with a sledge-hammer and walking is painful, I can't stop smiling. I have put Magic FM on and am doing my level best to bop around the kitchen to Kelly Clarkson's 'Stronger', safe in the knowledge neither of my sons will walk in and look at me as if I've lost the run of myself, or complain about the music I'm listening too.

I'm in such a good mood that I don't even mind that it's so far taken me thirty-seven attempts to get through to my GP surgery and none of them have been successful. The anticipatory high of my forthcoming date with Conal is clearly having a better mood-altering effect than any amount of HRT or anti-depressant could ever have. My patience this morning is unlimited. I am unfuckwith-able today.

I'm rewarded for my good mood by the phone finally connecting to a very stressed sounding receptionist who immedi-ately apologises for the difficulty in getting through. With immense magnanimity, I tell her not to worry and that it can't be helped. We chat amiably about the pressures on the system while she helps me arrange appointments for both Niamh and me to pop in together to discuss the menopause. I have to hold myself back from explaining how we're morphing into witches and this is our wise woman era in case she decides to have me sectioned.

With the two appointments under my belt, I'm free to get on with my work for a few hours, while still in my joyous little bubble of imminent dating.

All is good in my world.

I've already made the decision that I will be decorating the Christmas tree tonight, so while I'm working, I put Michael Bublé's Christmas album on and light a cinnamon-scented candle. The world of business-to-business marketing may not traditionally form a large part of seasonal festivities but today I am making the most of my good mood and channelling it into to some light-hearted content.

While it's not exactly the job young Becki dreamt of, it does allow me the occasional flourish of creativity and that's probably a large part of why I hang in here. If I do get the chance to write my own column for *Northern People* as well, then I'll really get to go to town with my creative voice. The thought makes me almost giddy.

It's quite impressive what a good mood can do when you're writing your top ten office Secret Santa gifts, or a list of dos and don'ts for the Christmas party. Yes, I have to sprinkle in more than a little *soupçon* of wanky corporate speak and plug some really boring/morally questionable sponsored ideas (a 'fun' app that monitors your productivity which I'm pretty sure can relate it back to your boss, anyone?) but I still get to add a little heart and yuletide warmth into the article. Businessmen and women everywhere will be weeping happy festive tears into their morning coffees after reading it.

Wired by my writing buzz, I do what only a fortnight ago would have seemed impossible. I attach two draft columns, and a list of six further ideas and I pop them in an email to Grace Adams at the magazine. I may never hear back from her, but at least I've tried. Becki would be proud that I tried.

Just before lunch, my mother calls and for once I don't immediately panic at seeing her number on my phone screen. It's a sad reality that ever since my father died, my heart threatens to beat out of my chest every time I see her name and number light up. I live in fear of answering only to hear the voice of a paramedic or doctor on the other end breaking the worst news – but not today. Today I just feel in my bones that everything is okay. This is just my mother calling me for a chat in the way that mothers often call their children to catch up. The worst that will happen, I tell myself, is that she will refer to Daniel as 'that dog' again or tell me she's stuck in the attic. If it's the latter, I will arrange a rescue and then tell her of my own attic escapades and use it as a warning story to stop her trying any of her tricks again. I broke my arse which is bad enough. She could break a hip and have to stay in hospital for months sharing a room with people who snore and break wind in the wee small hours. She would not like it.

'Mum, hi,' I say, wondering if I should let her know about my impending date or if I should leave it 'til after when I can tell her how it went.

'Rebecca Louise Burnside, I want to have a word with you,' she answers.

Shit. I'm in trouble. I know that voice. I fear that voice. It has the ability to reduce me to a ten-year-old version of myself knowing I have just sailed up Shit Creek and subsequently dropped my paddle by sneaking open my Easter eggs on Good Friday. I thought

I'd get away with my criminal endeavours by eating the back half of the egg, and propping the front against the box to look unsullied, only for Ruairi to rat me out before Peter had even denied our Lord for the first time.

I wonder if I should just hang up, turn my phone off, and deal with this drama later. I could tell my mum the signal went and hopefully by the time she gets through to me again – when I switch my phone back on, obvs – she will have forgotten about whatever it is that has given her the rage.

Of course that would go against my new policy of meeting things head on, so I take a deep breath.

'Yes?' I say. 'Is everything okay?'

'Well, no,' my mother says, her accent particularly well enunciated in the way normally only reserved for when she talks to doctors and priests. This must be very serious business indeed then.

'I've been talking to your brother,' she says.

Ruairi! I think. He must have grassed on me. I'm not entirely sure what he could've grassed on me about, but that isn't stopping this triggering my own version of PTSD anyway. Dear Reader, let me introduce you to PBWADD – Post-Brother-Was-A-Dick-Disorder. 'Whatever he says, he's lying,' I mumble. 'I didn't do anything wrong. He just always wants to get me in trouble!'

I know they say there are times when, as you grow older, you open your mouth and hear your mother's voice come out. I wasn't aware there would also be times I would open my mouth and hear one of my own children's voices as they tried their best to rat each other out.

'He tells me you were trying to book a holiday for me, for us,' she says in a voice that makes it sounds as if booking a holiday is the equivalent of taking a poo in the middle of her carpet.

'Yes,' I say, confused. 'Just a few days, maybe. To Donegal. Like we did when we were little.'

'Well, why would you be wanting to do that? And in winter? What would you do with yourself in Donegal in the winter? And the cost of it too. And you with those boys to put through university.' She sounds absolutely horrified and enraged. The strength of her reaction is flooring me.

'Because when we spoke recently about things you really enjoyed you said your happiest memories were the family holidays we went on when we were wee,' I offer. 'There's plenty to do in Donegal in the winter. A walk along the beach on a blustery day is hard to beat.'

'I'm almost eighty, Rebecca,' my mother says. 'There are lot of things that beat a walk on the beach on a cold day. In fact, almost anything does.'

'And it's not *that* expensive,' I cut across her. 'Besides, Ruairi said he would pay the majority and it's not like he's short of money, what with being so successful and everything.'

I know that going in with a comment praising her beloved eldest child in the hope of placating her is a bit of a manipulative move but needs must. Besides, I've no idea how else to go in. This is a nice thing I'm trying to do and yet she sounds mortally offended at the very notion.

'Maybe so,' she says, 'but do you not think you should've talked to me about it before you started making plans? I might've made other plans already for myself.'

As if, I think but I know better than to say it out loud. 'Well, we've not actually booked it yet. We were just looking at different options and we'd probably have run it past you,' I tell.

'Probably?'

She's really not happy. I need to fix this quick. 'Well, we would've, Mum. I promise.'

'And I would've told you there's no need because I already have a holiday booked, and I didn't need anyone to do it for me. There's life in the aul doll yet, you know.'

I am, for once, at a complete loss for words. My mother has booked a holiday. My mother who can't even go to Asda on her own, has booked a holiday?

'What? Where? With who? When?' The questions spill out of my mouth as quickly as they land in my thoughts.

'With Mrs Bishop,' she says. 'I was thinking about all the stuff you said about living life and trying new things and so I talked to Emily – Mrs Bishop – and she said she couldn't remember the last time she went on holiday so we thought, you know, why not? Long story short, we found a travel company online—'

'You found a travel company online? *Online*? You, who doesn't trust the internet not to steal all your money?' I interrupt, not sure whether to be impressed or terrified she has found some online crook who will, in fact, steal all her money.

'Yes. Online. One of the lovely ladies down at the Central Library helped us find our way through it,' my mother says and I immediately think that the lovely ladies in the Central Library must have the patience of saints. 'We found a company that specialises in holidays for the more senior members of society, and we booked a week-long cruise around the Canary Islands. We fly out at the start of February.'

I've never really understood the expression 'you could've knocked me down with a feather' before now. Nothing in this modern world is really *that* shocking. Except, I realise, for this.

'So you see, Rebecca, you don't need to be spending money or time that would be better devoted to your work, your youngsters or *that dog* on me and taking me on some holiday. I appreciate the thought but I'm well able to make my own plans and there's life in me yet. If you can go on a girly holiday, then so can I!'

The thought of my mother describing a break with Mrs Bishop as a 'girly holiday' is incredibly sweet. And even though she has just told me off for trying to do a nice thing for her, I can't help but feel a swell of affection for my mother and a real deluge of pride that she has worked this out without my help. Who would've thought my mother and Mrs Bishop had it in them? I only hope they're not about to unleash a whole new variety of Thelma and Louise-type mayhem on the world. Or maybe I hope they do.

'Of course you can do it,' I tell her. 'I think that's brilliant. Anything that distracts you from putting your affairs in order, or climbing into attics is a positive in my book.'

I hear a little laugh. It sounds almost girlish. Who would've thought that Pandora's Shoebox would have such a positive effect on my mother as well?

'Well, I'll still be putting my affairs in order,' she says, 'but I promise that I won't climb into any more attics. I'll leave those sorts of antics to you.'

'How... how do you know about that?' I ask.

'I have spies everywhere, Rebecca. Or maybe I just bumped into Niamh at the library. She was herding a group of rather boisterous school children. Fair play to her though, she kept them under control. She's a lovely girl, that Niamh. I've always liked her.'

'I'll be sure to tell her,' I say, also making a mental note to tell 'lovely Niamh' not to divulge any of my secrets to my mother in the future.

'How's your bum anyway?' she asks.

'Some lovely shades of black, purple and blue,' I tell her.

'Come over later. I'll give you your Arnica cream back. That will help.'

My mother – ever practical and always good in a crisis.

'I love you, Mum,' I tell her and I feel it in my very bones. So many times we say 'love you' out of habit but there are times, like today, when it's the truest thing we could ever hope to feel. I love my mum. All her quirks and annoyances too. I think of how she still has a kind word and a warm smile for everyone – even Daniel, begrudgingly – when her heart has been shattered by the loss of her life partner. She is a powerhouse. A woman who has been through hell with little to no complaining. A woman who went through the menopause before it was socially acceptable to talk about it. A woman who raised both me and my brother to be fairly decent human beings. Obviously, I'm more decent than Ruairi, but I can acknowledge he's actually done quite well for himself and he's not the worst. Even if he is a first-class tout.

'I love you too, Rebecca,' my mother says and I feel as coddled and loved as I did as a child.

'Now if you are coming over later to the get the Arnica, would you mind picking up a few things for me from the shops? And for Mrs Bishop too? Hang on, I'll get my list...'

39

THE NEXT ADVENTURE

The week sweeps by in a rush of Christmas preparations, work and a now very active group chat between Laura, Niamh and me. We have decided, for definite, that we will go to Amsterdam in the spring and we have already decided on a relatively small budget, and are building our itinerary of things to do and see – including eating a pot brownie. It's no surprise to any of us that Niamh is already a weed connoisseur. She only smokes occasionally, she says, 'when the thought of murdering Year 11 becomes increasingly tempting'.

Truth be told, I feel quite reassured to know someone with experience will be with us. If nothing else she will be able to stop me embarrassing the life out of myself by using the wrong terminology and sounding like the sad, drug-naïve case that I am. Niamh has also been able to educate us on the danger of 'taking a whitey' which, from what I can tell, involves over-indulging to the point of needing to boke and possibly thinking you've entered a whole new dimension. I've assured her I'll be grand. I've not met a brownie that could defeat me yet, but secretly I *am* nervous about trying something that has felt so illicit for my entire life.

The prospect of the holiday has put a much-needed spring in my step. It has distracted me from waiting to see if Grace will reply to me about my column idea. It feels like I have something tangible to look forward to – and I've realised that's not something I've had in a very long time. I haven't even minded trudging through the rain and sleet to take Daniel on his walks. I feel rejuvenated and not even my GP talking through the less pleasant symptoms of menopause is enough to bring my good mood down.

Both Niamh and I have had blood tests done to check our hormone levels, but given our age and our symptoms, our lovely GP has assured us that the perimenopause is very much upon us. Who knew it's only official full-blown menopause when your periods actually disappear completely? I certainly didn't. Just as I didn't know you have to go a full twelve months without bleeding to be considered out the other side.

We have been given a bunch of leaflets to read – including information on tablets, gels and patches, as well as pessaries to prevent vaginal atrophy, which sounds like it comes straight out of a B movie. *Attack of the Vaginal Atrophy* wouldn't look out of place on an illustrated movie poster of a woman running for her life, would it? Of course, when I said this to my doctor she looked at me as if I'm mentally ill, which only goes to prove it was a good call not to tell her about the Mayans and how I'm claiming my inner witch status.

Now though, I'm in my living room with my Christmas lights twinkling and I'm on my fourth cinnamon candle of the season. I'm dressed in a new frock, which Laura and Niamh helped me choose, and I'm feeling kind of into myself. It's black and cut just low enough to be enticing, but not low enough to risk a wardrobe malfunction. It ticks off everything on my checklist for what I want in a dress. It has sleeves, is made from slinky material – the kind that swooshes around your legs when you spin – and looks amazing with my favourite pair of red boots. It's not too formal but a step above casual. Teamed with my denim jacket I look age-appropriately hot. There is not a hoodie nor a pair of leggings in sight and my Crocs are tucked under my bed.

Niamh is a dab hand with a curling wand so she has managed to create a lovely tousled beach-wave look in my hair that I have never been able to achieve myself – no matter how many YouTube tutorials I have watched.

In the ten years since I last spent any decent amount of time with Robyn she has become very gifted at applying the kind of make-up usually only seen on celebrity faces at awards ceremonies. My lips are red. I have been contoured to within an inch of my life and my brows are, I'm told by Laura, 'on fleek', which garnered a groan of disapproval from my make-up artist.

'Mu-um,' Robyn says, 'I've told you before about trying to sound cool! All your phrases are about three years out of date, bruh! You sound like such a try-hard.'

'A try-hard who pays your pocket money and who is giving you money for that dress you want from Disturbia, *bruh*!' Laura mimics back and while the words are different, and the years have passed, I am reminded of the same way Laura and Kitty used to banter in our teenage years. They could be sharp with each other and call each other out on every little thing but there was no doubt that behind it all was love – and buckets of it.

'You're a ride, you know,' Niamh says, grinning at me. 'You always were but you look more so tonight.'

'Girls, I agree that Becca looks amazing but if we cannot talk about riding that would be super,' Laura says, before taking a long sip from her gin and tonic.

'God, sorry. I forgot what age Robyn is,' I say.

'I'm not worried about Robyn,' Laura laughs. 'I just don't want to think about rides or riding when it's my brother who's taking you out. No thank you very much!'

I can see her point. I'd have similar feelings about Ruairi.

'Fair enough,' Niamh says. 'Becca, you look beautiful and I'm so very happy to see you taking this step and going out on an actual date. You are far too gorgeous to be hiding from the world and you deserve to be loved...'

'Awwww!' Laura says, smiling. 'That's lovely!'

'I wasn't finished!' Niamh declares, and as I watch my two longest and best friends existing and laughing in the same room together, I feel a fuzzy warm glow that I really don't think is coming from the gin and tonic I've just downed to settle my nerves.

'As I was saying,' Niamh continues, 'you are far too gorgeous to be hiding from the world and you deserve to be loved, and loved well and often.'

Robyn lets out a peal of laughter as loud and dirty as her mother's used to be at the same age, while Laura cringes. 'You're on a warning, Cassidy!' she scolds.

Before she can say any more, my doorbell rings and Daniel decides it's his time to sing the song of his people loudly and ferociously as if warding away evil spirts, and potential love interests.

'Go get your man,' Niamh says. 'We'll tidy up and lock up here when we're leaving.'

'But you will be meeting us for breakfast in the morning to fill us in on all the gossip?' Laura asks.

'Unless she's otherwise engaged,' Niamh replies with a wink.

'Girls, pack it in!' I tell them, my heart beating at twice its usual rate. I'm so glad I put on an extra spray of deodorant as the nervous sweats are already on me. It has been more than twenty years since I have been on a first date. In fact, it's closer to twenty-five.

It's been at least a decade since I have been kissed – properly kissed. I can't allow my brain to think about all the other things I haven't done in at least a decade because I will freak out entirely if I do.

Kissing is enough to make my knees feel weak and my skin tingle and... what if I've forgotten how? What if I do it all wrong? Maybe it's changed in the last decade?

With shaking hands, I open my front door and see him. Tall, handsome him.

His dark hair, speckled with the occasional grey, is just long enough to fall in soft curls across his forehead. It's the perfect length of hair for running my fingers through when I pull him close for a kiss, I think before blinking and doing my best to focus on what is happening now and not just what I very much want to happen later.

'This isn't at all really weird and awkward,' Conal says, with a slight grimace and I freeze, wondering if I'm about to get dumped before we've even got going. 'Picking my wee sister's friend up for a date,' he continues. 'Who'd have thought it would happen?' He smiles and the way his eyes crinkle and how he tilts his head makes me weak with relief and longing.

'Not weird or awkward at all,' I say, with the same faux grimace. 'The big brother who was always telling us to get out from under his feet and to turn our music down.'

'In fairness, you three had the *worst* taste in music,' he says, shaking his head.

'Excuse me, but how very dare you!' I mock. 'Every single Take That song was an absolute banger.'

'The constant replaying of "Deep" by East 17 was something I could've lived without though,' he says, and his eyes meet mine. Who knew this chemistry between us was fizzing away deep under the surface all this time?

'Will we go?' he asks before nodding his head towards the currently closed living room door. 'I know my sister, and probably

Niamh too, are in there and most likely listening in to every word...'

'*Hi, Conal!*' they call in unison and he rolls his eyes.

'We're leaving now,' I call to my friends and they call their good-byes back as Conal O'Hagan takes my hand in his and leads me out of my front door and on to my next adventure.

Sixteen-year-old Becki Burnside would be so delighted.

40

TEN DAYS LATER

It's quite nice to have the house to myself for a bit. The boys have headed out with their friends for the evening, taking their noise and mayhem with them.

It has been non-stop since they've been home, between doing their washing, refilling the fridge (over and over again) and picking up soggy towels from the bathroom floor. I know I should make them do it all themselves but I'm enjoying feeling needed again. That said, I'll be glad when they go back to Manchester too.

The boys being at home has enforced a taking-things-slow approach to my burgeoning romance with Conal. It's probably a good thing. I don't want to make a mess of this and I think Conal is nervous too. Going slowly is giving us time to adjust and really get to know each other. But getting the chance for a good snog isn't easy and I really do enjoy snogging Conal. Our first kiss was everything I hoped it would be and I'd been delighted to find out I hadn't forgotten how to do it after all. We'd had a lovely meal together, followed by a couple of drinks and we laughed and chatted as if we were always meant to laugh and chat together. We'd touched on tougher times – talked of his grief and mine but it didn't feel like we were wallowing in it. We were just sharing the experience of having lost a parent. Conal and I, it seems, have a lot of shared experiences. We're both divorced. Both of us have two children. We both have dogs that have larger-than-life personalities and we both want to see more of the world.

By the time he'd walked me home, my heart felt lighter than it had done in years and I'd remembered what it was like to really, really want to be kissed by someone. What it was like to feel the hairs on my arms rise up when he took my hand. How the warmth of him beside me made me feel safe.

He didn't come in that night. We were determined to do this right and give us the best chance. But he did kiss me, on my doorstep, his breath warm, his hand tilting my face towards him. When his lips first brushed against mine I'd realised that even if the Waltons had fifty children, I'd be unable to talk my body out of wanting and needing more of him.

The next morning I'd started to write another column – Ten Ways to Take a Chance on Love in Your Forties. I was just saving it onto my desktop when my phone pinged with an email notification. Grace Adams at *Northern People* had emailed me back. She liked my column ideas. She wants to discuss my writing after the Christmas holidays. 'I think you could be just the voice we're looking for,' she'd written. 'I love the pitches. They need a little finessing but I've no doubt you'd be more than able for it. I really appreciate you sending these to me.' I had been practically radioactive with the glow of a woman who felt valued and visible for the first time in years. I'm so excited about it that it drowns out the nerves I feel at the thought of a proper face-to-face meeting with an actual magazine editor.

But even with my nerves there is no Christmas present I could want more. Apart from my boys being back under my roof, of course. With them here, the house feels alive again.

Saul is delighted to be back on familiar territory and has been enjoying living it up with his old school pals – all of whom have congregated back in Derry for the holidays. Adam, who would normally have been one of this gang of friends, has been much, much too distracted by his romance with Jodie. There's no shortage of snogging going on there.

Yes, their relationship is real and yes, it's serious. To the surprise of both Niamh and me, the big love affair has been going on longer than we could've guessed.

It appears, they sheepishly admitted, that it all started on one particularly hot and sultry summer night, which I don't want to give much thought to. Adam has even admitted to me that he has had a crush on Jodie since forever – but he'd put it out of his head because they had grown up together and he didn't want to ruin their friendship.

But that was before he'd realised that some risks are worth taking. That's a lesson I'm learning myself.

Right at this moment, I am in my happy place. I am curled up on the sofa, with a sleeping Daniel at my feet and the fire is burning while I catch up on the *Strictly Come Dancing* final, with a not-so-little glass of Baileys at my side. I don't think I have felt this serene in years.

But of course, just as I think about how relaxing this is, my doorbell bursts into life as someone rings it six or seven times in a row – waking a very unimpressed Daniel in the process. I jump, of course, and this knocks over my Baileys, which Daniel decides he quite likes.

As the doorbell keeps ringing, I've no choice but to leave Daniel to his libations and run to see what obviously life-threatening emergency is befalling us.

Please God, don't let it be something wrong with Mum, I think as I open the door. *I can handle anything else but something happening to Mum.*

As I open the door, I'm greeted by the sight of Niamh, her face sheet white, her eyes wide. Behind her I notice Laura running up the driveway. 'I got here as fast as I could,' she gasps as I look between her and Niamh, my heart now thumping.

Niamh pushes past me into the living room while Laura gives me a sympathetic look as she walks through the door. I'm worried now. Really worried. If it's not Mum, is it Conal? It's not the boys is it? I can't speak. I don't want to put my greatest fears into words.

As I follow my friends into the living room, Niamh sees the look of fear in my eyes. 'No one's dead,' she says. 'I should lead with that because you look like you might throw up.'

'Then what is it?' I ask, as Daniel plods over towards me and slumps at my feet. Just how much Baileys does it take to intoxicate a spaniel?

I look from Niamh to Laura – who looks as confused as I am.

'I just got a message to get over here as soon as possible,' she says.

Niamh is standing in front of my fireplace, rummaging in her bag while Laura and I look on expectantly.

'This!' she says, taking an item from her bag and waving it in front of me. 'This is what it is!'

I squint at it in the soft glow of the Christmas tree lights. Is that... Is it a pregnancy test? 'Not this again, Niamh,' I say. 'You spoke to the doctor. You got your results back. Your hormones are in the toilet and you are *not* pregnant!'

'Correct!' Niamh says, glaring at me. I wonder what I'm missing.

'*I'm* not pregnant,' Niamh says, slowly, and none of this explains why on earth she would have almost beaten my front door down just to tell me something we already knew.

'Is this just an announcement you're going to make once a week from now on?' I ask. 'Or am I missing something?' I ask, again looking from her to Laura and back again.

'Yes!' Niamh says. 'You are missing something. A very big something. Take a moment and think about it.'

Nope. Nothing is coming to mind. I grab the stick from her and look at it. I can confirm there are very clearly two blue lines on display. If Niamh isn't pregnant then who...

'Oh my God!' Laura says. Clearly the penny has dropped for her but it hasn't for me. If Niamh isn't pregnant then who could be... and suddenly it all falls into place.

'Becca, congratulations. We're going to be grannies,' Niamh says finally.

ACKNOWLEDGEMENTS

This might be my fourth novel published as Freya Kennedy, but it is the twentieth novel that I (the real me, Claire Allan) has published. To have reached this milestone is something I couldn't have dreamed of back in 2006 when I was writing book number one as a bit of a challenge to myself before my 30th birthday.

Nonetheless, here we are, and my thanks have to go in the very first instance to every single reader who has enabled me to do this for a living. Special thanks to those who have been with me from those early days and who have stayed loyal readers. I feel incredibly lucky to have you all in my life.

With that out of the way I want to acknowledge just how special this book is to me. Originally, I had intended making the last Ivy Lane book my last ever Freya Kennedy title – but as my forties progressed, I realised there was so much I wanted to say. When I floated the idea of writing this book to my agent, Ger Nichol, she was enthusiastic as always – and I am ever grateful for that enthusiasm. It inspired me to keep going – as Ger has done many times over the last twenty books.

I then floated the idea to the wonderful Caroline Ridding at Boldwood who shared in my excitement and offered me a further book deal. Thank you, Caroline for your continued belief in me. And huge thanks also to my editor Rachel Faulkner-Willcocks for your help and enthusiasm for Becca Burnside and her band of friends.

Indeed, thanks to all at Boldwood Books, including my fellow authors, for providing such a warm, welcoming and supportive environment to be published in. Thank you to the boss lady, Amanda Ridout, for creating something very special indeed.

Thanks to Candida Bradford for her keen eye and suggestions during the copy-edit, and Debra Newhouse for being a great proof-reader and cheerleader too!

This book was intended to be a love letter to women of a certain age – and also to my friends, family, home city of Derry and to many people whose lives have impacted on mine. They do say writers are magpies after all and this book has nods to the key moments and friendships in my life. Thank you to all those who inspire me daily.

The character of Rebecca/ Becca/ Becki Burnside was named after a nickname my beloved Granny, Anna Davidson, used for all the girls in our family. It seemed the perfect every-woman name to give to a character I hope will resonate with a whole lot of women. It is an honour to give Becki a full personality and back story.

Thanks, as always to my family – my parents, siblings, nieces and nephews, my husband and my children for just being there and being supportive.

Thank you to my friends – especially those who have been with me throughout this journey called life and who haven't run off screaming. Thank you for inspiration, the laughs, the tears, and the chipulary burns.

The star character in this book – Daniel The Spaniel – was named after the pet of a customer of Bridge Books in Dromore, who won the chance to name a character by supporting Bridge Books during Independent Bookshop Week last year.

Thank you to the booksellers, especially the independent stores who are invaluable when it comes to putting my books in front of readers. And of equal value, thanks to our librarians, especially those from Libraries NI.

Thank you to the reviewers, the bloggers, and the journalists who still talk to me even though they've interviewed me countless times by now. Sixteen-year-old me dreamed that one day she would be an author – I'm delighted she made it.

If you've enjoyed reading this book and want to enjoy the songs mentioned in it, you can also download The Fecking Fabulous Forties playlist on Spotify.

ABOUT THE AUTHOR

Freya Kennedy is the alter ego for bestselling thriller author Claire Allan. A former journalist from Derry, Northern Ireland Claire has published eleven novels. Now, as Freya, she is writing warm, funny women's fiction for Boldwood.

Sign up to Freya Kennedy's mailing list for news, competitions and updates on future books.

Visit Freya's website: http://www.claireallan.com/freya-kennedy

Follow Freya on social media here:

 facebook.com/ClaireAllanAuthor

x.com/claireallan

instagram.com/claireallan_author

bookbub.com/authors/freya-kennedy

ALSO BY FREYA KENNEDY

The Hopes and Dreams of Libby Quinn

In Pursuit of Happiness

Don't Stop Believing

The Fecking Fabulous Forties Club

WHERE ALL YOUR ROMANCE
DREAMS COME TRUE!

THE HOME OF BESTSELLING
ROMANCE AND WOMEN'S
FICTION

 WARNING:
MAY CONTAIN SPICE

SIGN UP TO OUR
NEWSLETTER

https://bit.ly/Lovenotesnews

Boldw☺☺d

Boldwood Books is an award-winning fiction
publishing company seeking out the best
stories from around the world.

Find out more at www.boldwoodbooks.com

Join our reader community for brilliant books,
competitions and offers!

Follow us
@BoldwoodBooks
@TheBoldBookClub

**Sign up to our weekly
deals newsletter**

https://bit.ly/BoldwoodBNewsletter

Printed in Great Britain
by Amazon

48796685R00169